RISE OF A QUEEN

KINGDOM DUET
BOOK TWO

RINA KENT

To kings & queens.

AUTHOR NOTE

Hello reader friend,

If you haven't read my books before, you might not know this, but I write darker stories that can be upsetting and disturbing. My books and main characters aren't for the faint of heart.

To remain true to the characters, the vocabulary, grammar, and spelling of *Rise of a Queen* is written in British English.

Rise of a Queen is the second book of a duet and is NOT standalone.

Kingdom Duet:
#1 Reign of a King
#2 Rise of a Queen

Don't forget to Sign up to Rina Kent's Newsletter for news about future releases and an exclusive gift.

FOREWARD

Quick note,

These special edition covers are for all the lovers of spice who prefer "Safe for work" covers! Enjoy!

XOXO,
Rina

Nothing is fair in love.

This is my kingdom. My territory.
I own everything and control everyone, Aurora included.
She shouldn't have barged into my world with no armour.
She shouldn't have caught my attention with no warning.
Alas, she did.
Then she thought she could disappear.
If a battle is what it'll take to protect and own her, I'll shed blood.
Wars aren't fair, and neither am I.

PLAYLIST

Epilogue—Normandie

What I've Done—Linkin Park

Everything I Wanted—Billie Eilish

Broken & Beautiful—Kelly Clarkson

What Have You Done—Within Temptation & Keith Caputo

Valentine's Day—Linkin Park

In My Remains—Linkin Park

Soul on Fire—The Last Internationale

I Hate Everything About You—Three Days Grace

Demons—Written by Wolves

Bottom Of The Deep Blue Sea—MISSIO

So Cold—Ben Cocks & Nikisha Reyes-Pile

Lonely—Nathan Wagner

Control—Zoe Wees

True Love—Coldplay

Sparks—Coldplay

Til Kingdom Come—Pop Evil

The Reckoning—Within Temptation & Jacoby Shaddix

Prayers For The Damned—Sixx:A.M.

You can find the complete playlist on Spotify.

RISE OF A QUEEN

ONE

Jonathan

Twenty-Two years ago

I'VE NEVER LIKED FUNERALS.

Especially when it's my mother's.

The pretentiousness and the fake sympathy, or even the real tears, are all useless. Why cry for someone who will never come back? They can't hear you, so the whole point behind crying is selfishness.

People don't cry for the dead. People cry because of the uncontrollable rush of their own emotions.

The grey clouds condense in the distance, forming one thick layer over the other until the air is nearly black. Looks like the sky might start weeping, too.

But why would it? Did it even know the woman lying in the casket?

The people surrounding it, throwing her favourite tulip flowers didn't know her either. They pretend they did, because she spent her entire life running between charities and spending money we didn't have.

Not that Gregory, my father, would've told her to do otherwise. He cared for her wellbeing enough to swallow the knife with its blood.

I take a sip of my small stash of whiskey that I stole from my brother, James, and let the burn soothe my throat. He'll probably kill me, but I don't need him drunk on this day, of all days. At least I'm in full control of my actions and myself.

Father is about to fall apart and if James does, too…well, fuck if I can carry them both.

I sit at the back of the cemetery, in front of a grave that appears a few decades old. Layers of dust cover the stone and the writing has been erased by the hands of time. Birds' waste clings to it like a second skin. One of the forgotten dead.

"There you are."

I don't lift my head as my best friend, Ethan, sits beside me. He's wearing a black suit and his light hair that he usually leaves haphazard is styled and neat.

At least he dressed up for the occasion. It took a funeral for that.

For a moment, he remains silent, his shoulder not far from mine as we both stare at the forgotten grave with its unpleasant appearance and the birds' waste.

It's me who breaks the silence, "Do you think her grave will be like this one twenty years from now?"

"Not if you have a say in it."

"True that."

"Are you going back there?" He hesitates, his voice taking a sympathetic turn. "Your father and James aren't doing so well."

"When have they ever?"

"They need you, Jon."

"They need false promises and a machine to go back in time. I have neither of those."

"So you're just going to stay here?"

"For the moment, yes. Screw off if the company bores you."

"Fuck you." He snatches my drink and takes a long pull. "I would never leave you on a day like this."

"Leave the sappy for Agnus."

"Fuck you again. I'll give you a pass for being a dick today."

"As if I would need your pass." I scoff as I yank back my bottle and down the liquid, revelling in the burn that coats my throat before settling in my empty stomach.

I've barely eaten today and that was only because I needed the energy to remain standing tall. For me, eating and physical activity aren't things that I enjoy, but I do them religiously anyway because I don't need my health to get in the way of my brain's plots.

"It's okay if you show emotions, Jonathan. You don't have to trap it all in."

"What do you do with emotions?" I tilt my head to the side, watching him. "Do you profit from them?"

His light eyes soften at the corners. "She was your mother."

"Is showing emotions going to bring her back? Should I go through an episode like James and trash the whole house, or should I collapse like my father so it's written in some record that I mourned her?"

"I get it. You want to be strong for them."

"It's not a choice, Ethan. I have to. My father can't plan his fucking day without her and James has always been a mama's boy. If I fall with them, nothing will bring us up again. The bank will take the house as collateral if none of us gets our shit together."

"Damn. Want me to help?"

"I have a plan."

He grabs the bottle and takes a sip. Ethan and I have never found trouble in sharing things. It's our modus operandi. "What type of plan?"

"You know Lord Sterling?"

"The one who holds a grudge against your father because your mother didn't choose him?"

"Yes, that one. Mother abandoned him at the altar and he still feels the humiliation to this day. That's why he's after everything Father's built, from the company to the house and even the summer home in Wales."

"Sorry fuck. What do you intend to do?"

"Find his weakness and hit him where it hurts so he backs the fuck off."

My father's heart condition isn't doing well. Ever since Mum fell sick, it's like he's aged ten years every day.

The doctor told me and James to try to keep him as far away from stressful situations as possible. I couldn't do anything about today, but the future is different.

I'm taking things into my own hands, and I'll force everyone who's brought my family down to pay. In blood if I have to.

"I like that." Ethan grins. "I'm in."

"No one invited you."

He wraps an arm around my shoulder and squeezes. "I invited myself and you can't kick me out. You're stuck with me for life, Jon."

"Is this my punishment?"

"Fuck you, mate." He stands up and offers me his hand. "Come on."

I take it, staggering to my feet and dusting the dirt off my trousers and jacket.

After downing one last swig from the small bottle, I let Ethan throw it away.

"Go first," I tell him. "I'll be there in a bit."

He tightens his grip on my shoulder one final time in an obvious show of comfort before he releases me and disappears to the other side of the cemetery. James probably needs Ethan's consoling more than I do. My brother's the type who feels too much, sort of like my parents.

I'm like our grandfather. It's not that I don't feel, it's that I find it hard, even impossible, to show those feelings.

Ever since Father's company started to struggle, I've known I don't have a choice in being who I am. I might've not finished university yet, but the courses of action I suggested have worked more than what Father has been doing for years.

He can be soft when it comes to business, and that's his biggest mistake. If you're not a wolf, you'll be eaten by wolves.

James couldn't care less about affairs. He's content with being a rugby star and spending his youth drinking and shagging his way through the female population.

I cross the distance from the forgotten grave to where Mother's burial is happening. I mourn her alone, not in front of people. I mourn the way she was too naïve for this world, the way she thought giving to others was her purpose of being, to the point she forgot about us sometimes.

There was no misconception about who was Mother's favourite between me and James. She always looked at me with a furrow between her brows whenever I hit her with facts she didn't appreciate, like how Father couldn't sponsor her charitable events anymore.

She couldn't relate to me, and we remained that way. However, she loved me, I guess. Like anyone would love the child whose morals they doubted.

Mother thought I was too cruel, when I was just too realistic for her liking.

Today, I'll be the rock James and Father need, and then I'll protect the house Grandpa left us.

I will protect the King legacy.

My feet come to a halt at a low weeping sound. I stand by the tree, half-camouflaged by the trunk, and tilt my head to the side.

A woman in a black dress and a matching veil covering her eyes kneels in front of what seems like a new grave, tears falling down her cheeks.

Her black hair is pulled into a conservative bun that doesn't go well with the designer clothes and shoes she's wearing.

Beside her stands a little girl no older than five years old. She's also wearing a long black dress that swallows her small body. A veil similar to the woman's, though sheerer, covers her eyes as well. Her ebony hair is tied in pigtails, falling on either side of her face.

As the woman—her mother, I assume—cries, the little girl fiddles with the veil, nose scrunching and lips thinning in a line. Someone doesn't like that veil.

When she finally manages to shrug it off, she bunches it in her small hands, hides it behind her back, then drops it to the ground.

I smile at the mischievous look in her dark eyes. From this distance, I can't tell if they're brown or blue, or a mixture of both.

As soon as she finishes her mission of getting rid of the veil, she leans over the woman and wipes her eyes with the back of her tiny hands.

"Don't cry, Alicia. She'll be reight," the little girl says in a brittle voice with a northern accent. Yorkshire dialect? "Our Mummy is happy in heaven."

That only makes the older woman cry harder, her sobs echoing in the air like an opera gone wrong.

So they're siblings, not mother and daughter. The age difference is too large, though. The older one must be at least twenty, if not more.

The little girl wraps her tiny arms around the woman's neck and squeezes her. "I love you, Alicia."

"I love you, too, Claire." The woman, Alicia, manages to say between hiccoughs, her arms caging the small girl against her chest.

They remain like that for a second before the girl, Claire, pulls away. "Hey, Alicia. I'm gonna make ya happy."

"Really?" Alicia ruffles her hair, a sad smile on her lips. Her tone and voice are more sophisticated than the younger girl's, hinting at a more refined upbringing. "How?"

"I'm gonna dance for ya." She points a thumb at herself. "I'm the best dancer in town."

"You are."

"Aye. That's right." She grabs her sister by the wrist. "Come on, lemme show ya. Not here, cuz I don't want ghosts to see."

"Okay, okay." Alicia staggers to her feet and follows the small girl's lead.

Claire discreetly looks back, and I think it's at the grave, but then she kicks something on the ground. The veil—she's trying to bury it.

Her eyes meet mine, and she freezes. The colour of her irises are blue, a deep dark one like the undiscovered bottoms of oceans. A mischievous smile pulls at her lips as she places an index finger to them.

I wink at her and her grin widens before her sister drags her out of sight.

After they're gone, I cut the distance to the grave they were visiting. Smiling, I crouch and take the tiny veil that's half-buried in the dirt. My smile vanishes when I read the name on the tombstone.

Lady Bridget Sterling

Beloved Wife and Mother

I couldn't miss that name even if I wanted to. She was Lord Sterling's wife—the one who committed suicide not so long ago.

My gaze trails to the path the two girls took. One of them is Alicia Sterling, the only offspring Lord Sterling ever had.

In that case, who was that small one? She called Lady Bridget her mother, so is she perhaps illegitimate? The northern accent fits in that theory if Bridget had a lover in the North.

She doesn't matter, though. The one who shares Lord Sterling's blood does.

Alicia.

I commemorate the name to memory for later, shove the veil in my pocket, and join the burial of my mother's.

People are everywhere like flies, their heads bowed. Some are sniffling, others are feigning sympathy they don't feel.

I come to a halt at the scene in front of me. James is patting the back of my rigid father, whose face is paler than Mum's skin is as she rests in her coffin.

Taking a deep breath, I join them, standing on the other side of Father. Gregory King has a slim built and his hair has been slowly balding over the years. His grey eyes and straight nose are the only things he shares with me and James.

My older brother is buffer than me with wide rugby shoulders and a build to match. He also has a charming presence that instantly makes him the more approachable of the two of us, even though I'm three years younger.

"You're late," my brother hisses at me under his breath. "They closed her casket."

"I'm here now." Not that I wanted to say goodbye. I already did that at the hospital, then kissed her forehead and covered her again with the sheet.

I don't know how to say goodbyes. Not when Grandpa passed away, and certainly not now.

"Well, you could've come earlier," James snaps.

"Or I could've just come now."

"Do not fight in front of your mother. You know she loathes that," Father reprimands, his eyes not leaving the casket as it's being swallowed by the ground while the priest says a few words.

Dust to dust.

Ironic.

The start is always the end, isn't it?

We remain long after she's six feet under. Everyone slowly says their condolences and leaves. Soon enough, it's only the three of us.

What remains of the King family, anyway.

Ethan says he'll wait for us by the car. I'm ready to go home and start taking action on how we should go from here.

Just when I'm about to voice that thought, a man in a striped suit walks towards us like he owns the cemetery and all the damned souls in it.

Lord Sterling.

Both James and Father tense at his view, but I glare at him, my mind filled with all the ways I'm going to destroy the fucker.

"I'm late," he speaks in his over-the-top posh accent. "I couldn't say goodbye to Anna."

"Leave," James snarls at him.

"Public property." He stares down his nose at Father. "Maybe now she'll realise she made a mistake by choosing you."

"Piss. Off." James starts to push him, but Father stops him.

"No can do. In fact…" He grins, baring uneven teeth. "You should expect a visit from the bank in a few days. I'm confiscating the house you love so much, Gregory. Maybe I can still smell Anna in it."

It's my turn to tower over the lord's tiny, round frame. "I'll destroy every bone in your body before you'll be able to do that."

"Show me what you've got. Though I'm sure it's not a lot." He makes a cross at Mother's grave. "Rest in peace, Anna."

And with that, he leaves.

I keep glaring at his back as he disappears. Fucker. I'm going to ruin him and everything he's ever cherished. I don't care if it's his home, his business, or even his damn family.

I will destroy him.

A thud sounds behind me as something large hits the ground. I freeze, my breathing stopping for a second.

"Father!" James's voice booms in the empty cemetery.

I turn around and life as I know it ends.

My father is on the ground, clutching his heart, face blue, and he's not breathing.

As James yells and curses and tries to bring him back without any success, I vow one thing.

Lord Sterling will be eradicated in the ugliest way possible.

Everything he cares about will be taken, just like everything was taken from me.

He ended my family and I'll end his.

Or what remains of it.

TWO

Jonathan

Present

WHEN SOMETHING BAD HAPPENS, I FEEL IT BEFOREHAND. It's one of the additional senses I have aside from predicting monetary income and international markets' values.

No one believed me when I told them decades ago that the Chinese and the Russians were the future. It's due to that very reason that I have the strongest partners in said countries.

The moment I left the company, I sensed something was wrong. I checked on Levi and Aiden—by checking, I mean, Harris confirmed that my son was in a class at university and my nephew was at a football practice.

Yes, I do have people following my heirs around to ensure their safety. I always have since they were toddlers. I've lost enough family members for a lifetime and I will not be taken off guard again.

I step into the silent house. Its eerily calm atmosphere is almost like the cemetery from that day at the exact moment before my father had a cardiac arrest and passed away. On the day of my mother's funeral.

He died of anguish, of fear of losing this house his father left him and the last reminder of Mother's presence.

Persian carpets extend in my vision and Greek marble flooring shines under my feet. The vaulted ceilings and the handmade ornaments decorating the entrance and the rest of the house's doors weren't something we could afford when my parents were alive.

I did this.

I returned this house to its initial glory from when my grandfather was alive. Gregory and James King didn't protect the family legacy, I did.

After everyone started doubting our position, I'm the one who transformed the King name into something people respect and speak of in a hushed tone, either due to awe or fear.

Coming this far wasn't done through pleasantries or being nice. The only reason I get to sit on the throne is because I've slaughtered everyone who looks at it, let alone dares to approach it.

I've seen grown men tremble and nearly piss their pants when I acquisitioned their companies. I've had them throw lawsuits at me, just so I would crush them in court and take everything they have—and more. I've had men offer me their wives and their daughters if I would leave their companies alone, and I took pleasure in erasing their names from the business world.

Compromise and mercy are terms I abolished from my dictionary the day my father dropped dead over my mother's fresh grave.

If I want something, I take it. Fuck the world and its weak people. If they've chosen to be in a position I can explore, that's exactly what I do.

If I find a chance to grow the King name, consequences be damned.

Only one thing matters: my family.

So why the fuck have I been thinking about Aurora ever since this ominous feeling gripped me?

She's not family. Far from it.

Still, I spend more time with her than I ever did with Aiden and Levi.

Her face is the only one I wake up to every day and fall asleep staring at every night.

She's the one whose black strands I stroke when her pupils move beneath her lids and she's struck by a nightmare.

That's when she's most vulnerable and can't put up her walls or hide from me. I get to witness her bare.

The more I see, the more I want.

The more I dig my fingers into her, the deeper I want to go.

It might have started with her body, but it's her mind that I want to invade and conquer.

Which shouldn't happen, because I make it my mission to not get interested in any other human being.

I didn't sign up for being consumed by Aurora, and I'll put an end to it...*eventually.*

I check the notifications on my phone. Since Harris, the COO, and I spent the entire day locked in my office going through possible companies to add to our arsenal, I didn't have time to send her the occasional email that usually implies how I'll fuck her that night.

Besides, she's the one who wanted a date, so I thought she would be the one to get in touch.

There's only a missed call from her in the morning.

It doesn't add up, considering she never calls me when she's at work.

Something tells me she's not home, either. Otherwise, there would be some music playing in the hall. She does that a lot, especially when her black belt friend is around.

"Dinner, sir?"

I lift my head from my phone and shift my attention to Margot. She stands with her hands intertwined in a respectful pose over her white apron.

"We'll eat outside." I slip the phone back into my pocket. "Have you seen Aurora?"

"She didn't come home, sir."

Huh. It's past seven. She couldn't have stayed at work this late—especially since she insisted on a date.

"If there's nothing you need..." She nods.

"Where's Tom?" He's a decent butler, but he's usually hanging on to her robes, waiting for an order. I'll send him to Aurora's flat and Moses will go to her work since she has no other place to go.

But there's also Layla's family restaurant. Harris will go there. She better not be spending time with Layla's brothers, or the night will take a dramatic turn that will end with my handprint on her arse.

I have no tolerance for other people in her surroundings, not even people I trust, like Harris and Moses. It doesn't matter that she's known Layla's brothers for a long time, as she likes to remind me. They didn't come into her life first—I did.

"Tom stepped out for an errand, sir. Is there anything I can do on his behalf?"

"Have him find me as soon as he's back."

"Yes, sir." As Margot disappears, I retrieve my phone and call Aurora again. She's still not answering.

I type an email.

From: Jonathan King
To: Aurora Harper
Subject: Where Are You?
Must I remind you of who demanded a date tonight? My time is gold, Aurora, so answer your fucking phone.

As soon as I hit Send, the screen lights up with a call from Harris.

"You're just in time. I want you to go to—"

"We have a situation," he cuts me off. Harris never cuts me off, which means this is serious.

"And?"

"I just got updated when we left the meeting. Maxim Griffin is giving an interview for the first time since his capture."

"What?"

Harris's voice continues in a grim tone, "From what I've seen, he's accusing his daughter, saying it's time she's brought to justice, too. There's an uproar from the victims' families and the media about this. It's not looking good."

Fuck!

"Where's Aurora?"

"What?"

"She must've seen it and that's why she disappeared. Find her. *Now.*" I head out. Moses is stepping out of the car, but when he sees the expression on my face, he slides back in.

"I'll get in touch with my men. Give me ten minutes."

"You have five, Harris. I don't fucking care what you have to do to find her. I need a location sent to Moses immediately."

I hang up without hearing his reply. There's no way in fuck I'm going to let her slip between my fingers now.

Aurora Harper sold her soul to the devil. It goes without saying that she'll never be able to escape me.

THREE

Aurora

DISAPPEARING ISN'T EASY.

I tried it before and it was like pulling my own teeth from my mouth. It's not about changing names and going blonde for a few years. It's not about cutting my hair and picking a different clothing style. It's not even about losing my northern accent.

Those are the easiest parts of disappearing. Everything else that's hard to change is the problem.

It's about altering the way I walk so people don't recognise me from afar.

It's forcing myself to become a right-handed person after living for sixteen years as a left-handed person. That's why my handwriting is rubbish, and when I'm exhausted, I switch back to my left hand without realising it.

It's stopping myself from eating the food I like the most so that I'm not recognised through it. Over time, I've lost all joy in eating altogether and it's become a chore.

It's about erasing my habits and everything I used to take for granted, one by each bloody one.

Disappearance is about rebirth.

When I first escaped the Witness Protection Program, I kept watching over my shoulder and under every bed I slept on. I searched the wardrobes and installed three locks on my doors. I never slept with my window open, even if it meant drowning in my own sweat due to summer's heat. For a few months, I moved from one motel to the other and covered my tracks in case anyone from back home was following me.

I stopped being Clarissa and threw everything about her life behind me. I stopped believing in superheroes and in love. I stopped dancing and singing in the shower.

I stopped living.

So when I find myself at the site of my rebirth again, I'm not surprised.

After watching the snippet of Dad's interview, being attacked by Sarah, and hearing the message Alicia left about her own death, I had no actual presence of mind to think.

I still can't.

My fingers shake, my knees, lips, and palms sting. I haven't stopped for a bathroom break and I survived on a bottle of water through the entire four-hour drive here.

I've returned to where I was born and reborn.

The cottage in the middle of the forest.

Dad's site of murder.

On the internet, there are articles about how this place is haunted and many curious teenagers film themselves inside it to prove they're fearless.

A few years ago, I gave up ownership of our house in town. I signed it over to a charitable association and they're now using it as a centre for disabled children. I had my solicitor make all the arrangements so that no one would know I was behind it.

However, I didn't give up this cottage. One, it's not really worth much, and just like back then, it's as if a part of my soul is still trapped in there, along with those dead women's bodies.

It's black outside except for the silver moon. Its ghostly fingers creep between the stilled branches and the silent, black earth. The silence is like that in a cemetery, long and deafening in its uninterrupted quiet.

A shiver claws up my spine as I watch the place where many lost their lives without being heard. Death reeks from every pebble and every tree. From the sky and the night. They stand witness to the time everything started and ended.

The moonlight casts a shadowy silver light on the old architecture that Dad built with his own hands. He was so good with them, his hands.

He knew how to snap necks, then fix me breakfast. He knew how to set traps for helpless animals, then brush my hair as if he was the most doting father on earth.

It's been eleven years, but it's almost as if I saw Dad dragging a dead woman across the ground only yesterday.

Time is…immeasurable in this place. It has its own metrics and its own haunted memories.

It's been a few hours since I arrived, but I haven't left my car. My fingers keep tracing my watch, back and forth, as if that will fill me with the needed courage. I told myself I would get out when I could control the trembling of my limbs, but that hasn't happened.

My hand is still quivering as I open the door and step outside. I follow the moonlight's trail, my unsteady heels crunching against the pebbles.

My ankle pulses with pain; I probably twisted it when Sarah pushed me to the ground.

I limp my way to the cottage, then stop in front of the door. The need to destroy it—or better yet, burn it—rushes to the forefront of my brain.

But that won't bring back the women who died. It won't bring back my life or everything I lost that day.

I do a detour and hobble to behind the cottage. When I came here eleven years ago, this place was circled by police tape. All eight graves were opened up and the corpses were taken for autopsy, and eventually the women had a respectful burial. However, only seven corpses were found—including the woman I saw that day. She was the last addition to Dad's collection.

The eighth grave was empty. He was already hunting for someone to fill it and I reported him before he could.

Now all the graves are closed. The black dirt is even darker under the silver moonlight. The eerily quiet atmosphere doesn't suggest that the earth was flipped upside down to hide murders.

I limp to where I remember the graves to be. Eleven years ago, I stood over each one and said their names. I apologised for not setting them free sooner and promised to shed everything I had in common with Maxim Griffin. Name, habits—everything down to any type of food we ever shared. That's why I barely eat anymore.

I do the same now. My limbs struggle to keep me standing as I stop over the first grave and speak in a low, brittle tone, "I'm sorry, Marissa Loyd. I didn't know you, but I know you had a bright future ahead of you. I'm so sorry he's making you flip in your new grave by doing that interview. If anyone should be buried here, it's him."

I drag my twisted ankle to the next grave and the next and the next. By the time I say all their names, exhaustion plays on my nerve endings and I'm about ready to collapse.

Being here is like reliving the past and allowing it to creep into the pores of my skin.

I've never forgotten the victims' names. Marissa, Giselle, Caroline, Selena, Mari-Jane, Hope, and Nora.

They're engraved in my mind like indelible ink.

I may be able to forget my own name, but I'll never forget the names of the defenceless women whom my father buried in nameless graves as if they were nobodies, erasing their existence.

My feet come to a halt in front of the eighth grave, and my heart jolts as needles form on my skin.

It's open. The grave that should be closed like all the others is open.

Oh, fuck.

Oh, shit.

Why...why is it open? It shouldn't be. It's like eleven years ago, when—

A rustle comes from behind me and I whirl around.

It's too late, though.

The last thing I see is a black mask before something slams into my face.

I fall backwards into the grave.

Just like back then. Just like when I was nearly buried alive.

I might've been able to escape that time, but it's different now.

It's finally over.

The world darkens as a tear slides down my cheek.

Why, Daddy? Just why?

FOUR

Aurora

Eleven years ago

Sweat trickles down my spine as I step over the yellow signs.

The flashlight that's gripped tightly in my hand outlines a clear path on the black dirt. The distant hoots of an owl echo in the otherwise silent night.

It's been a few months since the discovery of the murders, so the police eventually lowered the security around the crime scene. Currently, it's almost as if nothing happened here.

Almost.

Now that Maxim Griffin has been sentenced to spend the rest of his life in prison and the victims' families were able to give them proper burials, there's nothing left here.

Nothing except for the yellow 'Do Not Cross' tape.

I do cross it, not because I'm bent on breaking the rules, but because if I don't do this now, I won't be able to in the future.

My hair sticks to my face underneath the baseball cap I'm using to cover my identity. I went from one bus to another to finally get to where I am now.

The few hundred pounds I have from my savings will be able to get me a motel room and a plane ticket so I can fly outside of England. Not far, though. Maybe Northern Ireland or Scotland. Since I'll be seventeen soon, I'll have to figure out a way to forge the new identity I was given in the Witness Protection Program.

I'll figure it out. I have to. It's the only way I'll be able to escape the hell I've been living through during the last couple of months.

It's the only way I'll be able to start anew.

I wrap the coat around my body when a shiver goes through me, and I clutch the flashlight tighter. The graves in which Dad buried the women are still open.

Tears stream down my cheeks as I talk to them and apologise as I did to their families.

That's all I've been doing during the trials—apologising. No matter how much I do it, it doesn't seem to be enough.

Sometimes, when they hit or throw insults at me, somewhere in my brain, I feel like I deserve it. I'm the one who smiled and laughed and danced with the monster who ended the lives of their daughters, wives, and mothers.

I'm the one who didn't see the devil, even though he was right in front of me.

If I'd searched before, looked before, maybe I would've noticed it. Maybe I could've stopped him.

But it's useless now. It's already done, so all I can do is apologise.

When I reach the empty grave, I kick dirt in it. My stomps are fuelled with the rage and the injustice I've been living through. The lie. The smoke and mirrors.

"I hate you, Dad!" *Stomp. Kick.* "I hate you so much! I wish you'd killed me first. I wish you'd never let me see you like that. I wish I was never your daughter."

My throat burns with the force of my words, but the tears

won't stop soaking my cheeks and slipping into my mouth, making me taste salt.

I throw my head back and stare into the night, just like I did that day I begged for all of this to be a lie. A shooting star crosses the moonless sky, and instead of finding the beauty in it, a wave of grief hits me again. My sister loved shooting stars, but now, she's no longer here to enjoy them. Alicia used to tell me to make a wish whenever we saw one, but I said those don't come true, because Dad never let me believe in illusions. He never let me believe in Father Christmas or in the bogeyman or in the Tooth Fairy.

He forced me to live in reality and told me that actual monsters are scarier.

However, he made me believe in him—my superhero without a cape. Then he pulled the carpet from underneath my feet and left me as this shell of a person with nothing behind or in front of me.

I don't know what to believe in anymore. My own sense of self is starting to fade and I don't even have Alicia to talk to.

There's Jonathan and Aiden…

I shake my head frantically at the thought. I won't bring my baggage into my nephew's life. And Jonathan is scary—he'd probably be the one who'd chase me off.

As my tantrum against Dad withers away, only a bitter taste remains—the fact that I'm truly on my own in the world now.

The sound of the crunching of leaves echoes behind me. At first, I think it's one of the night animals who roam around here, but then I hear it again.

In the days when I used to hunt with Dad, he taught me how to recognise the noises animals make. We were marvellous stalkers and could find prey in no time.

Now that I know why he was that way, I want to bleach those memories out of my head.

There's something uneven about the sound coming from the bushes. It's a bit like…hesitation.

Sure, it could be an animal, but an animal's frantic movements would follow a pattern. If it were scared, it would've run by now. This one isn't running. It's more like he's…stalking. Similar to when Dad and I used to do it in the past. If anything, he's getting closer.

A shadow passes between the trees at lightning speed. I step back, my old sneakers crunching against the pebbles.

It can't be the police since they would've already caught me for trespassing on a crime scene. Or worse, sent me back to the Witness Protection Program, where I heard the officers discussing me in an unfavourable way.

I don't trust them.

I trust no one. Just like Dad always insisted I shouldn't. It's ironic that I've come back to his words now.

This leaves only a couple of other possibilities. The most probable one is that it could be a victim's family member. Or maybe one of the many people who sympathised with the victims and made the trial period a nightmare.

I inhale deeply and slowly, letting my ears capture their movements. They're behind the tree. But the thing is, my ears aren't reliable with the amount of ringing in them.

Wait. Could I be imagining the noises?

For months, I don't remember sleeping a full night. One, I've been scared they'll attack me in my sleep. Two, whenever I close my lids, all I can see are the victims' faces, duct tape, vacant eyes, and blood.

So much blood.

Sleep deprivation toys with the brain. Sometimes, I worry that either Dad or the families will come after me.

Tonight, it could be the latter.

I aim the flashlight in the direction of the trees where I suspect the shadow is lurking. "Who are you?"

No answer.

"If you want to take a jab at me, come out. You're neither the first nor the last." I'm proud of how my words are steady and confident.

I'm sure as shit not confident right now.

Those people and the hatred in their eyes frighten me. I always feel as if they want my head on a stick or wish I was buried six feet under like those victims.

"I'm here!" My voice rises. "I'm over here, so if you want to—"

My words cut off when the shadow runs towards me at supersonic speed.

I lift both my arms to protect my face. That's what they go for the most—the face. It's as if they want to erase anything that resembles *his* face. Mainly the eyes. The fact that I have my father's eyes has made me a monster just like him.

Something crunches against my ribcage. At first, I stare with stupefaction, expression frozen, not sure what's happened.

Then pain explodes in my side and hot liquid spills from me, soaking my coat, and when I look up, I see the shadowy form of a masked man snatching a knife away. A trail of blood flows from the wound and drips onto the dark ground. The dim glow from my flashlight turns the view gruesome, haunting even. The blood is nearly black—like a demon's.

Unable to carry my weight, my legs stumble and I twist my foot as pain spreads across my nerve endings and shoots straight to my brain.

Then I'm falling.

To keep myself from going down, my fingers dig into his mask and I pull, my nails scratching his skin.

I make out a tattoo on the side of his bald head. A dragon.

He hits my hand, and the flashlight slips from my trembling fingers. I follow soon after. My energy fails me and I drop backwards.

Straight into the eighth grave.

My head hits the dirt, and a metallic taste fills my mouth before blood gurgles out from it.

The dark shadow stands over my grave, the light from the flashlight forming a halo around him. His black-gloved hands rest over each other, the blood on the knife he still holds glinting under the moonlight.

He's watching me so intently, as if he's my father and I'm one of the victims he suffocated to death. He doesn't move, doesn't make a sound. He just…watches.

My eyes roll back, slowly closing. The last words I hear are Dad's.

When I see you again, either I kill you or you kill me.

FIVE

Jonathan

AURORA IS BACK IN HER OLD HOUSE.
  Not her flat, but the fucking place she escaped from as a teen to have her rebirth.

Fuck.

It takes us an hour to fly with my private jet from London Heathrow to Leeds Bradford Airport. An hour I don't fucking have to spare. And currently, Moses is driving us straight to that house, which is taking another thirty minutes I don't have.

Why would she come here, of all places? If this is a ploy to escape me, then she doesn't know who she's dealing with. She must've felt like she had some leeway just because she's spent a couple of months with me.

The fact that I claimed her as mine means something simple—she's not allowed to disappear.

Not even if it's to face her ghosts.

That part still doesn't make sense. Considering the way she completely cut herself out of Maxim's life, she shouldn't have returned here willingly.

It's like she's gutting herself by her own hands.

I know for a fact that she gave up ownership of her house in Leeds, so why the fuck would she come back?

Loosening my tie, I pull my phone, then dial Harris. "What else do you have on her from the time she dropped out of the Witness Protection Program?"

That period of her life is still a blur and I need to find out everything there is to learn about it. If she's keeping it under wraps, something important happened. Something she likes to keep between her and herself.

But here's the thing, she's not allowed to hide anything from me, including her demons.

Harris's unaffected tone comes over the line, "I told you, she forged an identity and her age and then flew to Scotland."

"What happened exactly between the end of the trials and Scotland? There's time that's unaccounted for. A week to be exact."

"It's…" He seems to check something. "Unknown."

"So make it known, Harris. I need a report of her every movement from back then." The fact that she even managed to forge an identity and make herself eighteen is already impressive for a girl that age. And not just any girl—a sheltered one. She didn't live in the streets or have a hard life prior to Maxim's arrest, so that survival instinct wouldn't have come easily for someone with her background.

But something tells me that's not all she's been through.

And I need to know everything about her—the nitty-gritty, the good, the bad.

Every. Fucking. Thing.

"Hold on." There's a flipping of papers from his side. "She was caught on a pharmacy's security camera near Bradford a few days before her trip to Scotland."

"Send me the footage."

I hang up, and almost immediately, my screen lights up with a video from Harris.

The black and white footage shows a girl dressed in a dark

hoodie, her hair sticking out from a baseball cap that's covering half her face. However, I recognise her, even though she's hiding.

She's holding her side and slightly leaning over so that the counter will carry her weight. When a female employee addresses her, Aurora tells her something.

Since there's no audio, I wait to see what she ordered. The employee returns and places some items on the counter. Pausing the video, I zoom in. Bandages, a bottle of antiseptic, and what looks like antibiotics.

I hit Play again, and my suspicions are confirmed when Aurora shoves a note across the counter with shaky hands and practically jogs out of there, still holding her side. Then, at the entrance, she stops and clutches the door for balance.

She remains there for a few seconds, her back bowing and her hand wrapping around her middle, before she raises her head and leaves the pharmacy. The video stops with her holding the door for an elderly woman. Part of Aurora's face is caught on camera and her lips are…bloodied.

She was hurt, and if my calculations are correct, she's clutching the same part of her right side where there's the knife scar and the closed eye tattoo.

The injury was from back then, from when she was fucking sixteen. Aurora was stabbed and she had to self-medicate and probably suture herself. That's why the scar is a bit messy.

The sense of pride I feel for her strength is doused by the need to ruin the fucker who dared put his hands on her.

So what if she's Maxim's daughter? She's not him. It's a fact I apparently need to incinerate into people's minds in the hardest way.

The car slows to a halt, pebbles crunching under the tyres in front of the crime scene. This is the cottage where Maxim used to suffocate women with duct tape, before Aurora reported him.

The night's air is chilly and seeps underneath my suit when I step out. Moses follows, holding a flashlight. His other hand is at the gun in his waistband.

He's an ex-intelligence agent and works as both my driver and security, if needed. For all these years, he's been efficient in warding off unwanted attention, and I'm counting on his skills in case something happens.

There are only two people I trust—Harris and Moses. It didn't happen arbitrarily, because I'm naturally distrustful. I tested their loyalty with underhanded methods more than once. I made them offers through my business associates and gave them the chance to stab me in the back and leave, but they never took it. That's why they've been with me the longest.

I push at the door of the cottage and a rotten smell hits me in the face. When Moses directs the light inside, we see the corpses of a rat and a rabbit, decayed and almost unrecognisable, their guts spilling out.

Since Aurora isn't there, I motion at Moses to follow me behind the cottage to where the burial happened.

The first thing I make out is a black shadow leaning over a hole in the ground. Upon seeing the light, he jumps and sprints in the direction of the woods.

"Follow him!" I bark at Moses.

He springs into action, his legs racing after the shadow.

I turn on my phone's flashlight and quicken my pace to the hole he was perched over. My extra sense kicks into gear, and I know, I just know something is wrong.

Sure enough, the sight I find in the hole makes me pause, my chest constricting.

Aurora is splayed on her back in the grave, her legs and arms lolling in awkward positions.

Her pink dress is bunched at the middle of her thighs, covered with dirt and...blood.

It's all over her clothes and her translucent skin. Her knees are scraped, her palms are bleeding, and her lip is busted.

Her eyes are closed too tightly, as if she's enduring the pain.

Fuck!

Fucking fuck!

If I'd known she would pull this, I would've had security follow her at all times.

Leaving the phone on the edge, I hop down to the grave and cradle her head in my hands. Dirt and dry blood smudges the soft skin of her face.

Aurora's body jerks in my hold and she starts scratching, clawing, and pushing me away.

Fuck me. Even unconscious, this woman has the strength of a warrior. She can protect herself, and she can do it so well. But that doesn't stop me from wanting to take all the pain away so no one dares come near her again.

So that she doesn't need protection anymore.

"I...am...s-sorry..." she mumbles. "S-so s-sorry... Don't...h-hurt me... Don't..."

"No one will hurt you anymore, Aurora. Not on my fucking watch." I run my finger on the cut in her lip. The fact that she's marked in this brutal way sits wrong with me.

Sits wrong? That's an understatement. The fury that pulses inside me is like a beast with no restraints.

I want to bring hell on the world that had her apologise for things she didn't fucking do. I want to eradicate the people who judged her without knowing her story.

She was sixteen. Just fucking sixteen, yet she abandoned the only family she had because she believes in justice above anything else.

No one, and I mean, no *fucking* one is allowed to treat her as if she's the perpetrator in this.

Moses returns alone, his brows scrunching. "I lost him, sir. He...seems well aware of the area."

I pick Aurora up and she whimpers, lips trembling. She must be having another nightmare. That's when she's most vulnerable and her walls crumble one after the other. When she's had them while sleeping in my arms, she's held on to me, her nails digging in my chest as if searching for an anchor she never had.

The fact that she's been a loner her entire life is so similar to me. The only difference is that I used it to rise up, while she had to run. She's had to suffer in silence, including during her sleep.

Soon enough, I'll make all her nightmares vanish, even if it's the last thing I do.

"Call Harris," I tell Moses. "We need to arrange an underground meeting."

If the fucker who attacked her today—which I assume is the same person who stabbed her eleven years ago—thinks he can escape me, he has no idea who he's up against.

He can fool fate itself, but he can never fool me.

I'll find the scum who did this to her, and I'll enjoy ending his life in the slowest way possible.

Aurora is mine, and I'll bring chaos to the world to protect what's fucking mine.

SIX

Aurora

MEATY FINGERS WRAP AROUND MY WAIST AND DRAG ME across the dirt. The black, merciless dirt.

It's my turn now.

I'm going to die today.

But…why? What have I done?

I try to struggle, to squirm, to scream, but not one muscle in my body moves. I'm trapped in my own skin where no sound comes out.

As the dragging continues, my head bumps against the hard ground.

He's here.

It doesn't matter that I can't see him. I know without a doubt that he's returned for me, and this time, he won't let me go. This time, I'm absolutely done for.

"Aurora…"

That voice.

My muscles relax into the dirt as it filters through my ears. It's not Dad's. It's…someone else's.

Someone I shouldn't be thinking about, but the remainder of my energy is rushing to the surface so that I can recognise him.

There's something about that voice. His presence and his entire aura.

Is he an illusion?

My shoulders shake. "Aurora!"

I startle into the clutches of wakefulness. My eyes snap open, and for a moment, I'm frozen in place. I'm in that grave, and now, I'll be buried alive. I'll be...

My eyes meet the steel-like gaze that I've grown used to in the last couple of months. Its grey is harsher and non-negotiable right now, only it doesn't seem to be directed at me.

Jonathan runs his fingers through my hair, stroking it back, and I almost want to purr like a kitten.

I'm not in that grave. I'm not anywhere near it. There's no black shadow after my life.

It's...over.

The sense of relief hits me like a soothing wave and I fight the urge to close my eyes and sink into the feel of Jonathan's touch.

It's comforting and gentle, and I know for a fact that tenderness isn't his thing at all, so I should soak in this moment as much as I can.

As I relax into the familiar mattress of my bed, I take in the rest of my room—the soft curtains and the large lamp on the side table. I try not to think much about the fact that he brought me to my room, not his. After all, he needs a punishment to let me step in there.

"Are you okay?" he asks in that no-nonsense tone of his. It takes everything in me not to scoff. Only Jonathan would ask if you're okay while being authoritative.

Still not finding my voice, I nod.

"You don't look okay." The stroking stops, and I groan before I can catch myself.

Jonathan is sitting on my bed, his large body looming over my small one, both like a comfort and a threat. The mixed signals give me whiplash, but I don't get to think about it as he retrieves a small first aid kit from the bedside table.

He touches his finger to my mouth and I wince as his skin connects with my cut. "I covered the scrapes on your knee and palms. I was going to apply ointment on your lip when you woke up."

Sure enough, my palms have small bandages on them. Since the covers are pulled up to my neck, I take a peek under them. The first thing I notice, along with the bandage on my knee, is that I'm dressed in a nightgown.

"Did you...did you dress me?" My voice is a bit hoarse, a bit weak, but it's nothing I wouldn't have expected.

"Who else would have?" His expression is unchangeable as he applies the ointment on a cotton bud. "It's not anything I haven't seen before."

I clamp my lips shut before I start arguing that I was unconscious, and I hate that I wasn't awake to watch how he stripped me.

Damn it. There's definitely something wrong with me.

Jonathan glides the ointment on my cut lip and I grimace at the sting of pain. Yet I stay completely still, afraid that any unwanted movement would ruin this moment.

Seeing Jonathan's gentle side always strikes me deep. It's like witnessing a passing unicorn and I need to soak it in. Maybe next time, I can film it and watch it secretly or something.

After he's done, he traces his fingertips beneath the cut, so he's almost touching my lips, but not really. I suck in a breath as goosebumps start a war on my skin, beneath the covers and under my clothes.

He retracts his hand faster than I want and organises the ointment and cotton back into the first aid kit. The sensation is weird. Not being touched by him, I mean.

Not that I've ever gotten used to being touched, but since he barged into my world, I've started to take it as a given. It feels weird that he's beside me, his woodsy, spicy masculine scent enveloping me, but he's not touching me.

I want to grab his hand and place it on my face again, or go back to sleep with that same hand around my waist.

However, there's something at the back of my head that stops me. No idea what—it seems as if I'm missing something.

But what?

"Now." He lifts his head, his merciless gaze zeroing in on me and holding me like a vice. "Tell me why the fuck you returned to Leeds."

My lips tremble as the memories strike me in the hollow place of my heart.

The interview. Sarah's attack. Alicia's message...

My eyes widen as I stare at Jonathan with what I'm sure appears to be a horrified expression.

Jonathan has been poisoning me, Claire.

I jump up to a sitting position, and my shoulders hit the headboard as I draw my knees up and pull the sheet to my neck. I'm about ready to do anything to put some distance between me and him.

Oh, God.

That's why I left. That's why I shouldn't have been found. Even the attack pales in comparison to the man sitting on my bed. The man whom I willingly gave my body to and was in the process of giving more than that. I fucking bargained for inserting myself into his armour.

At least the attack was straightforward. The black shadow was someone who felt wronged by my father and took it out on me.

This, though?

This man was giving me safety signals, and no matter how fucked up and wrong it felt, I started to believe in Jonathan King. I even started to believe that I could somehow unlock his emotional vault.

How naïve could I have been?

He killed my sister.

The realisation hits me like a thunderstorm, like that day I fell to my knees in the middle of the road, struggling to breathe through my tears.

But this time, I don't bother to look up and ask for all of this to end. It won't.

This is the reality I have to face. The fact that the man I've been giving myself to every day is my sister's killer.

What's stopping him from killing you, too?

A shudder snaps my shoulders together, and perspiration covers my skin, causing the nightgown to glue to my flesh.

"What is wrong with you?" Jonathan's brow creases. His beautiful face twisting in disapproval. That face is the devil's. Just like Dad's.

"N-nothing." If he knows what's going on in my head, he'll finish me off sooner rather than later. I need to be as smart about my survival as I always have.

"It doesn't look like nothing, Aurora."

"It is."

He grips me by the ankle and I yelp when I fall, my back meeting the soft mattress. I'm splayed in front of his savage eyes as he plants a hand at the side of my face and speaks in a low, chilling tone, "Better opponents have tried to fool me, and it's always failed. So how about you tell me why the fuck you scooted away from me just now?"

The need to fight him pulses into me like second nature. The survival instinct that's been my modus operandi since I was sixteen claws its way to the surface. However, I don't act on it for two simple reasons. One: Jonathan will easily overpower me. Two: I'm injured and fighting would be the dumbest move.

Smart. I have to be smart.

"I...I just need to rest."

"Try again, wild one." He sounds clipped and fierce. He knows

I'm lying to him, and honestly, I have no clue how to fool someone like Jonathan or if it's possible to do so.

All I know is that I need him the fuck away. I will not end up like Alicia. I will not let him suck the life out of me, then eventually kill me.

I escaped one of the most notorious serial killers, and I can escape him, too.

Smoothing my tone, I say, "I really just want to sleep. I'm exhausted."

His knuckles touch my forehead and I suck in a breath through my teeth and release it through my nose.

To my dismay, it's not because of fear. Far from it. My body hasn't gotten the memo that Jonathan is a real danger to my life and I need to stay the fuck away from him. My stupid skin is still tingling like it does every time he touches me. I'm still getting caught in his orbit as if it's the only place to be.

A line slowly forms between his brows. Whether it's because of worry or that he doesn't approve of my expression, I don't know. It could be both.

"You're a little warm, but the pill will take effect soon."

"W-what pill?" Oh my God. Did he already start poisoning me?

"Painkillers. The family doctor came to look at you earlier and prescribed it. He also said the bruise at the back of your head isn't serious and will eventually disappear."

Now that he's mentioned it, something tingles beneath my hair at my nape. It's from when I was hit, but I've forgotten about all of that. Compared to the real danger hovering over me, that one doesn't even register.

Is it sad that I consider an attack less dangerous than this situation? Probably, but my brain has been trained for survival, so immediate danger always gets my attention first.

"Can I sleep? It must be late, right?"

"Three in the morning."

"You brought the doctor over this late?"

"It's his job, and he knew my demands when he agreed to become the family doctor."

"Is there anyone you consider a human instead of something you buy?" I don't know why I asked the question when my main focus should be to get him the hell out of here.

"You." The word, although calmly spoken, sets every part of me on fire. Not only my cheeks and my chest, but also the thing that's thumping loudly inside said chest.

"You already bought me," I murmur.

"That's what I thought, too. Turns out, it's far from the truth." He straightens, and I hate how I mourn the loss of his proximity and the way I cling to his airy, sensual scent.

It'll all go away with time. I have to believe that.

"Go to sleep." His voice is soothing, warm. Probably the warmest I've heard from him. "I'll be here."

"No, you don't have to—"

"I'll stay. No negotiations," he cuts me off. "Besides, you *will* tell me why the fuck you went back there."

"I just want to be alone."

"We all know what happened the last time you were left alone, so the answer to that is no." His features harden, darkening by the second. He shoves a hand in his pocket and when he speaks again, his voice is on the verge of breaking all hell loose, "The thought of what that fucker could've done if we hadn't come in time…"

He trails off as if the words fail him to describe that possibility.

A shiver grabs me by the throat at the thought of what could've happened. Would I even be sleeping here if that black shadow had gotten what it wanted? They tried to bury me alive in the past, so maybe they wanted to finish what they started this time.

Jonathan drops onto the chair. "I'm staying."

Shit.

He really is, and I really need to go. I don't know where, but I'll figure it out as soon as I'm out of here.

I always do.

My mind goes into overdrive trying to think of ways to get him to leave. Water and a covered bowl of what I assume is soup sit on the bedside table, so I can't ask for either of those.

Think, Aurora, think!

"My pillow," I blurt.

Jonathan is still watching me with that unnerving focus that makes me feel like I'm under a researcher's microscope. "What's wrong with your pillow?"

"I want the one from your room. This one isn't soft."

"You used to sleep on it just fine."

"That was a long time ago. I'm not used to it anymore." Then I speak in a slightly bratty tone, going for the low blow, "My head hurts."

That works.

He stands, but instead of leaving, he leans over and brushes his lips against my forehead. A shock wave grips my limbs and it takes everything in me not to melt. That's...that's the first time he's ever done something like that.

There's an unrivalled intimacy about a forehead kiss—the feeling of his lips on my skin, the care in it.

God. Why is he doing that now of all times?

"I'm glad I was there before you were hurt badly. Doesn't mean I'm letting it go, though." He straightens, expression blank. "I'll be right back."

I watch his retreating form, even after the door closes behind him. The skin where he kissed me still tingles, burning and sending me all the wrong signals.

Shaking my head, I jump up. The world starts tilting, but I plant my feet wide apart until the dizziness slowly retreats.

I don't have time to waste. Jonathan will return soon, and I can't be around when he does.

Since the door doesn't have a lock, courtesy of the tyrant, I push the coffee table against it. My palms sting and blood soaks the bandages, but I don't stop until it's firmly fixed against the door.

I shove my feet into the first pair of shoes I see and quickly make a rope out of any sheets I can find.

Using the front door is out. Jonathan is the type of freak who has cameras in the hallways, and since I'm sure there's someone who's watching them at all times, there's no doubt they'll catch me.

My balcony, however, overlooks the garden from where the staff's back entrance is visible. During my snooping sessions, I didn't find any blinking cameras around here.

After securing the rope to the foot of the bed and testing that it can carry my weight, I throw it down. It doesn't reach the ground, but it's close enough. I'll take anything that shortens the distance of my fall.

This isn't the first time I've done this. I escaped this way from many motels in Scotland. Oftentimes, I had no money to pay for the night, and there was no way in hell I was going to sleep on the streets or in parks where anyone could find and attack me.

After I grew up, I sent those motels cheques, but at the time, jumping from second and third floors were part of my everyday life. I'm a bit out of practice, but I can make it.

The doorknob moves, and I stiffen.

He's back.

Not that I didn't suspect he would be, but shit, it's too soon. I have to do it now.

"Aurora. Open up!" His voice booms from the other side and then a bang sounds at the door from his attempt to shove it open.

My spine snaps upright as if it's about to break.

It's now or never.

I grab the end of the rope and just like that, I jump.

My hands and legs wrap around the sheet in a lethal grip as I slowly slip towards the ground. I don't look down, because that will fill me with fear worse than what's already whirling inside me.

It takes me longer than I'm used to in my mission to slide down the rope. Part because Jonathan's freaking mansion is too high and part because it's been a long time since I last did this.

My palms scream in pain, blood soaks the sheets, and my knees burn as the early morning cold air hits me in my bones.

By the time I reach the end of the sheets, my legs dangling down and my hands gripping it tightly, I know I have no choice but to jump.

It's a steep one, and my legs will fucking hurt. But if I do it right, I won't break any bones. *Hopefully.*

Though a broken bone would be worth it if it means I'll be out of here.

Inhaling a deep breath, I close my eyes and let go.

This is it.

I'm free and alive and no one will take those from me.

I've fought so, *so* hard to get here, and if I can make it here, I can make it anywhere.

Then, instead of feeling the sharp sting of my legs hitting the ground, I'm enveloped in steel-like arms.

The sense of failure seeps straight under my ribcage and squeezes my heart.

My breathing hitches as I meet Jonathan's raging grey eyes. "Fascinating, Aurora. Fascinating indeed."

SEVEN

Aurora

F OR THE FIRST TIME IN MY LIFE, MY ESCAPE PLAN FAILS BEFORE it even starts.

As I stare at the fury emanating off Jonathan's features, I know, I just *know* that there's no way in hell I'll ever be able to escape.

I'll end up like Alicia.

Roaming the halls. Hallucinating. Poisoned.

Dead.

A rush of life shoots through my bubbling veins and I push at his chest with my bloodied palms, my limbs flailing about. I'm acting straight out of irrational anger and the need to stay alive. Gone is my logical, strategic side—it was killed when I didn't hit the ground and fell back into Jonathan's cage. "Let me go!"

My fight is futile. It's like he doesn't feel my fists against his shirt or my scratches against the skin of his collarbone. It's almost as if he's waiting for my fit of anger to subside and for me to go slack.

I don't.

I squirm and wiggle and push and punch. I use every trick under the sun to get away from his merciless grip.

The silent treatment greets me as he walks me back to the house. No, no...

My energy heightens and I kick my feet in the air in an attempt to make him loosen his hold.

All I get is a harsh squeeze on my outer thigh. *Ouch.*

We pass the statue of the Virgin Mary carrying the little angel as they both cry, and a scary sense of foreboding goes through me.

A realisation, too.

That statue represented Alicia's life in the King mansion. She was crying and no one saw her. She suffered and no one helped her.

If anything, her husband and life companion poisoned her. He killed her.

He *killed* my sister.

Angry tears fill my eyes as I elbow and claw at his side. I know it won't get me anywhere with his strength, but as long as I can breathe, I'll fight.

I'm a fighter. A survivor. I've come this far, and I won't allow Jonathan to dictate my end.

It doesn't matter that my palms keep bleeding. The sting and the burn will eventually go away once I'm out of here.

Margot appears at the entrance, wearing a long nightgown. She must've gotten out of bed due to the commotion.

"Help me, Margot! Help!" I scream at the top of my lungs.

She opens her mouth, then closes it while she watches the scene like it's out of a freak show. I'm struggling in Jonathan's hold while his face is stone-cold as if it's made of fucking granite.

"Sir...?" she asks, almost uncertain.

"Go back to sleep, Margot," he tells her in a firm tone that accepts no negotiations, his attention focused ahead.

"No!" I squirm. "Nooo!"

I stare behind me at Margot, hoping against all hope that she'll follow and somehow help me out of the tyrant's clutches.

She's not there.

No one is.

It's only me and him.

By the time we reach my room, my energy has waned, but that doesn't make me stop. I *can't* stop. If I do, that means I'm admitting defeat, and I would never do that.

I hate how easily Jonathan overpowers me with a squeeze of his big hand around my thigh or arm. I hate that I'm so small in comparison to his frame.

I hate *him*.

I hate him so much, not only because of what happened to Alicia, but because I was about to instil my trust in him.

I was fucking falling for him, and for what? For this betrayal. For this…desolation.

It's like my feelings are trapped in a state of hyperawareness and it's almost impossible to sort through them.

All I know is that I need to leave. *Now.*

"Are you done?" he asks in that closed-off tone of his. His features are blank and the lack of reaction, the fact that I can't read past his façade, is more frightening than if he'd lashed out at me.

Jonathan isn't a man to be taken lightly, and to be caught under his thumb means danger. However, that doesn't stop my innate need to run.

"I'll never be done. Lock me up again and I'll try to escape until I finally do it." I punch him one more time for good measure.

He places me on the bed and I scramble away like an injured animal.

In fact, I am.

The bandages covering my palms are soaked in blood. My knees and lip sting, and the back of my head throbs.

However, that's nothing compared to being stabbed, crawling out of the grave, and suturing myself.

If I could endure that, then I can endure this.

Jonathan stands in front of the bed, both hands in his pockets, appearing like a warlord sampling his prisoner of war. There are a few scratch marks on his neck and collarbone, and blood stains on his light blue shirt.

I try to hold on to my hate for him, but I don't like inflicting pain on others. That's so similar to my dad, and I promised myself to never be like Dad.

No.

I'm only defending myself like any injured animal trying to escape. It's only natural that I'd scratch, bite, and claw.

Jonathan stares down his arrogant nose at me. The storm brewing in his grey gaze is a force not to be reckoned with. "Measures are already in place, so you will not be able to escape, and even if you do, I'll find you in no time, Aurora. Now, why don't you stop fucking around and tell me what's with the show you're putting on."

I lift my chin, refusing to answer.

"You won't talk? Is that it?" Jonathan lowers his knees to the bed, dipping the mattress.

I hold my ground, meeting his unfeeling eyes with all the bitterness and hate in mine.

His knees are on either side of my legs as he cages me in and lifts my chin with two lean fingers, trapping me with his savage eyes.

At a naïve moment, I imagined that I was seeing myself in those eyes. That's far from accurate.

There's no way I'd be able to. His gaze is bland, lifeless, and only filled with the purpose to hurt or to be obeyed.

Or both.

His philosophy is that he'll hurt whoever doesn't obey him. That he'll make them disappear as if they never existed.

Is that what happened to Alicia?

Despite my attempts to regulate my breathing, it's chopped off and I'm straight out panting as if I've just returned from a hike.

"What was that stunt all about, Aurora?"

"I want to go out," I blurt.

"Go out where?"

"I want to go to visit Layla."

"At three in the morning dressed like that?"

I stare down at myself and realise I'm only wearing a thin nightgown that outlines my breasts and stops above my knees. I hadn't thought about that earlier, but now, I'm starting to feel self-conscious. It takes all I have to speak in a semi-neutral tone, "She's a night owl. She wouldn't mind."

"Try again."

"Just let me go, Jonathan!"

"That's not how it works. You live here, and that includes abiding by my rules. That means, no jumping from the second fucking floor when you're injured. In fact, even if you aren't. That nonsense won't happen again."

The anger in his tone lands on my skin like whips. It's even more painful than his clutch on my jaw.

He releases me and I suck in big gulps of air. It doesn't last long as he pulls the first aid kit and undoes my palm bandages. I wince when the bloodied cloth is ripped off my skin. Despite his lethal expression, he's not harsh about it, but the flesh is cut deeper than I anticipated.

"Were you even fucking thinking?" He examines my palms with disapproval as he soaks them with the disinfectant.

The sting makes me sink my teeth into the cushion of my bottom lip and I inhale through my nose until they're finally clean. There are a few cuts positioned both diagonally and horizontally.

Jonathan wraps new bandages around the wounds and I stare at him from beneath my lashes, my body tightening for the next fight-or-flight mode.

I've had too many rushes of adrenaline for one day. I feel like I'm going to collapse from the force of them.

But it's not like I can order my body to shut down. Survival has always been my natural gift.

After he's finished with my palms, he checks my knee. Seeming satisfied with the bandage, he leaves it alone and pushes the box away. However, he remains looming over me like a threat, his brows still drawn together, and his expression is that of destruction.

It's like when I first re-met him. When I didn't trust him. Why the hell did I think I could trust him?

"What's going on, Aurora?"

"Nothing."

"You want to tell me you escaped to fucking Yorkshire, got attacked, pushed me away, then jumped by a rope made from sheets for *nothing*?"

Not finding anything to say, I purse my lips.

"I thought so," he continues, his closeness doing shit to me I'm not supposed to feel right now. Why the hell do I keep inhaling him in?

And why on earth do I want to erase those scratch marks on his neck? He deserved them.

Right?

He grabs my jaw, nearly swallowing it in the palm of his hand. "Here's how it'll go, Aurora. You'll tell me the truth, and I'll decide how to deal with you afterwards."

I clamp my mouth shut.

"Last chance." His fingers dig into my cheeks. "You won't like how I'll react if you keep this tantrum up."

"The only truth you need to know is that I hate you."

"Wrong answer." He releases me with a shove and I fall back on to my elbows.

My heart hammers at the dark promise in his voice, and I hold my breath, waiting for his next move.

Is he going to punish me?

Spank me?

I hate how my thighs throb at that thought. Screw that and screw him. I'm getting out of here the first chance I get.

It may take me a day or two, or however long it does, but it's not like Jonathan will remain by my side for eternity.

He's a workaholic. Come morning, I have no doubt he'll piss off to screw more lives over. That will be my chance to escape.

Jonathan stands in front of my bed, his monster mask back on as he slips a hand in his pocket. "You'll remain in this room until you talk."

"W-what?"

"You're the one who'll choose if it'll be hours, days, or weeks." He tilts his head to the side. "Or even months."

"You can't lock me in. That's kidnapping!"

"If that's what you want to label it." He turns to leave but stops and throws over his shoulder, "And don't try to jump from the balcony again. I have my security surrounding the perimeter."

"You can't keep me here, Jonathan!"

"Then fucking talk." His threatening tone slams into me and remains behind him as the door closes.

That's when I hear it. The sound of my freedom being stripped away.

The sound of a lock.

Shit. Fuck.

I run to the door and test the doorknob, and sure enough, it's locked.

After kicking it, I jog over to the balcony where the sheet rope is still hanging, and sure enough, two buff men dressed in black stand there.

My legs fail me, and I slip to a sitting position. Two realisations hit me at once.

One. I failed the only escape I could've had from here, because now that Jonathan knows of my intentions, he'll make sure I never have the chance to repeat it.

Two. I have a weird sensation that I'm reliving Alicia's fate all over again.

EIGHT

Aurora

I DON'T SLEEP FOR THE ENTIRE NIGHT.

I can't.

It's like I've been pushed back to eleven years ago, to those safe houses and in police custody. My body is scratched and my existence is humiliated.

Back then, I couldn't sleep much, and now, it's the same.

Survival is a bitch.

The moment it kicks in, all your brain is attuned to is the need to appease it. To fucking survive.

The game I prayed to never play again is back, and this time, I can't drop out of the Witness Protection Program or forge a new identity.

I'm stuck in a gilded cage, and if I stay here for more, my fate will be just like that of Alicia's.

That's the only thought my brain is able to conjure up. That if I don't get out of here, I'll die.

I spend the long dawn and early morning hours searching around the room for a way out.

My phone isn't here; I lost it somewhere. The landline is busy, which means Jonathan must've suspended it. I left my laptop in the car, so that's out.

Every now and then, I spy on the buff blokes through the window in case they change position and I get a chance to escape.

They don't. Both remain standing there as statues.

Not that I expected less from Jonathan's level of control freak.

Around eight in the morning, I'm in my wardrobe, searching for something, a modern device or anything I can use to call for help.

The door opens and I startle, my injured knee hitting the wood panel. I wince, using my other leg to stand upright and bending the hurt one.

Jonathan waltzes inside, carrying a tray of food and wearing his impeccable suit as if this is an ordinary morning.

I can't help feeling relief at how his shirt is clean, not smudged with blood like earlier. It hides most of the scratches, but there's a long one that peeks from the edge of his collar.

I swallow at the view. It's reddened compared to when I last saw it. Not that I should be sorry. He's the one keeping me against my will.

"You haven't slept." He places the tray on my makeup console, flips over the coffee table I used to block the door during my failed escape, then slides the plate across it.

"Do you have a camera in here, or something?" I study the corners of the room because I wouldn't be surprised if he does.

"Not currently, no. But that's a good idea."

Damn it, there I go putting ideas in his messed up head. I bite my tongue to stop from spouting nonsense. That will only give him the upper hand more than he already has.

"Sit down." He motions at the sofa with a tilt of his arrogant nose. "Eat."

"No."

"Do you want me to shove the food down your throat, is that it?"

"I want you to let me go."

"Are you going to sit the fuck down and eat, or will I have to do it?"

I jut my chin and realise my mistake too late. Jonathan reaches me in a few long strides and throws me over his shoulder as if I'm a sack of potatoes. A squeal rips from me as my world tips upside down, my hair falling to his thigh-level. Blood rushes to my head from this position, and I hit his back over and over, ignoring how my palms sting.

"Stop that or it'll reopen your wounds."

"Then let me go." I hit him some more.

Slap.

I freeze as fire erupts in my arse. My thighs clench, and I can feel the wetness coating my knickers.

Shit. Fuck. *No.*

This can't be happening. Why the hell am I still turned on by this? I shouldn't be. He...he's going to hurt me, to kill me. Like he did with my sister.

However, a part of my brain is numbed to that fact as if it doesn't exist. A part of my brain horrifies me because that idiot doesn't think Jonathan would ever hurt me.

That part felt no threat when Jonathan walked into the room. If anything, it was something completely different that I don't like to name.

"There. Good girl, though you're not acting like it lately." He slowly drops me on the sofa and I scoot to the edge, pulling the nightgown down, nearly ripping the straps.

Jonathan's head tilts to the side, eyes devouring my chest in that purely lustful way. "I like the view."

I stare down in horror and sure enough, in my attempt to cover my legs, I exposed my breasts and a hard rosy nipple peeks through. I let the cloth snap back into place and glare at Jonathan, who seems…slightly disappointed.

The moment ends when he points at the food.

"No."

"You haven't eaten since yesterday."

My stomach growls as if agreeing with his statement. I ignore it and the embarrassment that comes with it.

"I wasn't joking about shoving it down your throat, Aurora. You know I can do it, so don't make me act on it."

"You don't get to keep me against my will, then force me to eat as if I'm a prisoner, okay?"

"You're not a prisoner. You get to walk out of here any second you like if you tell me what the fuck is wrong with you since last night." His voice turns lethal with every word and I know that he's losing his patience.

Jonathan and patience aren't on the best of terms, even on good days, let alone on bad ones. He's used to getting what he wants with a snap of his fingers and now that he isn't, he'll get more ruthless with every moment I remain silent.

But on the other hand, if I tell him about the message Alicia sent me, I'm never getting out. That's like accusing him of murder, and someone like Jonathan won't let anyone throw something like that around. He'll smother it in no time.

Forget about the six-month deal. He'll have me follow my sister as soon as he deems necessary.

"So what's it going to be?" he asks with that sharp tone.

I stare at him, bemused.

"The food, Aurora. Are you going to eat or should we go with my plan?"

I glare at him as I grab a piece of toast. If I'm going to get out of here, I'll need every bit of my energy, so I won't refuse the food that's able to give me strength.

My palm stings when I close it around the bread and I flex it a little to alleviate the pain.

Jonathan seems to notice that, too. He sits beside me, and I attempt to scoot away, but I'm already at the edge. His thigh touches mine, and I try to ignore the warmth or the woodsy scent emanating from him like it's his second skin.

He takes the toast from between my fingers, puts butter on it like I usually do, then brings it to my mouth. I try to snatch it back, but he keeps it out of reach.

"I can eat on my own."

"Not after you injured your palms and reopened the wounds."

"But—"

"Stop being fucking stubborn. Open that mouth and eat."

I purse my lips, once again feeling like a child being reprimanded. It's the damn authoritative tone, I swear. The way he lashes it out with that firmness has always gotten to me.

Deciding to pick my battles, I slowly open and take a tentative bite of the toast to not trigger the cut on my lip. Jonathan also detects that fact since he places it back on the plate.

God. Is there anything this man doesn't notice? He's so attuned to details, it's insane.

He uses the knife to cut it into small pieces, but he doesn't use the fork to feed me. No, he goes with his bare hands. Every time he slips something in my mouth, his lean, masculine fingers scrape against my skin, and a shiver overtakes me.

It's like we're back to the days when we used to have breakfast together as he wrenched one orgasm out of me after another.

I hate that I'm thinking about it.

I hate that it feels weird to not sit on his lap like usual.

Snap out of it, Aurora.

The food melts in my mouth before I'm even able to chew properly. My stomach stops making sounds as Jonathan fills it with everything on the plate.

He keeps feeding me, and I keep eating. I tell myself it's to get my strength back, but each time his fingers brush against my skin, I shudder.

"Is it because of the attack?" His cool voice drifts around me like a lullaby.

What? A lullaby? Jonathan? This must be the lack of sleep talking. Jonathan and lullabies are as far apart as they could be.

I continue chewing on a piece of egg to give me an excuse to not speak. My hands lie limp on my lap as if they don't know what to do. Usually, they would be picking food while Jonathan's fingers are busy with other parts of my body.

The balance is off, and the fact that it'll never be the same again fills me with a sudden sense of grief.

"Or is it Maxim's interview?"

My blood runs cold at that, and I stop chewing for a second before resuming. Of course, Jonathan doesn't miss it.

"I assume it's both." He cocks his head to the side. "Do you think you're eligible to have another rebirth to escape this?"

I clamp my lips shut.

"You cannot have a rebirth when you didn't finish the first one, Aurora."

My voice is calm, considering my internal mess. "What do you know about rebirths when you were born with a silver spoon hanging from your mouth?"

He scoffs. Jonathan scoffs. The entire motion is so weird that I take some time to commit it to memory. "If anyone here was born with a silver spoon, it's you, wild one. Just because that spoon was snatched from your mouth in your teens doesn't mean it wasn't always there. Maxim gave you everything you wanted, didn't he? You were his spoiled little princess."

"Stop it."

"That's why you failed your rebirth, Aurora," he continues as if I haven't said a word. "You can't be reborn if you still can't get out of his shadow."

"I am *not* in his shadow."

"It looks that way, though. What did I tell you about how he'll reappear? That he doesn't like being forgotten. Are you that surprised he's dragging you with him? It's his way to retaliate for what you did eleven years ago, and if you keep giving him leverage, he won't hesitate to use it against you."

His words have the impact of a natural disaster. Sudden and wreaking. It's not that I haven't thought of it that way before, it's that I always thought I'd escape my dad. That I don't live in the shadow he cast over my life.

That's why I changed everything we used to do together. I even dyed my hair blonde at some point, and I hate the blonde me. She was a coward and a thief who jumped from motel rooms.

"How about you?" My voice is steady but low in volume.

He pauses cutting an avocado. It's been secretly becoming my favourite new food. "Me?"

"If I keep giving you leverage, won't you also use it against me?"

"I don't want to, but I will if you force me."

"Me? Force *you*? You're the one who's forcing me right now."

"Keep your voice down."

"Or what?"

"You don't want to know the answer to that." He shoves a piece of avocado in my mouth, shutting down my protest. "And I'm not forcing you. If I did, you wouldn't have a choice, but you do."

I swallow the piece, commemorating its taste to memory. Who knows if he'll take this small luxury away? Jonathan enforces the most sadistic type of cruelty. He makes you get used to things, then snatches them away as if they never existed. "Is that what you tell yourself to sleep better at night?"

"I'm well aware of who and what I am. I don't have to delude myself, Aurora. You do."

"W-what?"

"You've been squirming and rubbing your thighs since I sat beside you. It doesn't matter how much you tell yourself you don't want me or you don't want to get out of this situation. You and I both know your body doesn't lie."

"That is not true." I'm thankful my voice doesn't betray me.

Jonathan tilts his head, and I expect him to try and prove me wrong like he always does.

Pushing my buttons and cementing his supremacy is one of his control-freak methods that he doesn't hesitate to use.

So I'm surprised when he stands. "Follow me."

"To where?"

"Do I need to throw you over my shoulder again?"

I jerk up, not wanting to feel whatever the hell I did when he spanked my arse earlier.

He steps into the bathroom, and I stop at the threshold.

"Are you waiting for an invitation?" he asks in a clipped voice, his nostrils flaring.

"Why are we here?"

He reaches into the cabinet and retrieves another first aid kit. Now that I think about it, he seems to have those everywhere. Almost like he's expecting to injure himself in every room he walks in. Which is weird, considering that Jonathan is far from being the clumsy type.

He retrieves something from the box and closes it. "You need to shower."

"I can do that on my own."

"Not with your injuries."

Before I can protest, he appears in front of me and wraps what seems like a plastic waterproof bandage around both my palms.

He then kneels and I'm momentarily stunned by the fact that Jonathan is willingly kneeling at my feet. It's a sight I never thought I'd witness in my lifetime.

His fingers strap a similar plastic thingie around my knee. I resist the urge to close my eyes as his skin lingers on mine for a second too long.

Then he runs the water in the bath, and I remain there, torn between escaping back to the room and having him chase me—and inevitably ruining whatever gentle side he's showing—and staying there.

He pours the bath product, the apple-scented one, and the smell fills the bathroom's space.

When he's satisfied with the temperature, he lets the water run. He faces me as he removes his jacket and tie, hangs them on the towel hanger, and rolls the sleeves of his shirt to above his elbows.

He's barely showing any skin, but watching him revealing his arms is like a porn show all on its own. The only reason I don't look away is because I refuse to lose my ground.

Or that's what I tell myself, anyway.

"Remove the nightgown."

I lift my chin up and don't comply. If I follow his order, it'll feel like I'm agreeing to whatever madness he's planning.

"If you want something done, do it yourself."

"What did I say about that attitude, Aurora?"

I huff, but the sound soon vanishes when he grabs the straps, his fingers gliding over my skin along with them as he lowers them down my body.

Staring at a fixed point in the bathroom, I pretend my flesh isn't tingling and my face isn't heating with the mere effect of his presence.

Soon enough, the nightgown pools at my feet. His gaze slides down my nakedness as if it's the first time he's seen me.

His fingers stroke over my scar and the tattoo, and something in his eyes and the way his lashes flutter against his cheek tells me he knows exactly how I got it.

The weight of his attention on that part of me is like reliving the time when I struggled to move from one corner to the other to get to the pharmacy, buy medicine, and suture the wound.

It was a mess, but I managed to close it. However, when it became worse, not better, I didn't have someone like him to tend to it, and I was so clueless about self-care back then.

"You closed it yourself." His thumb slides across the skin with a deceptive tenderness. "You had an infection, too. It must've hurt. You must've been feverish."

"H-how do you know that?"

"It's the same attacker, isn't it?" His attention drifts from my scar to my face.

The way he's looking at me, that focus, and the anger that... somehow doesn't seem to be directed at me, overthrows me.

I push him away and storm to the tub. In my haste to get inside and hide my scar and the tattoo, I slip.

My shriek fills the bathroom, but instead of hitting my head against the edge, I'm held steady by a strong hand.

"Easy." The tenor of his voice is that of care.

No. He shouldn't care. He *doesn't*.

I flop under the bubbles, hiding my nakedness from sight. The water is cool on my skin, not too hot and not too cold. It's the perfect temperature—as usual.

Jonathan is silent as he retrieves the apple-scented shampoo and pours it on my head.

I try to zone out, but the way his fingers glide through my hair in slow, measured strokes robs me of my breath.

He doesn't even seem bothered by the stubborn knots at the back of my head. Since my hair is long, I always have the hardest time washing it.

Yet he takes his time with the knots, one by one, until my hair falls smoothly to my back. He holds it above the water as he rinses it, then ties it at the top.

Jonathan isn't the type to show tenderness, so it's definitely not to be taken for granted when he does.

But now that he's doing this under these circumstances, I don't know how to react. Is this a ploy? A game?

He grabs the sponge and uses it to lather my body. He doesn't linger on my nipples and barely touches me between my legs. His only intent seems to be to bathe me. That's all. I'm the one who struggles not to close my thighs when his fingers trail down my stomach.

The bath is finished way too soon, and he rinses me, stands me up, then wraps me in a fresh, soft towel.

It's too harsh against my heated skin. He might've not touched me in a sexual way, but my body has already gotten the signals. My nipples are hard and pointy, and my core keeps freaking pulsing.

Stop it, damn you.

As he dries me, Jonathan takes his time running the towel against my aching nipples. I nearly topple over as I swallow the moans trying to slip through.

The spark in his eyes suggests he knows exactly what he's doing to me and is doing it on purpose.

"You'll talk, Aurora. If I have to use your body against you, I will."

NINE

Jonathan

I F YOU WANT SOMETHING DONE, YOU SHOULD GET YOUR HANDS dirty.

I don't do that—usually. I have no problem crushing people with lawful methods. I even like seeing them struggle to turn the law to their favour and fail.

The law stands with the strongest. And in this world, that's me.

However, when lawful methods don't work, it's time to go to the other side of the wall.

Harris has been coming up blank with the identity of Aurora's attacker, even by using the intel given to him by our top-notch security company.

Since the law-abiding security team didn't bring anything, I find myself at the Rhodes estate.

The duke of the house, Tristan Rhodes, has agreed to my offer, as he should, considering I gave him a discount I wouldn't present to anyone else. His family is returning to business in the near future and he needs any push he can get in the right direction.

I'm willing to enter a profitable partnership with him for what he'll give me in return.

As Moses drives down the long, undulated road, Harris watches out the window, his calculative gaze lingering on the countless security guards stationed in each corner covering almost every surface of the property. Their grim faces and the metal glinting from their sides hint at the damage they can cause if they choose to attack.

"This is like a crime lord's house, not a duke's." Harris faces me, his tablet lying on his lap for the first time in…well, ever. "Maybe we should consider other ways."

"Its similarity with a crime lord's residence is what makes it useful. I will not waste more time."

The man who fucking stabbed Aurora will be brought to his knees in front of her sooner rather than later.

Harris scrolls through his tablet. "Okay, let's go through the information we have one more time. Tristan and his cousin, Aaron Rhodes, are the only remaining members of the once-powerful Rhodes family. They spent most of their childhood and teenage years in a boarding school after a fire that wiped out the rest of their family, *but* there are rumours."

"That they were betrayed and the fire was instigated. That information is going viral in the aristocratic community. Many say that Tristan and Aaron are back for revenge."

"Correct, but I've been doing some more digging and…" He lifts his head and readjusts his glasses with his index and middle finger. "It's rumoured that they're trained in combat, which shouldn't be the case since they've never been in the military."

"Perfect. That means Tristan knows the people I need and won't waste my time."

"It means they're dangerous, sir. Doing business with them is one thing, but getting involved in their secret lives is an entirely different territory."

"If it gets me what I want, I don't mind."

"How about your principle of not taking risky decisions?"

"Risky decisions need to be made sometimes for better opportunities. Besides, Tristan is a businessman before anything else. He knows how to speak the language of profit."

The car comes to a halt, and I step out, buttoning my jacket.

This isn't the first time I've been here, but I usually come to the Rhodes estate with either guests or Ethan's unwelcome presence to conclude business deals.

A security man motions at me to go into the northern wing. There are four wings in the estate, and Tristan always welcomes his guests in this one.

The other wings sit majestically in the distance—eastern, western, and southern—forming a massive rectangular shape. Despite the effort Tristan and Aaron have spent in turning this place into what resembles a palace, there's a certain haunting quality to the Rhodes estate.

It's probably because of the fire and the number of people who lost their lives in it.

It reeks of death; I can smell it no matter how many flowers and perfumes are used to mask it.

A statue of a knight on a black horse sits majestically in the middle of the reception hall. Another statue, a black jaguar with blue gems as eyes, stares down his nose at me.

That's another weird quirk of the Rhodes'. They actually raise live jaguars as pets.

I follow the security man up the sweeping marble stairs until we reach Tristan's office. He stops, straightening as if he needs to be presentable for the task, before he knocks on the door.

"Come in," Tristan's levelled voice reaches us from the inside.

The buff man opens the door and nods at me to go in. As soon as I enter, the door closes. I have no doubt the security team member will stay in front of the office in case I pose a threat to his employer.

Not that I would. He's an ally, and I take good care of my allies.

Tristan isn't behind his large desk. He's casually sitting in the lounge area, reading from a newspaper. He's wearing a dark blue striped suit. Italian. Interesting. Nobles usually prefer English cut suits, but Tristan is an exception to his title in many ways.

He and his cousin have black hair and dark eyes that differentiates them in a crowd. Although Tristan is in his mid-thirties, he has the mind of someone much older. The most fascinating part is that he doesn't like to show it—almost as if he's living a secret life, as Harris suggested.

Upon my arrival, he neatly folds the newspaper and slides it onto the table, showcasing his family crest ring that rests on his index finger. Taking his time, he stands up and buttons his jacket. "Jonathan, welcome."

I take his hand in a firm handshake. "Your Grace."

"We're past the titles' nonsense. Tristan is enough." He motions at the chesterfield sofa across from him. "Please."

I unbutton my jacket and sit down, acutely noticing that the contact he said would be waiting for me isn't here.

"Do you want anything to drink?"

My gaze discreetly takes in my surroundings, so I commemorate details in case there's a need for an escape plan. I might consider Tristan an ally, but I never allow myself to get too comfortable. "I'll take cognac on ice."

"Excellent choice." He strides across to his minibar and pours us both a drink. And while I know he prefers scotch, he returns with two cognacs.

That's a good tactic to show how open-minded he is, and to put me at ease in return. Only, I never leave myself unprotected.

He pauses near the open balcony that's directly opposite me before he settles across from me. Well, well…

"Have I shown up early?" I take a sip of my drink.

"No, not at all. Perfect timing as usual, Jonathan." Cradling the drink in his hand, he leans his elbows on his knees. "I just thought we could talk about your needs before I put you in contact with my man."

"I need someone to be found."

His expression doesn't change, but I sense how his mind is calculating. He's a bit like me in how he masters which emotions to show and which to keep buried. "We'll need more than that. Background?"

"Not much, except that he must've lived in Leeds or North Yorkshire for a while, or he could've visited them often." After all, Moses lost all trace of him because he knew the area more than Moses did.

"How about your reason for wanting to find him?" He motions at my neck. "Does it have to do with that?"

The scratch Aurora left on my neck. It was like a cornered kitten trying to find a way out.

"Could be."

"And?"

"Is knowing the reason necessary?"

"I'm afraid, yes, Jonathan. Let's just say my man doesn't like—" he makes air quotes "—'boring' missions.

"It's related to Maxim Griffin's murders." That's all he needs to know.

Tristan raises a brow, appearing impressed. "That's certainly not boring."

"I assume you've heard about Maxim."

"Who hasn't? Let's just say he's weak for choosing helpless victims."

"I'm in." The voice reaches me before a man saunters in from the balcony. I figured someone was out there, but I thought it could be one of Tristan's endless security folk.

The man standing in front of me has a sophisticated aura about him. He's wearing a designer shirt and trousers. No jacket or tie— which means he's not a businessman but likes elegance. His hair is styled, and his features are sharp but not in a criminal kind of way, more like how models look. He's certainly not what I expected from what Tristan said about him.

According to the duke, this man was a key player in the Russian mafia in New York. What I found impressive about his background is the fact that he killed for a living for a long time and his speciality is tracking and finding.

His face is definitely not what I had in mind. I thought I would find a buff man with mean, angular features.

He's certainly not that. Moreover, he appears to be younger than Tristan, barely in his early thirties. The only thing that hints at his true nature is the sparkling in his light blue eyes. Mentioning Maxim's name is a deal sealer for him.

Killers and their need to outsmart each other is a translation of their egos. They like knowing they're the smartest and strongest alive.

It's something I'll use to my complete advantage.

"Jonathan, this is Kyle." Tristan motions at him. "An old associate of mine."

"Associate?" Kyle scoffs. His accent is standard English, but there's something in its undertone that I can't quite pinpoint. It's like he learnt to speak that way but had to shed another accent. A northerner, perhaps? Scottish? Irish? "Stop the nonsense and tell him we used to kill together."

"Kyle." Tristan glares at him.

"What?" Kyle sits beside him and snatches his drink. "I didn't know it was a secret."

"It's safe with me," I say. Not that I didn't suspect it. The Rhodes family has always given off vibes, especially Tristan's cousin, Aaron.

"It better be." Kyle takes his time to savour his drink. "Or else we'll have to…you know…shut you up with other methods."

"You're not allowed to threaten my guests, Kyle."

"I'm just putting it out there." Kyle is the type who speaks with complete nonchalance, appearing almost bored, but he knows exactly what he's doing.

Not that he rattles me. No one does.

Or more accurately, no one aside from the woman who's locked in her room because she was trying to escape.

I can't believe she attempted to fucking jump right after she was attacked. My chest constricts whenever I think of what could've happened if Moses and I had been even a few seconds too late.

Or if I hadn't been there to catch her.

The fact that she changed so suddenly has been sending my mind into overdrive. I barely slept last night. Every time I closed my eyes, her vulnerable fainted state came to mind.

It doesn't help that my bed feels empty without her. It shouldn't, but it fucking does.

Pushing that thought out of my head, I focus on Kyle. "Can you find who I'm looking for?"

"I can find anyone."

"Tristan will forward you all the information we have." I take a drink. "I want him alive."

Both Tristan and Kyle smile at that. But the sadism that shines in Kyle's eyes is nothing like I've seen before. It's almost as if he finds a sick pleasure in it. "I love it when they're alive...at first."

"What's the time frame?" I ask.

"As long as it takes. I'll be in touch when I find your guy, or girl, you never know."

"Name your price and I'll pay."

"I don't need money." He stands. "Once the mission is complete, I'll take payment in the form of a favour."

I don't like that idea. Money is more about cutting loose ends, but a favour could be anything. However, since my choices are limited, I nod.

"Perfect. Looking forward to this." He heads to the balcony. "And here I thought England was boring."

"There's a door," Tristan says in a semi-exasperated, semi-resigned tone.

"Doors are dull." And with that, Kyle jumps from the balcony.

Tristan shakes his head, then smiles at me. "You can trust Kyle with this. He's one of the best."

"I'm counting on that."

"May I ask what you intend to do with this man once you find him?"

"Make him wish he was never alive."

Because no one, and I mean no-fucking-one, touches what's mine and lives.

I reach home somewhere after seven. Harris stays at the company to send me updates about an upcoming merger.

Usually, I'd remain with him, but my attention is constantly robbed by the wild presence I left at home. Although there's security and Margot is to bring Aurora meals, I don't trust she won't do something stupid.

Aurora is not only like an injured animal. She's also trapped, and they tend to bite any chance they get.

A tiny woman in baggy clothes is shouting at the front gate guard. Layla. Of course. I knew she'd show up here and create a ruckus over her friend's disappearance.

I motion at Moses to stop, and he obeys. The front gate guard nods at me in acknowledgement.

She points a finger at herself. "*I'm* talking to you. Pay attention, or better yet, let me in."

"Not going to happen, Miss Hussaini," I speak to her through my window.

She whirls around and narrows her fierce eyes on me. "Johnny! Where's Aurora? What have you done to her?"

"Done to her? What makes you think I've done anything to her?"

"She would never skip a day at work without telling me first, and she hasn't answered my calls and texts for more than forty hours."

"That's oddly precise."

"That's because she's never done it."

"She's a bit unwell and needs rest."

"Unwell how?"

"Sick, tired, or both."

"Then tell your bloke here to let me in so I can check on her."

"I'm afraid that's not possible at the moment."

"Why not? Unless you did something to her!" She gasps. "I swear if you don't let me see her, I'm going to call the police."

"You won't be able to do anything to me, Miss Hussaini, but if you're stupid enough to call the police, I'll bring your family to the ground."

She lifts her chin. Layla is Aurora's friend, all right. "I'm not afraid of you."

"You ought to be." I let the window go up, slowly muting her shouts. She's screaming about how she'll take this to social media and spouting every threat under the sun.

The gate opens and Moses drives in. The guard holds Layla as she tries to bolt after me.

There's loyalty in that woman. I like it. But I also meant it about crushing her if she goes against me.

I step into the house, ready to find Aurora and make her talk. It's long overdue. Surely, she also doesn't like to stay away from her company and her weird friend.

"Sir?"

Margot's hesitant voice stops me at the base of the stairs. She's standing there with a silent Tom.

"Yes?"

Her skin is pale and she swallows a few times but doesn't say anything.

My inner alarms go off at the same time. "What's going on, Margot? Did something happen to Aurora?"

I checked in a few hours ago to make sure she'd had her lunch, and Margot didn't mention anything.

"What's going on?" I say with a stern voice when neither of them speaks.

It's Margot who finally does. "After I brought her lunch, Miss Aurora has...been..."

"What?"

"Screaming. Breaking things. The crashes could be heard from downstairs. She's calmed down a bit now, but it was so similar to..."

Tom shakes his head at her, and she clamps her lips shut.

But I know who she was going to compare her to, even if she didn't say the words.

So similar to Alicia.

Fuck.

I loosen my tie as I ascend the stairs, then turn the key in the lock. The scene I see in front of me is utter fucking chaos.

The coffee table is turned upside down, clothes are thrown on the ground, some torn, and the lamp is broken in pieces at the side of the bed.

I step inside and close the door, pocketing the key.

Since Aurora's nowhere to be found, I expect her to be in the bathroom. I'm a few steps in when she darts behind me, towards the door.

I grab her by the wrist, careful not to hurt her injured palms. The bandages are already bloodied, which means she's reopened her wounds.

Again.

Not that it should be a surprise with the amount of damage she's caused. This fucking woman has no care whatsoever for her own safety.

She thrashes against me, her face red and her loose black hair flying in all directions.

I grab her by the throat and push her down against the mattress. My body overpowers hers as I hover above her. "Stop."

She squirms, one of her hands hitting me across the chest, but the other remains inert by her side. Her face is pale—minus her flushed cheeks. Her lips are cracked and have lost their natural rosy colour, and the cut on the side of them is bloodied as well. Her deep blue eyes are frantic, pupils dilated—could be due to lack of sleep or her angry fit or both.

"You're reopening your fucking wounds, Aurora. What is wrong with you?"

"*You.*" She's breathing harshly—so much so that her words are muffled with her breaths. "If you don't let me go, you'll regret it."

"Is that so?"

"Don't underestimate me, Jonathan. I lived on the streets for way too long. I can cause you damage."

"Then why aren't you?"

She lifts the hand that was limp by her side only moments ago. I thought she was only bleeding because she reopened her wound, but turns it out, she's been squeezing a shard of glass. She points it at my neck, her breathing still chopped and uneven, but her eyes are blazing with sure determination.

This fucking woman has no thought for her safety whatsoever if she was holding a shard of glass against her already wounded palm. Or maybe an injury or two doesn't matter to her as long as she gets to run.

She's an expert at that.

Running the fuck away.

"What are you going to do with that, Aurora? Are you going to slice my throat?"

"I will if you don't let me go."

"The only way I'll let you out is if you fucking talk, so you might as well go for it."

"I can't stay here."

"Why not?"

"I just can't." Her voice breaks.

"Try again."

"Let me go, Jonathan, please."

"No."

"I'll hurt you."

"Do it."

"I really will."

"Fucking do it then."

She pushes the shard against my throat and I see the widening of her eyes before I feel the sting of the cut.

Then my blood flows to her face.

TEN

Aurora

H OT LIQUID LANDS ON MY CHEEK, MY NOSE, MY MOUTH, AND I taste metal.

Blood metal.

Oh my God. Oh my God.

My hand shakes uncontrollably and I release the shard of glass, letting it fall to the mattress. The blood mars the white sheets, soaking them red.

No, no…

Flashbacks from that day slam into me. The bloodshot eyes, the vacant look, the blood that trickled down her arms.

It's happening again. It's coming back.

Jonathan pushes off me, sitting on the bed, groaning. That manages to finally jerk me out of my daze.

Oh my God. I did that to Jonathan. I…I sliced his throat.

"Oh my God…" I breathe out loud as I straddle his lap and wrap a quivering hand on the wound in his neck. "I'm so sorry, so *s-so* sorry, I…I d-didn't mean it, I only wanted… I'm s-so sorry…"

"I'll survive," he says it with enough ease that it should soothe me. It doesn't. All I can focus on is the blood seeping through my fingers, covering them. I did that. Just like Dad.

I'm just like Dad.

Oh, God.

I'm going to throw up.

"Hey…" Jonathan's soothing voice echoes in the air. "Look at me."

I can't. All of my attention is on the trail of blood that is seeping through his cut and slipping between my fingers. The blood that I brought out. What was I thinking? This is Jonathan. How could I cut him?

"Aurora." His fingers stroke through my hair, then slowly slide to my chin, lifting it and gently guiding me to stare at him.

I'm trapped in those eyes I spent weeks and months getting lost in. Eyes I was going to turn vacant just like my dad did to those women.

"It's just a graze."

"It's not!" My voice shatters, tears falling down my cheeks. "I'm just like him, aren't I?"

"No, you're not."

He grabs a tissue from the side table, removes my hand, and wipes his neck. "See, it looks worse than it is."

Now that it's not covered with blood, the cut isn't long, but it's there, and it's still bleeding. The more blood comes out, the harder the tears leave my eyes.

"I'm going to fix it," I say through sniffles. "I know how."

I crawl to the first aid kit on the bedside table, then go back to straddling Jonathan's lap. Although I expect him to push me away, and he has every right to, he doesn't.

Jonathan leans on one hand as the other goes back to stroking my hair.

I retrieve the disinfectant and clean the wound with barely

steady hands. I can't stop crying, even when the blood dries. By the time I place the gauze on his skin, I'm a sobbing mess.

Jonathan pushes me back so that I'm sitting on my haunches on his thighs and changes my bandages. He glares at the cut on my palm from when I clutched the shard of glass earlier. The fact that he disapproves of how I reopened my wounds, and then made them worse, is loud and clear in his dark gaze.

"Hurt yourself again and I'm tying you the fuck up, Aurora."

A sniffle is my answer. I couldn't talk even if I wanted to. My attention keeps filtering back to the gauze on his neck, to the blood that's soaking the collar of his shirt.

"How do you know how to do it?" he asks in a quiet tone.

"W-what?" I manage through tears.

"You said you know how to fix it." He pours disinfectant on my palm, but I don't even wince. He pays special care to wipe his blood from between my fingers and from under my nails.

That makes me cry harder, feelings of shame and regret haunting my words as I try to speak, "I w-was stabbed when I was young and I-I sutured my wound myself."

I don't know why I'm telling him this. Maybe, like him, I'm trying to get my mind off the present.

"Why didn't you go to the police?"

I shake my head frantically. "I didn't trust them. I still don't. They hated me and would've probably accused me of doing it to myself. I…that's why I didn't go to the hospital either, because they would've reported me. Besides, if the perpetrator was a victim's family, I didn't want to hurt them. They'd experienced enough pain for a lifetime."

"There." He drops my bandaged palms to my lap, and I soak in the comfortable feeling when the wounds stop pulsing. He then wipes what I'm sure is the mess on my face with a wet piece of cotton.

My brow furrows. "What?"

"There's the reason why you're not Maxim. He wouldn't give

a fuck if people suffered as long as he got his gratification. You got stabbed and remained quiet to protect others."

"But I c-cut you." The words burn in my throat.

"You were cornered, and I'm certain you won't do it again."

"How can you be so sure?"

"I just am."

My chin trembles. "I-I'm so sorry, Jonathan."

"Stop apologising."

"But—"

"If you don't, I'm going to spank you."

My insides liquefy at that promise. This feeling of utter surrender to the lust I have towards Jonathan is the reason I trashed everything. I tried to get anyone's attention so they would open the door and I'd get to flee.

The fact that he could use my body against me scared me. It still does, but now, I feel like I'm suspended in an altered reality. Now, I don't have the right to think about anything past the fact that I hurt him.

I could've killed him.

I could've lost him once and for all.

"Jonathan, I—"

"Shut up, Aurora."

"But I—"

His hand wraps around my throat and his lips capture mine. My words and tears come to a halt and my thoughts scatter into thin air. Something tells me I shouldn't do this, but that reason can be damned.

I moan into his mouth as he claims me whole. He tastes of cognac and coffee. I love this taste on him so much. The fact that it's mixed with his woodsy, spicy scent feels as if I'm diving deep into him.

My tongue meets his, keeping up with his pace—or trying to, anyway. He's too intense for me to maintain the same rhythm.

Having his fingers around my neck adds to the lethal feel of his sheer presence surrounding me like a vice.

Still kissing me, he flips me over so I'm lying on my back on the mattress in the midst of the chaos of thrown clothes, towels, and sheets.

His mouth leaves mine, and I breathe heavily, my lips are swollen and raw, but I want more. I need the confirmation that he forgives me, that he sees that I didn't mean to hurt him.

Jonathan's fingers tighten around my throat, and I clutch his hand, not to remove it, but to keep it as leverage. I need to hold on to something, and it's strange that he's the only thing I can turn to.

"Don't cry again." His voice is hard yet tender at the same time. "Those eyes aren't made for tears."

Before I can make complete sense of his words, he crawls down my body and flings the nightgown to my waist.

I didn't bother with underwear after my morning bath, and I'm glad I didn't.

An appreciative groan comes from Jonathan's lips as he slides his fingers through my folds. I've forgotten what it felt like to be dead down there. Jonathan made me bury that part of me with every orgasm he's wrenched out of me.

Now, I don't even need pain. I just need his presence and my entire body flames back to life.

He releases my throat, and before I can protest, he settles on his knees at the foot of the bed and starts to open my legs.

They widen of their own volition as his fingers slide from my core to my inner thighs, leaving a wet trail.

I'm falling into that sensation when Jonathan's tongue does a long swipe. My back arches off the bed as a zap of pleasure sparks down my spine.

He holds my thighs in a merciless grip as he thrusts his tongue inside me. At first, it's slow, almost as if he's sampling me.

I've never allowed anyone to go down on me. It felt too intimate and just wasn't something I was willing to give up. Just like, before I met Jonathan, I'd never gone to my knees to suck a man off. However, Jonathan has burnt through my inhibitions one by one like it's his God-given right.

The foreign sensation causes my lips to part in a needy whimper.

"Fuck." His head peeks up from between my legs. "You're the best thing I've tasted."

And then he's back to feasting on me. Gone is his unhurried pace. Jonathan thrusts in and out of me with a rhythm that lique-fies my limbs. My nipples turn into hard pebbles, straining against the nightgown's material.

I grip his hair with both hands, fingers digging into his skull as he ruthlessly devours me. There's no other description for it. Jonathan doesn't only eat me, he claims me. He owns my body, but he doesn't stop there. In a way, it's like he's also coming after my soul.

The detonation sneaks up on me and grips me in its ruthless clutches. I brace the sheets for leverage, nails sinking into the cloth as more of my arousal coats his face.

If that bothers him, he doesn't show it. Not one bit. Jonathan goes on and on, lapping his tongue against my most intimate part. The feel of his stubble adds friction I didn't know would be this pleasurable. He does one long sweep from the bottom of my slit to the top, then he does it again.

He doesn't stop until I'm a quivering mess on the bed. "Ohh…J-Jonathan… Aaah…"

My words end on a gibberish sound as I come all over his mouth. My legs are boneless and my spine tingles due to the force of my orgasm.

Jonathan climbs atop of me, his hand wrapping around my throat as his lips find mine again. It's almost as if our mouths were never separated. This time, his tongue smears mine with my own juices.

The intimacy kills me, but it's not only that. It's the fact that Jonathan is kissing me without me having to somehow manipulate him into it.

It's the fact that he ate me out even after I hurt him.

It's all of him.

My fingers curl in his hair, gripping it as hard as he's holding my neck.

He removes my palm, gently stroking the bandage and shaking his head. "You'll reopen your wound."

A sniffle tears from my throat as I murmur against his mouth, "Why would you care?"

His expression doesn't change. "Why wouldn't I?"

The words leave me in a haunted whisper, "Because you killed my sister."

ELEVEN

Aurora

THE MOMENT I SAY THE WORDS, THEY HANG BETWEEN US LIKE the blade on a guillotine.

For a minute, I stare wild-eyed at Jonathan, not sure why I think he'll chop my head off.

Wait. Is he going to?

His expression doesn't change, but the lust that covered his features disappears. Instead, I'm faced with his stone-cold expression. The ruthless one.

The one meant to hurt.

I instinctively push back against the mattress. I might not be scared of Jonathan, but his silence snaps my shoulder blades together. It's like I can't breathe normally when he's this close yet feels far away.

So far away.

His hand is still wrapped around my throat and I gulp, expecting him to squeeze the life out of me.

But that part, that stupid little part that's slowly eating my heart, is serene, peaceful almost. That part believes that Jonathan would never hurt me. He snapped at me for aggravating my wound, after all. He wouldn't do anything to me.

But that part keeps forgetting what Jonathan did to Alicia.

"What are you talking about?" The neutral tone of his voice and the fact that he's not getting off me is pushing my thoughts in all different directions. I don't know whether he's bluffing or genuinely asking.

I could deflect or backpedal, but someone with a strong perception like Jonathan would read straight through me.

Not knowing what to say, I turn my head away and stare at the broken lamp on the side of the bed. Maybe if I study it hard enough, Jonathan will get bored and leave me alone.

I scoff internally. The chance of Jonathan leaving me alone is probably as impossible as the likelihood of that lamp magically repairing itself.

His fingers caress the pulse point in my neck in a deceptive type of softness. I have no doubt he'll squeeze anytime he chooses to.

"Your time is up, Aurora."

My frantic gaze slides back to his. "U-up?"

Is he going to kill me?

"I'm done waiting for you to talk. You will do it right now."

Oh, so it's not actually 'up' as I thought. A rush of relief floods me, and I hate how light my chest feels.

When I remain silent, Jonathan's fingers squeeze lightly, almost as if he's reminding me of his power. "If you don't talk, I'm liquefying H&H."

The relief settling at the bottom of my stomach slowly disappears. "You can't do that!"

"I can and I will. For the record, your black belt friend was here earlier and she made the mistake of threatening me, so I might be in the mood to ruin her life."

Oh my God. Lay! I should've known she'd get her claws out if

I disappeared on her. Not that her claws can do anything to a man like Jonathan. She'll only end up hurting herself.

Shit.

Knowing Jonathan, he'll also go after her family to drive the point home.

"I hate you," I snarl at him.

"You didn't hate me when you came all over my tongue."

My thighs clench at the reminder of the pleasure he brought out of me not too long ago.

"Now, fucking talk, Aurora. What's with the nonsense about Alicia?"

"Fine, let me up."

"So you'll throw one of your tantrums? No."

"I'm uncomfortable."

"Liar." His lips twitch. "You've been rubbing your thighs together."

"Which means I'm uncomfortable."

"You're aroused, not uncomfortable. You think I can't tell the difference?"

Damn him and how observant he is.

I take in a deep breath, but it comes out chopped and broken—just like the whole chaos in my chest.

Being cornered is one of the feelings I loathe the most. I've fought so hard to escape my father's shadow, but I've never managed to.

Even though Jonathan has threatened everything precious to me, there's a vile need to tell him everything. To just spill it out and…be out there for the first time in my life.

I know it's dangerous and that it'll probably come back and bite me in the butt, but I'm so exhausted. My body is full of bruises, cuts, and a healed scar that still hurts.

It could be due to the physical pain, the lack of sleep, or both, but I murmur, "Ever since the first day I came here, I've been receiving messages from Alicia."

"What type of messages?"

"Recordings on flash drives. It seemed like her will to me. At the beginning, she said that if I got them, it meant she was dead. Then she went on to tell me that someone wanted to kill her. She also said that our mother told her to cut all connection with me. In the last message, she was crying and told me…"

"What?" I expect him to squeeze my throat for good measure, but his fingers loosen until he's almost caressing me.

"She…she said you were poisoning her. You were trying to kill her."

I expect him to deny it, to tell me I'm wrong, but he continues studying me with that calculative gaze of his. I wait for his words with bated breath, but they never come out.

"So?" I whisper.

His face is covered in that blankness that I can't get past, no matter how much time I spend with him. "Where are those recordings?"

"In my car."

"Where in your car?"

"In my glove box." I'm bemused. "Why is that the main point here?"

He pushes off me, and the skin where his fingers were wrapped around my neck is suddenly hollow and desolate.

The fact that he stopped touching me so suddenly feels wrong. Why does it feel so wrong?

I try not to focus on that as I follow his movements and sit on the edge of the bed beside him. Jonathan places a phone to his ear. "Moses. Search the glove box in Aurora's car and bring me the flash drives in there."

Why would he need them?

Wait… "Are you going to get rid of the evidence?"

Jonathan hangs up but keeps his phone in his hand. His expression is still that bland one, but something about it bothers me.

The emotions he's hiding behind his façade seem wrong. "There's no evidence, because that nonsense didn't happen."

"Alicia said you poisoned her in order to kill her." I probably shouldn't be accusing him this openly, but it's out there now, so I might as well hear his take on it.

"I want to hear it for myself."

"More like you want to destroy the evidence."

"If I wanted to kill Alicia, I would've done it right after she gave birth to Aiden. I wouldn't have waited until eight years later."

"Why would you even want to kill her? She was the softest person alive."

"She was, and that softness ruined her." The warmth in his tone takes me aback. It's the first time he's actually talked about Alicia without his usual impersonal touch.

"What happened, Jonathan?"

"Why do you want to know?" He narrows his eyes on me. "So you can engrave me in your head as your sister's killer?"

It's the exact opposite. Despite hearing Alicia's message, a rebellious part of me refuses to believe Jonathan hurt her or would hurt me. That's why I want him to talk, so that I'll be able to murder that part of me.

"I told you my side of the story. It's your turn, Jonathan."

"Is that why you ran away and tried to escape?"

I bite my bottom lip.

"You don't trust me?" Though his voice is calm, there's an angry undertone to it.

"I trust my sister."

"You shouldn't. At least not blindly. She was mentally unwell."

I puff my chest. "My sister was not crazy."

His mouth twitches at the corner. "And you wonder why I call you wild one. You look the part right now."

"If you expect me to stay still while you badmouth my sister, you have another thing coming."

"I'm not badmouthing her. I'm stating facts that she tried her hardest to hide from you and the world."

I inch closer to him until my thigh nearly touches his. "What do you mean?"

"Alicia's father was the King family's arch enemy. Lord Sterling was out to destroy my father and any legacy he left behind because my mother didn't choose him. After my parents' deaths, I decided to destroy him."

I gasp. "Is that why you married Alicia? For revenge?"

"Yes."

"How could you do that to her? You tyrant! Brute!" I curl my palm to punch him.

Jonathan cuts me a sharp glare. "Reopen your wounds and I'm tying you the fuck up, Aurora. I meant it earlier."

The thought of being helpless causes a shudder to overtake me. I let my palms fall to my sides, but he doesn't stop glaring at me, the sense of injustice on my sister's behalf enveloping me whole. "Why would you do that to her?"

"She knew."

"W-what?"

"I told her about my reasons from the start."

"And…she agreed?"

"Indeed."

"But why did she?"

"Because she hated her father for your mother's death and wanted to bring him down. She didn't have enough power to accomplish that, so I lent her that power and gave her the ability to see her father on his knees. He came to our doorstep, begging us to loan him money to save his business. I made sure no one else would, so his only solution was us."

"And?" I scoot over, and this time, my thigh touches his. I want to watch his expression closely as he tells me about the past. But it doesn't change much, except the part where he seems trapped in another timeline.

"She gave him money."

"Oh."

"She was that soft."

"Did you…" I trail off, the question catching in my throat.

"Go ahead, ask. If you don't voice your question, you might never know the answer."

"Did you ever love her?" My words are small, barely audible.

"I thought I did, in my own way. Alicia was my wife, the mother of my only son, and she did everything I asked without giving me attitude about it." He stares down his nose at me, driving the point home.

"Well, sorry I'm not a replica of her."

His lips pull in what resembles a smile. "That, you aren't. So far."

"What do you mean by so far?"

Jonathan's phone vibrates and Moses's name flashes on the screen.

He puts the phone to his ear, listens without speaking, then hangs up. The line between his brow creases as he stares at me in a strange way.

It's the second time Jonathan has looked at me like this—like he's seeing a ghost. The first time was at Aiden's wedding.

"What is it?" I murmur. "Why are you looking at me like that?"

"There were no flash drives in the car."

"Of course there were. I put them in there myself. Are you sure Moses didn't get rid of them?"

"Moses would never do something without my order."

"They're in the glove box. I'll go check myself."

He grips me by the arm, disallowing me from leaving his side. His expression falls, almost like he's disappointed, but in what? And why the hell do I hate that he's directing that expression at me?

"Why the hell do you keep looking at me like that?" I snap.

"Are you sure you received those messages?" His tone, although not harsh, feels like a slap across my face.

"Of course I did! Do you think that I…I made it up or something?"

He says nothing, but that expression doesn't disappear. If anything, the line in his forehead deepens.

"I received recordings from Alicia, Jonathan. I did!"

When he continues his infuriating silence, tears form in my eyes—angry ones. Why the hell is his disbelief affecting me so much? All I want is to reach out and erase that look off his beautiful face. I don't want him regarding me that way, not now. Not ever.

"Paul!" I snatch his phone. "I'll call the concierge of my building. He's the one who contacted me whenever I had a wooden package that contained a flash drive. I'm going to put it on speaker so you can hear that I'm right."

Energy bubbles in my veins as I unlock the phone using Jonathan's fingerprint and punch in Paul's number. I learnt it by heart from how much I manically checked to see if I'd gotten a new message.

Jonathan doesn't stop me as I place the phone between us while it rings.

"Hello," Paul's voice comes from the other side.

"Hey, Paul. This is Aurora from 19."

"Hello, Miss Harper."

What's with the formality in his tone? Anyway, that's not what's important right now. "Paul, remember when you used to call me whenever I received a small wooden box?"

"I'm sorry, Miss?"

"The boxes, Paul. The ones you pulled from under the counter and said they didn't have a sender address on them, and you usually found them in front of the building."

"I'm afraid I don't know what you're talking about, Miss. I've never seen such packages. Besides, you already directed all your packages to your new address."

"There were boxes." My voice rises as my hold tightens around the phone. "I received the first one two months ago and the last one came yesterday."

"I didn't see you yesterday, Miss. I took the day off for my dentist appointment."

No, no, no…

"Stop playing with me, Paul." My voice is brittle, but it's also on the verge of breaking all hell loose.

"Excuse me, Miss?"

Jonathan takes the phone from my fingers, even as I try to fight for its possession. "Thank you."

Two words. Two mere words and then he hangs up. His gaze trails up to my face as if I'm an injured animal on its death bed.

"Stop looking at me like that." My voice cracks.

"Like what?"

"Like you think I'm insane. I'm not."

"All right."

"I am *not*. I received those packages."

"Okay."

"*Stop* it." I hit his chest. "Stop it! Stop it! I'm not crazy, okay?"

Jonathan prisons both my hands against his chest, stopping my tantrum. They lie limp in his hold, exhaustion and confusion rearing at my nerve endings.

"You need rest, Aurora. You haven't slept properly in two days."

He stands up and reaches for me, and I pull back, leaning on my hands.

"You'll aggravate your wound." He places one hand on my back and the other underneath my legs and carries me in his arms.

I don't fight. I feel like if I do, I'll really be labelled crazy.

And I'm not. I had those vocal messages from Alicia. I don't care what Jonathan or anyone else says about it.

He quickly crosses the distance between my room and his upstairs. The entire time, I keep watching his face, the way that line remains between his brows.

God damn that line. Why the fuck isn't it disappearing?

Jonathan places me on his bed, then softly pulls the cover to my chin.

But he doesn't join me. He doesn't even attempt to. And the

realisation that he won't share a bed with me slices me deeper than I'd like to admit.

"Sleep, Aurora."

"I'm *not* crazy."

"I never said you were."

"But you believe it. You're thinking about it right now. I can tell." I clamp my lips shut to not spout all the nonsense my brain is bubbling with. That will make my case harder, not easier.

"We'll talk in the morning."

"Where are you going?"

"I need to make some work calls."

Work calls, my arse. More like he's avoiding me. He won't even look at me like before anymore, will he?

Refusing to think about that, I direct my thoughts to something else.

"I want Layla." I jut my chin. "You said I could get out and meet whomever I want."

"She'll be here when you wake up in the morning." He reaches a hand, which usually means he'll stroke a stray hair off my face, but instead, he readjusts the cover, not attempting to touch me. Then he retracts his hand and leaves.

As the door closes behind him with finality, a tear slides down my cheek.

I am *not* crazy.

TWELVE

Aurora

S HE'S LIKE ALICIA.
    Just like Alicia.
    Do you remember when she used to make things up?

It's not only a resemblance in their features. They must've inherited the wrong genes from their mother.

The voices collapse and blend together. I think I can catch them, but the moment I reach out a hand, I fall.

Down.

Down…

I jerk awake, sweat covering my skin. For a second, I can't figure out where I am, but then, soon enough, the familiar sensual scent fills my nostrils. Woodsy and airy. A strange sense of peace envelops me like a cocoon.

Jonathan's room. It's dark since the curtains are drawn, but I can feel it without having to search hard.

I vaguely recall strong arms wrapping around me from behind in the middle of the night. Or was that also a play of my imagination?

My breathing turns harsh and shallow as I recall what happened last night and the way Jonathan looked at me.

Why did he look at me like that?

I feel like I'll be old and grey and I'll never forget the disappointment in his eyes, and was it also…disgust?

The door barges open, and I squint as the light in the hallway hits me.

"Your knight in shining armour is here, mate!"

I smile despite myself at Layla's voice. I've never been so happy to see her in my life as I am this moment.

She's wearing baggy trousers and a hoodie on which is written, *If You're Happy and You Know It, Stay Away*. Her expression plummets when she focuses on me. "What happened to your palms and lip?"

"I fell."

"F that. It was Johnny, wasn't it? I'm going to sue his arse. I'm dragging that dictator into court."

"It wasn't him."

She narrows her eyes, slowly approaching me. "Are you protecting him or something?"

"Why would I do that? Now, come here. I missed you."

She practically jogs my way, then engulfs me in a hug. It's the first time Layla has ever initiated a hug and I know not to take it lightly.

"I was so worried about you," she speaks into my neck. "I was legit planning to stab Johnny in the throat so I could see you."

I already did that.

My heart falls at the reminder of blood and the cut and everything. Circling my arms around her slender back, I hug her and we remain like that for a while as I fight the tears trying to break loose.

I sniffle, and Layla pulls away. "Hey…what's wrong?"

"Everything?"

"It's that piece of S, Johnny, isn't it? I'm totally kicking him in the nose."

"Stop it, Lay."

"What do you mean by stop it? He locked you up!"

"No, I mean, yeah, but it was complicated. I need to ask you about something."

"There's nothing complicated about locking someone up. That shit is no bueno, mate. And then the arsehole forbids me from coming here? Yeah, not going to happen. Not in this life."

"Lay, focus."

"What?"

"When I first moved in with Jonathan, did I tell you about the packages with no sender I used to receive at my old flat's address?"

"I think you said something about changing your mailing address because it was annoying to go back and forth."

"That's not what I'm talking about. Did I mention a flash drive and Alicia's messages? I said I agreed to Jonathan's deal because I wanted to know the truth behind her death."

"You did, totally, and I said, don't do it, but you went on with it anyway. No one listens to Layla."

"You remember the messages." My voice is so full of hope, it's pathetic.

"I have no clue about any messages. You said you hold a grudge against Johnny because you think your sister died because of him."

"I never mentioned the voice messages I received?"

"No."

"Shit."

"What voices messages?" she whispers, as if this is a conspiracy theory.

"N-nothing." I don't want Lay to also think I'm crazy.

Am I? I'm not, right?

She fixes me with that overdramatic scrutinising look she learnt from detective shows. "What are you hiding from me? Spill."

"I will. J-just not now, okay?" I pause, then blurt to deviate her attention, "Did Jonathan call you?"

"Yup. Seven in the morning like a damn alarm—not that I slept. I spent the entire night plotting his demise. He thought he could lock you up and have his happily ever after? Nuh-uh, not happening."

Not that she could've done anything to him, but the fact that she didn't give up on me warms my heart.

"I even brought backup."

"What type of backup?"

She grins with pure mischievousness. "Johnny doesn't get to chase me away, then call me over as if I'm his lap dog."

"What did you do, Lay?"

"Relax. I only shuffled his cards with the one person he hates."

Recognition settles in. "*You didn't.*"

"Totes did." Her grin widens. "I brought my Daddy."

I jump to my feet. "Lay! What if they go against each other?"

"You think they would? Oh em gee, I should've stayed to watch."

"You're..." I point a finger at her, lost for words.

"The best?" She flutters her lashes. "Your ride or die?"

"I'll deal with you later."

"Mate, wait!" she calls after me, but I'm already flying down the stairs, not bothering with shoes.

If my vague memories from last night were real, Jonathan barely slept. It was close to four in the morning when he spooned me from behind. The last thing he needs is a quarrel with Ethan at the start of his day.

There's no doubt in my mind that they'll go at each other's throats. Ethan might act cool, but he doesn't hesitate to take a jab at Jonathan—in fact, he makes it his mission. As for my tyrant, well, he has no tolerance for Ethan whatsoever and he doesn't shy away from showing it.

He even projects that hostility at Elsa, just for the fact that she shares DNA with Ethan.

Sure enough, clipped voices filter in from the main lounge area at the entrance of the King mansion.

"You're not welcome here, Ethan. Leave."

"Layla is worried about Aurora and I can't leave without making sure she's safe."

"Her safety and her entire existence are none of your fucking concern." Jonathan's voice turns eerily calm but with a threatening undertone. "Don't look at her. Don't talk to her. Don't fucking breathe near her."

A chuckle comes from Ethan. "And if I refuse?"

"Let the answer to that be a surprise."

"Are you threatening me, Jon?"

"Don't call me that."

"What? Jon? That's what I used to call you back in the day."

"You lost the right to call me that a long time ago, you fucking bastard."

"I lost my wife, too." Ethan's tone hardens.

"Not before she locked up and tortured my son, whom, should I remind you, *you* kidnapped."

"That's because *you* burned my whole fucking factory, Jonathan. People died. Aiden didn't."

"Alicia did."

"So did Abigail. So did I, for nine years, in case you forgot."

I arrive in time to find the two men standing toe-to-toe with each other. Jonathan's the first to look my way.

His eyes instantly darken to a terrifying colour. I remain frozen in place from the mere force of it.

What? What is it?

I stare down at myself and realise that not only have I come down barefoot, but I'm also wearing the flimsy nightgown from last night. My hair must appear like a mess and so must my face.

In my attempt to stop whatever war they were going to unleash, I've shown up like this.

Layla catches up to me, panting. "People with long legs suck."

"Why didn't you tell me I came down looking like this?" I hiss at her.

"I tried. You didn't listen."

I'm about to say something else when a large presence appears in front of me.

Jonathan.

I don't know why my heart skips a violent beat whenever he looks down at me with those steel eyes. It's like I'm the only thing that matters in his environment and he doesn't hesitate to show that fact.

Then why did he regard me last night as if I were insane?

Shooing that thought away, I take a moment to appreciate how elegant and larger than life he appears in his black tailored suit. Seriously, if he ever considers a career in modelling, he'll ace it—like everything in his life, basically.

I never knew I had a thing for men in suits until Jonathan came along. Or more accurately, he's the only man in a suit that I have a thing for.

Though *a thing* is putting it mildly. My nipples tighten against the thin nightgown at the view, and something tells me it's not due to the cold air coming from the entrance.

Jonathan removes his jacket and wraps it around my shoulders, and then he picks me up and carries me in his arms.

Just like that.

Just like it's a given.

A soft gasp leaves me, but the sound is swallowed by how warm he feels, how good he smells.

Will I ever get used to this? Worse, will I ever forget about this?

Layla makes a face at Jonathan's back, obviously still holding a grudge about the way he chased her away. Ethan's lips pull up into a mysterious smile as he watches us like a cat who's caught a mouse.

Jonathan takes me back to the room, his strides firm and purposeful. He walks with the same confidence he exudes—there's no hint of doubt. But this time, it's almost as if he's angry.

He lowers me to the ground, my bare feet getting swallowed by the plush carpet, then he kicks the door shut.

When he faces me, I'm pinned in place by the darkness in his gaze.

It's almost as if he's been saving it and he's now unleashing it.

By the time he speaks, his voice is clipped and non-negotiable. "Don't you ever, and I mean *ever*, show up dressed like that in front of Ethan or any other man. Is that understood?"

The possessiveness in his tone turns my skin hot and tingly.

"I said, is that fucking understood, Aurora?"

All I can do is nod.

Seeming satisfied with the answer, the edge slightly leaves his features. "Why did you come down anyway?"

"I…I didn't want you to fight with Ethan first thing in the morning."

The slight ease vanishes and he closes down like the vault he is. "Worried about *him*?"

When I don't answer, he reaches me in two long strides and wraps a hand around my throat. "Are you?"

"No."

"Then what is it?"

"I…you…you barely slept last night." My lips tremble. "Right?"

His expression is unreadable, and I expect him to confirm that I'm insane, but he loosens his hold on my throat. "Right."

Right. I didn't make that up. He *did* sleep beside me. He wasn't disgusted with me to the point he didn't want to touch me.

Does that mean I didn't make up those voices either?

"Come on." He takes me by the wrist so as not to hurt my palm. "Let me help with the shower so you can get ready."

"Get ready for what?"

"Don't you have to go to work?"

A long breath leaves me. Not because he's giving me back my freedom—because, in a way, I knew Jonathan would keep his word—but because of the fact that he didn't bring up the part where he thinks I'm crazy.

But then he stares at me over his shoulder and gives me that look again.

The pity.

The disappointment.

He...he's going to get rid of me, isn't he?

Just like Alicia.

THIRTEEN

Aurora

E VEN THOUGH I GO TO WORK, I CAN'T CONCENTRATE.
All I keep thinking about is those voices grating on my nerves and whispering things like:

She's losing her mind, just like Alicia.

What makes it worse is the way Jonathan looked at me. And then he didn't attempt to touch me during my shower today. His movements were anything but sexual with the sole purpose of helping me bathe.

Usually, his hands wander all over my body and he demands I beg him to finger me or bring me to orgasm.

Not today. He had no interest in me, even when I stood fully naked in front of him. I pretend that doesn't slice through me and leave a wound worse than the ones covering my body.

Being the sole focus of his touch just to lose it all of a sudden is harsher than I ever thought.

After the shower, he helped me dress, then disappeared.

Just like that. No words. No orders for later per his usual.

Just...*nothing.*

The coldness I felt when he walked out the door was like being shoved into a freezer and locked inside.

Is that what he also did with Alicia when she started losing her mind?

Not that I am. I'm *not.*

Though coming all the way here to prove my theory is probably pushing it.

I went to my old building during my lunch break, where Paul insisted that there was no package and he didn't see me on that day. Shelby, my grumpy neighbour, wasn't there for me to hold him witness. When I asked Paul where he was, he said he was having trouble with the law and was solving it at the police station.

Then, after I left, a scary thought assaulted me. What if the attack with Sarah never happened? I mean, how would she know where I lived, even if she saw me in that charity event?

Did she see me? Was she there or did I make her up?

All those thoughts have been throwing me for a loop. I feel like I exist outside of my body, and I can't find a way to go back in.

Except for this stupid, irrational action.

I'm standing in front of Aiden and Elsa's house in Oxford, hand gripping my watch. Elsa sent me the address when I last saw her in an attempt to invite me to dinner. I've always refused because Aiden seems like he wants to chop my head off.

Today, I drove the whole way here. And although I spent almost two hours on the road, I still haven't exactly managed to gather my thoughts.

The rain pours as if the sky is revolting against the world. The dusk has come and gone, and the early evening adds to the gloominess of the heavy downpour.

I'm soaked in seconds during the small trip from my car to the front door. My hair sticks to my temples and water forms rivulets down my face.

When I came up with this idea, my only angle was that, aside from Jonathan, Aiden knew Alicia the best. He would've noticed if there was something amiss with his mother.

I press the doorbell with hesitant fingers as doubts creep in, the most prominent of all being that Aiden doesn't like me. Why would he talk about Alicia in front of me when he thinks I'm an impostor?

This was a bad idea, after all. If I leave now, they'll probably chalk up the ringing bell to a child's prank.

Before I can run away, the door opens. Elsa appears on the threshold wearing shorts and a sleeveless top. Her long hair is held up in a neat ponytail and her face is soft and beautiful, even without an ounce of makeup. Upon seeing me, her lips widen in a gorgeous smile.

"Aurora! What a lovely surprise." She wraps her arms around me in a hug, uncaring about the fact that I'm soaked.

"I'm sorry for coming without notice."

"Don't be ridiculous. You're always welcome here." She ushers me inside. "Come in. The rain got you."

"Thank you." I remain in the entrance so that I don't drip all over the shiny wooden flooring.

Their house is nothing like the King mansion. It's smaller, homier, and has elegant but personal decor, like the small house figurines and the painting of Aiden and Elsa on their wedding day. Astrid must've done it—it has her special, unconventional touch.

The size and the feel of the house makes me wonder if Aiden wanted to exchange the big, empty, and cold King mansion with a place that he considers home. A place where he can start anew with Elsa.

"Why are you standing there?" Elsa motions behind her. "Come inside."

"I'm good here." I clear my throat. "Is Aiden around?"

"Yeah, he—"

"Sweetheart?" His voice filters in from the top of the stairs. "What did I say about opening the door? I'm the only one who does it. No one gets to look at you in those tiny clothes."

"There he is." Elsa shakes her head and whispers, "Sorry about that."

"You don't need to apologise." A small smile grazes my lips, remembering how Jonathan acted this morning in front of Ethan.

Like father, like son.

My smile falls when Aiden joins his wife and watches me with a furrowed brow. Like her, he's wearing cotton trousers and a simple white T-shirt. His black hair is tousled, and I can't help staring at the small mole at the edge of his right eye—the only physical feature he inherited from Alicia.

He places an arm around Elsa's waist and pulls her to his side, almost as if he wants to protect her from me. "What are you doing here?"

She elbows him. "Is that a way to treat our guest? She came all the way from London during this rain."

"She's not my guest." He continues to study me, probably waiting for an answer to his question.

"I…I want to ask you something."

"We have nothing to talk about."

Elsa pulls away from his hold, glaring him down, even though he's way taller than her. She then takes my hand and leads me inside and seats me on the sofa, despite my attempt to protest.

By the time she brings a fluffy towel and wraps it around my shoulders, Aiden has followed after, his hands in his pockets. His grey eyes narrow on me as if I'm a liability he needs to get rid of.

"I'll go get you something hot to drink." She smiles at me, then stares at Aiden. "Be nice."

"I'm anything but nice, remember?" He gives her an undecipherable glance, and although I can't quite read it, Elsa's cheeks redden.

It's fascinating how they can understand each other with a mere look.

That's how Jonathan made me sit on his lap or lie on my

stomach. Sometimes, he didn't have to say a word, and even if he did, it was because I was acting out to hear his commanding tone.

I shut the door on that thought and him. Jonathan is the last thing I need on my mind right now.

He doesn't want to touch me anymore. He thinks I'm insane. Dickhead.

I try to erase him by focusing on the scene in front of me.

Elsa runs her fingers up Aiden's chest and whispers something in his ear. His left eye twitches, but his expression remains the same as she disappears around the corner.

Aiden watches her back, then his attention snaps to me—dark and unreadable. Just like his damn father.

He sits opposite me, and I tighten my hold on the towel.

"Get on with it," he speaks in his stone-cold tone. "The faster you do, the sooner you'll be out of here."

What a great host. But I don't say that. "When you were younger, did you notice something wrong with Alicia?"

I'm almost sure he's taken aback by the question, but his features quickly return to their normal coldness. "What is this about?"

"Margot said Alicia had episodes where she roamed the house during the night and made things up. She also scribbled over books and walls and—"

"Shut up." Aiden's jaw tightens.

"Tell me, please. I need to know."

"Why? So you can pity her? Feel sorry for not being there? What is your angle exactly?"

"Because I might be becoming like her," the words leave my mouth in a haunted whisper.

My fingers shake until the towel nearly falls. My teeth start to chatter, but it's not due to the cold.

Aiden regards me for a second too long, not speaking. I'm not sure if he's weighing the words he'll say or just making sense of mine.

"What gave you that idea?"

"I think I'm having hallucinations. Things I swear happened aren't real, and I'm starting to doubt the things that did happen."

"That does sound like Alicia." His voice is calm, low. He rests his elbow on the armrest and leans his head on his knuckles. "She had nights where she insisted she saw ghosts. She wrote about them and even sang them a lullaby. Levi and I thought it was fun, but Uncle James, and especially Jonathan, forbid us from seeing her when she was in that state."

"Was it…bad?"

"Not when I was young, no. She used to read to me and circle words she thought were interesting. I think she got too bad too fast as I grew up." His fist clenches. "And Jonathan did *nothing* to help her."

I see it then. The grudge. The pain.

It was unnoticeable at first because, like his father, Aiden traps his feelings in a vault. It could be due to his abnormal childhood, losing his mother while being so young, or being raised by a control freak like Jonathan. It could be all of them.

The fact remains that Aiden blames his father for Alicia's death. Just like I did in the past. I thought he didn't protect her and that, because of his disregard, my sister died too soon.

"Was Jonathan too negligent?"

"To her physical needs? No. But to her emotional ones?" He scoffs as if that's all the answer I need.

"I'm so sorry."

He pauses, lifting his head a bit. "What are you apologising for?"

"Not being there when she left. It would've been different."

"Don't flatter yourself," he says, but there's no harshness behind it. "It wouldn't have been."

"It would've. For both of us."

Maybe if I'd been there, I would've somehow filled the emotional gap between him and his father. Maybe they could've anchored me after losing the only two people I considered family.

Maybes are too cruel.

The fact that those things didn't happen and never will hurts worse than physical pain.

"You're not her," Aiden whispers.

"I know. I never wanted to be."

"No. You're *not* her." There's no accusation in his voice. It's more like...sadness? "You won't fall like she did."

"What makes you think that?"

He hesitates. It's the first time I've witnessed Aiden hesitating. "Jonathan never looked at her the way he looks at you."

My breath shortens at his words, but before I can say anything, Elsa saunters in carrying a mug of hot chocolate and places it between my stiff fingers. The warmth dissipates some of the cold, but it doesn't fight off the tremors.

I don't miss how Aiden's eyes follow Elsa's every movement as if she's the magnet to his steel. It's like he's physically unable to keep his attention off her.

"You have to change your clothes so you don't catch a cold," she tells me. "We're different sizes, but I'll see what I can find."

"No, I better go." I start to stand, but she gently sits me back down.

"Nonsense. You can't drive back this late and in the midst of this rain. Stay the night."

"I'll be fine."

"Jonathan won't mind if you spend a night out." Elsa peeks at her husband and asks in an unsure tone. "Right?"

"He would." Aiden lifts a shoulder. "But stay anyway."

Both Elsa and I freeze, unsure if we heard him correctly. Did Aiden just tell me to stay over?

Elsa is the first to recover and grins at him wide, her nose scrunching. "Totally. Let me get you some dry clothes."

Fifteen minutes later, I'm wearing one of Elsa's dresses. She's one or two sizes smaller and I'm taller than her, so the cotton material tightens around my breasts, stomach, and hips, and it doesn't even reach my knees.

Still better than wet clothes. I also change my bandages to dry ones. Jonathan's voice about not reopening my wounds echoes in my ears the whole time.

Then he looked at me that way. Like he thought I was crazy. Like he was disappointed in me.

I can't chase that look out of my head, no matter how much I try. I also can't stop thinking about his platonic touch this morning.

It could be that I'm being petty, but I opt not to tell him where I am. He's not my keeper. He doesn't need to know where I'm spending my night.

I join Elsa in the kitchen, and to my surprise, she's only Aiden's sous-chef. His movements are organised and precise, and he knows his way around everything.

"Do you always cook?" I try, expecting him to ignore me.

He nods but barely pays me any attention. Well, that's a start, I guess.

"I'll tell you a secret," Elsa leans in to whisper. "I don't cook, like at all. Aiden doesn't let me."

"Well, I'm not so good at cooking myself," I murmur back. "No one should allow me near a kitchen."

We both laugh, and Aiden throws a glance that suggests he's not happy to be left out of our conversation.

We try to help him out, but he shoos us away, so we make the table, which is situated near the lounge area.

Elsa and I sit there, sipping wine and staring out the large window that the dining table overlooks. The droplets of rain running down it form long lines and the streetlights give the view a cosy feel.

It is a peaceful night, and I should enjoy it. I could if my heart would stop sinking like an abandoned ship.

"I'm sorry if I interrupted your plans," I tell Elsa.

She slides the glass of wine on the table. "More like Aiden's plans, but they're everyday plans, so he can wait."

"Are you sure he won't hate me more?"

"He doesn't hate you." She bites her lower lip. "I mean, you're the woman who tamed Jonathan King. Anyone would respect you for that—Aiden included."

"I didn't tame him." Far from it. If anything, whatever we had has been destroyed since my hallucinations.

"Have you seen the way he's possessive of your time and attention?"

"That's because he's a control freak."

"Well, that he is, but it's more. I can tell."

"You can tell, how?"

"It's in the little things, you know?"

"The little things?"

She takes a sip of her wine and leans her head on her palm. "Okay, so here's one. When we sit for family dinners, Jonathan doesn't touch his food until he makes sure you're not only settled, but you've also started eating."

"He just likes everyone seated."

"Jonathan?" She laughs, the sound throaty. "He couldn't care less about us. He only started that habit when you joined our dinners."

"Oh."

"There's also the way he watches you so you'll eat or how he snaps at Aiden or Levi whenever they address you. It's like he doesn't want your attention divided from him."

"He snaps at everyone."

"Not usually. Jonathan is the type who issues orders in the calmest, most frightening way. And he doesn't actually snap at Aiden and Levi—at least, not when Astrid and I are there." She grins. "You brought colours to his previously bleak world. I can feel it."

Her words are supposed to lift my mood, but it flattens at the reminder of what recently happened.

Before Elsa can go on, Aiden re-joins us with plates of pasta and meatballs.

Elsa's cheeks are red, and mine must be, too, considering this is our second glass of wine.

She tiptoes and kisses Aiden on the mouth, smiling. He deepens it, uncaring for having me as an audience. His arms wrap around her waist and he grabs her by the small of her back as he tongues her with intense passion.

I sigh into my glass of wine, watching them—probably like a creep. At least Aiden shows his emotions freely in front of Elsa. His father is stone-cold and demands punishment for every kiss and night in his bed.

He did kiss you and sleep with you without a punishment last night.

That was before he looked at me that way, so it doesn't count.

Elsa pulls away, her cheeks coloured crimson. Aiden's eyes are blazing as if he'll push her on the table and take her right here and now. That was probably their plan for the night before I interrupted.

As if reading into his intentions, Elsa flops onto her seat, forcing Aiden to do the same. At first, the meal is spent in awkward silence, but Elsa brings up uni and a debate club that Aiden and his best friend named Cole attend.

She complains that they're only there to make everyone's lives hell.

Aiden counters that not everyone is boring like her politically correct colleagues.

That gets them both talking and arguing in an adorable kind of way. Or more like, Elsa argues. Aiden seems to rile her up on purpose just to get on her nerves.

"Can you believe this?" Elsa asks me. "Did you have people like this at uni?"

"My best friend, Layla. You met her at that charity. She's so argumentative and doesn't like to be ignored. She's tiny, wears a religious scarf, and appears clueless and soft, so when she made a ruckus in debates, everyone kind of looked at her in awe."

"She seems so cool," Elsa says.

"She is." I'm so proud of that little bugger.

Aiden takes a bite of his food. "Invite her for dinner at Jonathan's someday."

"She and Jonathan don't get along." I pick at my pasta. "She's always threatening to practice her black belt karate on him."

He smirks. "Even better."

"She does that?" Elsa speaks in a slightly spooked voice.

"Yeah, I swear she has no fear for her life."

Elsa is about to say something, but the bell rings. She starts to stand, but Aiden gets up first, puts two hands on her shoulders, and sits her back down.

"There's no way in fuck someone is going to see you drunk."

"I'm not drunk," she argues.

He pinches her reddened cheek. "Uh-huh."

Aiden disappears around the corner before she can say anything.

She leans over. "Tell me more about your friend whom Jonathan hasn't killed yet."

"She calls him Johnny." I giggle, then slap a hand over my mouth. Apparently, I'm also drunk.

I try to never get drunk, because that messes with my senses, and I can't protect myself if I need to, but I guess I feel safe here.

That's...both weird and comforting.

"No way! And he lets it happen?" Her gaze trails behind me. "Jonathan."

"He can't really stop her." I giggle again and don't bother to suppress it. "She's fearless."

"No," Elsa whispers. "Jonathan is here."

I turn around, and sure enough, my tyrant has come to find me.

FOURTEEN

Aurora

F OR A MOMENT, I THINK IT'S A PLAY OF MY IMAGINATION. However, the image forms clear in front of me. My blurry vision slowly takes him in from bottom to top. The sophisticated shoes, the pressed suit, the big, masculine watch that gives off the same hard vibe as him.

And then his face. Those sharp features and defined jawline that are meant to cut. His hair appears slightly damp, which means he got caught in the drizzle outside.

It's only when I'm trapped in his steel eyes that I finally breathe. Or maybe I stop breathing altogether.

I cut off eye contact before I see that look. The one he gave me last night and this morning. The look that guts me open without him having to say a word.

Jonathan slides into the chair beside me with utter confidence, as if Aiden and Elsa's dining table is an extension of the King mansion. It takes everything in me not to stare at him some more, get lost in him some more. Just… more.

Aiden joins his wife, but before he can sit down, Jonathan's authoritative tone makes him pause. "Where's my plate?"

"You weren't invited. There's no more food."

Elsa starts to push her pasta in her father-in-law's direction. "You can have mine."

Aiden presses his palm over hers, gently stopping her. "Nonsense. I'll get him a plate."

Jonathan raises a perfect brow. "I thought there was no more food."

His son narrows his eyes on him for a beat before he disappears into the kitchen.

"How did you find me?" I whisper what I'm thinking.

This is another reason why I don't drink. My inhibitions kind of disappear, and sometimes, I don't know when I'm thinking aloud.

"I always know where you are." He removes his jacket, places it on the chair beside him, and loosens his tie. "You don't really think you can escape me, do you?"

I should focus on what he's saying, but my entire attention is robbed by the way his lean, masculine fingers glide over the tie, wrapping around it. Tugging on it.

Why am I not that tie?

As if answering my thought, Jonathan's knuckles glide over my cheek, turning up the heat a notch. "You're warm. Have you been drinking?"

I motion at my half-empty third glass. "A little?"

His gaze holds mine, and I'm caged in the moment. It's like he's taking me hostage, and I can't, under any circumstances, find a way out.

Not that I want to.

Aiden re-joins us and places the plate in front of his father— not so gently, might I add. Jonathan takes a moment before he drops his hand from my cheek.

"What is this supposed to be?" Jonathan asks as he stares at the pasta with meatballs.

"Food. Eat it." Aiden pauses. "Or don't."

"You made it?"

"So what if I did?"

"Is it edible?"

"It is," both Elsa and I say at the same time, then we break down in giggles.

Jonathan throws me an indecipherable glance before he takes a tentative bite of his food. Although Aiden pretends to be focused on his plate, his gaze keeps filtering back to his father.

The latter says nothing, but he keeps eating, which means he likes it. Jonathan is a tyrant and picky in everything—food included. He wouldn't have continued if he didn't like it.

Elsa asks Aiden to pass her the salt, and he says no because it's not good for her health. Elsa tells him he's being too much.

While they're busy arguing, I lean over to Jonathan until his woodsy scent smothers me and murmur, "Tell him you like it."

He turns his head so his lips are mere inches away from mine. His attention remains on my mouth as he whispers back, "What was that?"

I gulp at the heated look in his eyes. It's so different from the one he gave me this morning. Maybe that one will never appear again? Or is this wishful thinking because I'm drunk. "The pasta. Tell Aiden you like it. That would mean so much to him."

"How do you know that?"

"I just do."

Even though he doesn't show it—and never would—Aiden does care about his father's approval, in a way. There's just a deep hole between father and son that's almost impossible to mend, and after talking with Aiden, I'm certain it started after Alicia's death. Instead of fulfilling child Aiden's emotional needs, Jonathan brought him up to be just like him. Impenetrable, hard, controlling. In his mind, he probably wanted his son to be the best, like everything about his own life. However, I don't think Aiden knows that. I feel like he thinks his father doesn't care about him in any other way, except for the fact that he's his heir.

Jonathan does, though. I hear him every other day asking Harris for updates about Aiden and Levi. From the outside, it might seem like an extension of his control freak nature, and to some extent, it is, but he also makes sure they're fine and protected. Jonathan is the type who brings the world down if anyone so much as bothers his family. He just doesn't express it. In turn, Aiden doesn't know it. There's a huge gap between father and son, and it'll take a long time to resolve the pile of miscommunication cluttered in their relationship.

But baby steps, right?

I pull away before Jonathan brushes his lips against mine. From the way he's staring at me, I don't doubt that he might actually do it.

It's not only because of PDA, but I'm also kind of worried about my reaction in my drunken state. Who knows if I'll start clawing at his clothes right in front of his son and daughter-in-law?

"It's different from Margot's." Jonathan pauses eating to pour himself a glass of wine. "It's good."

Both Elsa and Aiden halt their banter about the salt and stare at Jonathan as if he's grown a few heads.

I wouldn't be surprised if this was the first time the tyrant ever complimented Aiden. He can be so heartless sometimes.

Okay, most of the time.

Aiden clears his throat but remains silent.

It's Elsa who grins like a proud mama. "He cooks the best food *ever*."

"Maybe he can cook something for the family dinner next time." Jonathan is speaking to Aiden, but he stares at me over the rim of his glass, and I pretend I'm not the subject of his attention.

"Only if Levi does," Aiden says.

"Make it a competition, then." Jonathan takes a sip of his wine. "Aurora and I will be judges."

Elsa points her glass of wine at herself. "How about me?"

"Your and Astrid's votes aren't subjective. You're forbidden from voting."

She appears disappointed, but she touches her husband's bicep. "I'm sure Aiden will win."

"We'll see."

I'm about to reprimand Jonathan for being his usual aloof self, but the sadistic spark in Aiden's eyes stops me. He likes the challenge his father is throwing his and Levi's way.

The King men surely think differently. It's like they bond over battles and wars.

As a confirmation to my theory, after dinner, Aiden does the dishes, then sits with Jonathan around a coffee table on which there's a glass chessboard. It's similar to the one at home, where Jonathan has taught me how to play.

Or tried to, anyway. I usually end up straddling his lap or splayed all over the chessboard as he fucks me.

I fight the flush that covers my skin but fail. Thank God for the wine; otherwise, my arousal would be clear.

Both Jonathan and Aiden's poses are similar, their grey eyes sharpened as they think of ways to bring the other down.

As Elsa and I finish our no-idea-how-many glass of wine, my attention is robbed by Jonathan's pure masculine beauty. He leans both elbows on his knees and forms a steeple at his chin with his fingers. Those long fingers that I can't stop staring at—or at him.

It takes them both a long time to make a move because, I assume, they calculate like hell before attempting it. When Jonathan slides a piece forwards, he's so sure and confident. There's no question that he'll win. Aiden might pose a threat, but it's still too early for him to beat his father.

That doesn't stop the younger King from trying, though. He grew up to be a force not to be trifled with.

Be proud, Alicia. Your boy is now a man.

"They're so alike," Elsa whispers from beside me. We're snuggled on the sofa opposite them, sharing a soft blanket.

"I know," I murmur back. "Does Jonathan always come over to play with Aiden?"

"We've been living here for fifteen months, and this is the first time Jonathan has stepped foot into our house. I thought he'd never come over, so thank you for bringing him. I know it means a lot to Aiden."

"I didn't bring him."

"Yes, you did." She grins and it appears child-like, considering her drunken state. "Told you. You're the colours in his life."

Am I, though?

After all, he's been disappointed in me since last night. Even the alcohol isn't able to make me forget about that part.

We watch them some more as we talk about university and the differences between my experience of it and hers.

When my eyes droop, Elsa leads me upstairs and into the guest room I changed my clothes in earlier.

There's a bed, a half-empty antique wardrobe, and a tall side lamp. It's simple, beautiful, and cosy.

"Sorry it's not much." Elsa brings out blankets from the wardrobe. "I haven't had the chance to properly decorate it. Aiden said we'd never have guests, because he'd kick them out."

"Sounds like Aiden."

"Tell me about it." She rolls her eyes and motions at the fresh towels and the silky nightgown on the bed. "Let me know if you need anything else."

"Thank you."

"I'm the one who should thank you for coming into our lives." She hugs me, her coconut scent mixing with the wine. "Thank you so much for giving Aiden a chance to not only move on from Alicia, but to also find some middle ground with his father."

"I did nothing."

She pulls back, a smile on her flushed face. "Yeah, you did. Aiden had a weird relationship with Jonathan and, deep down, it's because of Alicia's death. The fact that you're trying to mend it means a lot to him. He doesn't know how to be grateful, so I'll do that on his behalf."

The devotion and affection she has for her husband warms my heart. Age really doesn't matter. They might be barely twenty, but they share the connection of an old couple in complete harmony. "Aiden is so lucky to have you in his life, Elsa."

"And Jonathan is lucky to have you in his."

I wouldn't be so sure about that.

After Elsa leaves, I strip off the dress and underwear to put on the nightgown. It takes me several minutes due to my drunken state. I trip and catch myself, only to trip again.

"Stupid clothes," I mumble.

You know what? Who needs a nightgown? My skin is on fire anyway.

I kick all the clothes away, slip under the covers, and close my eyes.

Much better.

It doesn't take me long to fall asleep. I dream of strong hands twisting my nipples and fingers slipping into my pussy. My back arches off the bed as a moan falls from my lips.

The fingers angle inside me, hitting my sweet spot. I writhe in their merciless hold, needing more.

Oh. There. Just there.

He curls his fingers deeper inside me. "Here?"

My eyes snap open at the familiar voice.

It's not a dream. It's Jonathan.

FIFTEEN

Aurora

M Y MOUTH OPENS IN AN 'O' AS I FALL INTO JONATHAN'S
presence.

He's spooning me from behind, his firm naked chest covering my back. The pads of his fingers trace my areola with expert slowness. My nipples are so hard, they ache with the need to be stimulated.

His other hand hovers over my pussy, teasing my wet folds, but not touching. My skin is hot and tingly, and it's not because of the alcohol—at least, not all of it.

"Jonathan?" I breathe out. "What are you doing here?"

"What does it look like I'm doing?" His voice is husky with lust as he pounds two fingers inside me in one go and tugs on a nipple.

I arch against him, my breathing crackling as a moan rips through the air. My moan. It doesn't matter what state I'm in. My body is so attuned to his, so used to his domineering touch that I come alive in an instant. This is our normal—no matter how fucked up that is. That's why the platonic treatment from this morning messed with my head.

"No...I...I meant h-here...in this room?"

"Apparently, Aiden has one guest room and he thinks that's too much." He pauses, and I nearly curse my idiotic question. "Why? You have an objection?"

"N-no..." my voice ends in a whimper as he curls his fingers inside me, triggering a low thrumming at the bottom of my stomach.

"I thought so." He releases my taut nipple to pull my hair to the side. His hot lips latch onto the hollow of my throat, sucking the sensitive skin into his wet mouth. A zap of pleasure shoots straight between my legs as if he's feasting on my pussy.

"Oh... Holy...shit...J-Jonathan..."

I don't know if it's the alcohol or his touch or the damn friction, but my entire body is so turned on and about ready to burst with all the sexual pleasure pulsing inside me.

"You did something wrong, Aurora," he speaks against my skin, his light stubble adding to the unbearable stimulation.

"I-I did?"

"You ran away from me."

"I-I d-didn't."

He bites on the skin on my throat and I push back against him in need for more. "You're in Oxford, which means you did."

"H-how did you find me, anyway?" I doubt Aiden would've called him.

"I have my ways."

The realisation seeps into my dazed brain. "You...you have people following me like you do Levi and Aiden?"

No clue why I haven't thought about that after he magically found me in Leeds. Only, there's nothing magical about the situation. It was all calculated. Jonathan and his control freak, methodical brain knows no limits.

"Did you really think I'd leave you alone after you were attacked?"

"No?"

"No. I chased you before, and I'll chase you again if I have to."

"You chased me." I don't know why I repeat the words. It's almost as if I'm trying to commemorate them to memory.

"I did."

"W-why?" I clench around his fingers when he pulls them out, but he only does that so he can thrust them back in.

"Because you're mine." His hoarse whisper against the shell of my ear drives me over the edge.

Just like that. No warning. No preparation.

This orgasm isn't slow-building or submerging. No. It explodes all over my skin and detonates inside me.

I tilt my head back and capture Jonathan's lips as the wave invades me. It could be the alcohol or the bursts of excitement he's initiated in me, but I don't stop to think about my actions as I kiss him.

Or rather, he's the one who takes full control of it. The man's kiss is as commanding as he is. His tongue swirls against mine, dominating my every breath and confiscating my thoughts in the process.

He'll probably punish me for initiating the kiss later, but I don't care. Not now. He's looking at me with lust instead of disappointment and I want to drown in that. I want to snatch it away and hide it somewhere.

His fingers are still inside me, his thumb lazily stroking my clit. Small bursts of pleasure cause a shudder to overtake me.

He doesn't stop kissing me; it is as if it's the first time he's doing it. Unlike the way he handles my body, Jonathan's kisses aren't as experienced. It's almost like he didn't like kissing before. They're firm, though, his kisses, and filled with so much confidence that they turn me boneless.

The need to get lost in him further burns hotter and brighter. I reach behind me and wrap my fingers around his cock that's nestling against my back.

Jonathan grabs a handful of my arse cheek in his big hand

before he slaps it. I yelp, my lips momentarily leaving his. "You cannot run away from me again, Aurora. Is that understood?"

"Mmm," I mumble, eyes closing so I can go back to kissing him. I'm addicted to his lips, to the way he kisses, savage and all-consuming. like he intends to fuse us together.

He spanks me again and my eyes fly open. "Is that fucking understood?"

"Mmm," I whine this time.

"I mean it, Aurora. If you leave again, I won't only chase you to Leeds or Oxford. I'll flip the world upside down to find you."

"What if you can't find me?" My voice is still aroused, but it's low as my deep-seated fears trickle in. "What if I disappear?"

"Then I'll burn the world that forced you to disappear and resurrect you from its ashes."

"You...will?"

"You think I'm not able to?"

"It's not that." If anyone is capable of that, it's Jonathan. I have no doubt in my mind that he'll make anything he wishes happen.

"You don't seem to understand what it means to be mine. It's not only about how you belong to me, or that I'll cut off the dick of any bastard who looks your way and shove it up his arse. It's also about how I'll protect you from the world and yourself if I have to. It's about burning your obstacles so you can leave the shadows and shine like you were always meant to. You can provoke or test me or even give me that fucking attitude, but you do *not* get to run away from me."

Tears gather in my eyes and I blink them away, whispering, "Okay."

"Okay, what?"

"Okay, I won't run away from you, Jonathan. Looks like I'm stuck with you."

"You sure as fuck are." His voice is filled with possessiveness and something else as he grabs my arse tighter.

I love the feel of him behind me, cocooning me, almost like he's caging me from the world.

But…tonight, and after what he said, I need more. I don't want to be stuck in a position where he barely, if ever, sees my face.

Placing a hand on his cheek, I turn around, and I'm surprised that he loosens his hold on my pussy and arse to let me. Usually, whenever I attempt to wiggle away, he pins me in place and fucks me from behind.

It's the only position he's ever used to take me.

Our heads rest on the same pillow. My nose nearly touches his, and my nipples brush against the fine hairs on his chest with every torturous breath from my lungs.

For a moment, we stare at each other in silence, but my heartbeat thuds louder, thrumming faster against my ribcage. It's almost as if it wants to leave and go to him—the man whose undivided attention is on me.

His cock nestles at the bottom of my stomach—hard, enormous, and so ready. He grips me by the hip and pulls me against his groin.

"What do you want, Aurora?" The arousal with which he says my name wrenches a moan from me.

"Will I be punished for it?" I whisper.

"We both know spanking isn't a punishment for you. You get off on it."

"Then why did you punish me with it?"

"Because you made the deal."

"I don't want this to be for punishment." My words are so low and…vulnerable.

"Then how do you want it?"

"Do it because you also want it."

"Do what?"

I brush my lips against his, then murmur against them, "Fuck me while I look at you."

One moment is too long sometimes.

But other times, one moment is all it takes for a change to take place.

Jonathan flips me underneath him and my legs part of their own accord. Then he grabs me by the throat and thrusts deep inside me.

I push off the bed due to the force of it, eyes rolling to the back of my head. It doesn't matter how wet or ready I am. Jonathan is big and having him inside me always hurts so good.

There's so much power and pent-up energy in his shoulders. It's almost as if he's been waiting for this moment as long as I have.

My legs wrap around his lean waist, my hands grabbing his wrists for balance.

I try to meet his thrusts, going up while he comes down, but it's impossible. There's an animalistic need in his moves, a current, a storm that cannot be stopped or prevented.

I'm caught in the path of his natural disaster, in how he makes me feel whole without even trying to. He only has to be himself with his controlling, unapologetic, and oddly protective self.

Just *him.*

Jonathan slows his pounding, coming out almost entirely before ramming back in. White dots form at the edge of my vision as a sheen of perspiration covers my skin.

"Are you mine, Aurora?"

"Mmmm, y-yes…yes!" I manage through the tiny air space he's giving me.

"Now, scream it." He slaps my arse, hand squeezing tighter around my throat.

A loud moan fills the air as I fall to pieces around him, the waves scattering them farther apart.

That both scares me and consoles me.

On one hand, I know that Jonathan won't prevent me from gathering those pieces. If anything, he'll help put them back together again. On the other hand, I recognise that I don't want anyone but him to touch my pieces ever again.

Not that I allowed anyone in the past.

Jonathan grunts as he spills inside me, his seed warming my walls. This time, he doesn't curse because he came inside me or didn't use a condom.

This time, he kisses my nose. "Good girl."

SIXTEEN

Jonathan

DURING THE NEXT FAMILY DINNER, AIDEN AND LEVI DO COOK, and they give their all into it, too, messing up Margot's kitchen in the process.

They don't even allow their wives to help them. As we all sit for dinner, my son and nephew glare at each other across the table with that competitive streak that's always existed in the King household.

James and I used to compete with everything when we were younger. Then, as we grew up, he became dull and started forfeiting. That's why I found my competitive fix in Ethan— whose throat I will cut if he ever shows his face here again.

The fact that he saw Aurora in her nightgown is his first and final strike. No one gets to look at her dressed like that. Actually, even if she wore traditional religious clothes like Black Belt, I still wouldn't like it if anyone looked at her.

She's sitting at my left. Levi only gave up his place after some dramatic bitching about how he's always pushed out and some other nonsense.

I study her closely as she takes a bite of the beef. It's not about how her lips wrap around the fork—though that in itself is a sight to behold.

Since we returned from Aiden's house a week ago, I can't stop watching her. Not that I've ever been able to. But now is different. The fact that she could—and would—slip into a black hole is a possibility that could become a reality.

I could blame the way she mixed up facts on lack of sleep or the attack back in Leeds. After all, she was under a lot of stress during that couple of days. What's concerning me, however, is how she hysterically insisted that everything did happen.

That's how Alicia's decimation started. She said someone was following her, then that 'ghost'—as she called him—sent her voice messages and whispered things to her. However, whenever I asked her to show me, she couldn't find them.

The doctor said it was hallucinations due to stress. She became neurotic, and gradually, her mental health deteriorated. She hid her pills and it only made her state worse.

Unlike Aurora, Alicia didn't insist she wasn't crazy. She didn't scream at me or hit me or anything like that. She just…pulled back. With time, she stopped talking altogether and dived into her internal world, where she never really allowed anyone in—except for maybe Aiden sometimes.

My son thinks I could've provided for her emotionally, but he doesn't know that she never allowed me to get close. Just because she let him in didn't mean she let me. He thinks she cried because of my neglect, but she cried whenever I tried to talk to her. She cried when I asked her to take her pills. She cried when she returned from Leeds and wrote in her scattered journals that she missed Clarissa already. That she wanted to kidnap her baby sister and take her and Aiden to a place no one could find them.

She said the three of them would be happy without the 'ghost'.

Then she burnt those journals for no apparent reason, as if she didn't want anyone to read them.

She became paranoid to the point that she sometimes refused

to eat for whole days because the 'ghost' could've put something in her food.

Not once in our married life did Alicia come to me, or even attempt to talk to me. Forget the physical aspect. Due to her mental state and the meds, she became asexual, and withdrew from me. She told me to have mistresses, but I never did, because that meant disrespecting the mother of my son.

The only women I touched were long after her death.

The sole presence Alicia leant on was Aiden. He was her anchor, in a way, and when he disappeared because of Abigail, her state of mind spiralled out of control and then...she died.

That simple.

Could I have done better? Probably. But there was a wall between me and Alicia; sometimes I thought she wasn't the same woman I first saw in the cemetery, and others, she appeared just like her, broken and lost.

I have a lot of regrets when it comes to Alicia, and there's no way in fuck I'll repeat them with Aurora. It doesn't matter that she's showing the signs.

This time, I won't leave, even if she pushes me.

"So?" Levi leans forwards as if he's about to jump across the table.

"Out with it." Aiden sounds more impatient than excited. "And before you say anything, remember, you spent the night at my house."

"Hey!" Levi snaps his fingers at him. "Not fair. She could've spent the night at mine."

My son glares down his nose at him. "Who said anything about fair? I'm going to crush you, Lev."

"Cut down on your delusional pills, little Cousin."

After eating from both plates, Aurora wipes her lips with her napkin. "I'll go with nil."

"You can't go with nil," Levi protests.

"Yeah, pick one." Aiden motions at the one on the right—his. "That one."

"I'm sorry. I can't choose." She smiles in a soft, bright way. "Both are one of the best steaks I've had."

Levi puffs out his chest, but soon after, his along with everyone else's attention turns to me. Five pair of eyes watch me as I savour the meat. They're well-cooked, to the level of what I prefer, so that's one point for both.

"Any day now, Jonathan." Aiden taps his fingers on the table's surface, letting his impatience show.

He takes after me in that department—I was never one for patience. Aiden's problem is that he can be volatile. Not as much as Levi, but it's there. He'll learn to school his reaction better as he grows up.

"Yeah, Uncle. Suspense doesn't suit you." Levi's sense of sarcasm is too similar to James's. Sometimes, it feels as if my brother is sitting beside me, not his son.

"Neither," I say.

Elsa's and Astrid's expressions fall. They were waiting for the result as much as their husbands.

Aurora kicks me under the table. Hard. The pointy part of her heel digs into my calf and remains there, but a smile plasters on her face for everyone to see.

Fuck me. This woman has a fire in her, and she's not afraid of showing it whenever she deems necessary.

I suppress a groan as I place my fork on the table. "They're both good. I won't pick one."

Aurora's heel eases off me, but not before she rubs her leg against mine as if she's soothing the pain. Her touch is gentle, caring—another side of her I've gotten infuriatingly used to.

Before I can grab her leg and keep it there, or better yet, have her sit on my lap, she retreats from me and focuses on the others.

Levi grins at Astrid, who strokes his shoulder as if she's proud of him. Elsa takes Aiden's hand in hers and a smug look fills his gaze. "Though, for the record, Jonathan liked my pasta the last time. That makes me the winner."

"Nonsense." Levi points a finger at me. "You're spending the night at my place next time, Uncle. I won't take no for an answer."

"You, too, Aurora. Please come over," Astrid tells her.

"We would love to," Aurora says.

No, I wouldn't love to. The only reason I spent the night at Aiden's was because she was there.

Ironically enough, that'll be how she'll make me spend the night at Levi's. Not sure if she's doing it on purpose, but the smallest ways she's affecting my life are starting to have a much larger impact.

It's like she came into this family with a purpose and won't stop until she achieves it.

After dinner, Aiden and Levi insist on making me watch their chess game. They won't quit until one of them is considered the winner this night. Winning is in their blood, and I'm proud of the way they grew up—mishaps and all.

I sit across from them on a chair in the lounge area. Each of them occupies a sofa, with the glass chess board between them. I'm vaguely focused on their moves. While neither of them wins against me, their games are sporadic. Usually, the less distracted one beats the other.

A glass of cognac is cradled between my fingers, but I haven't been drinking. My focus is on the woman who's standing over the table in the other part of the lounge area. Her dark green dress clings to her slim figure and that arse I spanked right before dinner. It's part of the reason why she's currently standing, not sitting.

It was due to her attitude after an email exchange.

From: Jonathan King
To: Aurora Harper
Subject: Do Not Wear the Red Lipstick for Dinner Tonight.
Refer to subject.

From: Aurora Harper

To: Jonathan King
Subject: Do Not Wear the Red Lipstick for Dinner Tonight.
No.

From: Jonathan King
To: Aurora Harper
Subject: Do Not Wear the Red Lipstick for Dinner Tonight.
Don't fucking push me, Aurora. That red lipstick is meant for me and me alone. No one else is allowed to see it, not even my son and nephew.

From: Aurora Harper
To: Jonathan King
Subject: Do Not Wear the Red Lipstick for Dinner Tonight.
Oops.

Attached is a picture of herself. She wasn't only wearing the red lipstick, but she was also biting her lower lip while wearing a revealing dress that showed so much of her cleavage, she nearly flashed me her nipples.

One, I became as hard as a rock.

Two, I planned the murder of every last bastard who could see her like that.

Could, because there was no way in fuck she'd go out like that in front of anyone.

From: Jonathan King
To: Aurora Harper
Subject: Do Not Wear the Red Lipstick for Dinner Tonight.
Change your clothes and remove the lipstick. Now.

From: Aurora Harper
To: Jonathan King
Subject: Do Not Wear the Red Lipstick for Dinner Tonight.
Or what?

From: Jonathan King
To: Aurora Harper
Subject: Do Not Wear the Red Lipstick for Dinner Tonight.
Or that arse will turn red. If you're in the mood to sit at all tonight, change.

From: Aurora Harper
To: Jonathan King
Subject: Do Not Wear the Red Lipstick for Dinner Tonight.
I guess you have to come home and make me.

I went home and did just that. Then I grabbed her by the throat and fucked her against the wall, smearing the lipstick all over her face until she screamed my name.

I haven't missed the way she calls my house a home now, either. For someone who never actually belonged anywhere, it's a huge deal that she's picking my place as her home.

Maybe she meant what she told me once—the part about not running away anymore. But for some reason, I can't seem to fully trust that promise.

She's currently talking to Elsa and Astrid. While their conversation is far enough away to not disrupt the boys' game, I can almost hear Aurora talk about her next design.

She's been focused on that lately, working from home until late and even inviting Black Belt over. She said her peculiar behaviour is one of her inspirations. Sometimes, I catch her observing my wrist or measuring my watches as if planning for something.

From the outside looking in, it appears as if she's moving on from the attack, Maxim's reappearance, and everything that transpired afterwards.

But it's too soon. The possibility that she's bottling something—or everything—inside is what's keeping me on the edge. That's never a good sign and will eventually backfire.

"Your obsession is showing, Jonathan." Aiden focuses on me for a second, smirks, then slides his attention back to the board.

"Can you blame him?" Levi waggles his brows. "What's up with her knee, though?"

"Why the fuck have you been looking at her knee?" I rip my gaze away from her to glare at my nephew.

"It's innocent, Uncle."

"Innocent or not, do *not* look at her. That applies to you, too, Aiden."

My son lifts his shoulder. "I don't take orders, Jonathan."

"Well, you will now. Is that understood?"

"Does that mean you'll beat him up? Can I watch? Or maybe participate?" Levi's gaze sparks.

Aiden flips him off discreetly, but I see it.

"I must admit. I like this side of you, Uncle. It's more human. You weren't this way with Alicia."

"No, he wasn't." There's no maliciousness in Aiden's voice, as if he merely intends to relay facts. "Is it true that she's becoming like Alicia? Aurora, I mean."

I take a sip of my drink, letting the burn settle in before I speak, "How do you know about that?"

"She told me so herself."

"Since when did you two start to talk?"

"Since I can use her to bring you down."

My lips twitch. "Maybe in the next life, son."

"Whatever." Aiden twirls a knight chess piece between his fingers. "So is she?"

"Perhaps."

"Well, shit." Levi's voice lowers. "Is it genetic?"

"No clue yet, but probably."

"I'm surprised you haven't taken her to the doctor." Aiden kills one of Levi's pawns with his knight.

"Yeah, Uncle. Doctors are your modus operandi, aren't they? First Alicia, then Dad, then me."

"If there's need for outside help that's exactly what will happen." I take another sip of my cognac.

"Why didn't you do it with her, then?" Aiden motions his head in Aurora's direction.

"She would throw a tantrum."

Levi chuckles. "Whoa. Has the great Jonathan King finally met his match?"

"Looks like it." Aiden gives me an undecipherable glance.

"Don't you have a game to focus on? Your right is exposed, Aiden. Your queen is in jeopardy, Levi."

Both their demeanours sharpen as their attention shifts back to the chessboard. Now that they realise the other party is aware of their weakness, they need to give their all to win the game.

The women soon join us. Elsa slides beside Aiden, and her blue eyes sparkle. She's just like Ethan; they seem demure, but deep down yearn for challenges and wars. Her father is way worse, though.

Astrid sits close to Levi and points at a chess piece. Even though he's concentrating, he answers each of her questions.

There's a moment of hesitation before Aurora stands beside my chair. She's far enough away that her apple scent is barely noticeable. That scent, which I've never paid attention to before, has become a fucking addiction. Smelling it means she's there, close, and all mine for the taking. Having it all over my bed means she's beside me, holding on to me with her dainty hands as if she needs me.

I grab her by the waist and pull her close. She gasps as she falls at the edge of my chair. She attempts to wiggle away, because in her politically correct mind, she doesn't like the kids to see us close. She feels like she's taking a role that's not hers.

If they have an issue with her, that's their problem, not mine. Aurora is here to stay. I don't fucking care what anyone says or thinks.

My fingers dig into the flesh of her waist, and she must

realise that there's no escaping me, because she releases a long sigh and remains still.

Soon, she'll stop fighting or trying to run away from me.

Soon, she'll be safe from both the world and herself.

But to make that happen, I might have to take a measure that she won't like.

SEVENTEEN

Aurora

SOMETHING IS WRONG.

This feeling has been a constant over the last couple of days. It could be because Jonathan didn't spank me hard enough and has disappeared from my side when I wake up in the morning. He's usually there the entire night, sometimes holding me through the aftermath of my nightmares, and other times staring at me as if he's making sure of something. What, I don't know.

Needless to say, after that night at Aiden's house, I've been sleeping in Jonathan's bed. My room was cleaned up and appears as good as new. However, each time I end up there, even to grab my things, Jonathan grabs me by my hand and leads me back to his room.

Not that I've wanted to spend any nights alone after those voices I dreamt about.

He still spanks me as 'punishment', but we both know it's so much more than that.

It's our connection.

It's something that fills his eyes with possessiveness and mine with raw lust.

Sometimes, I wake up with his face buried between my legs. Other times, he fucks me into the mattress with his hand around my throat. He then sleeps with his cock deep inside me just so he can pick up where he left off in the middle of the night.

He exhausts me, but at the same time, he completes me in the strangest way possible.

There's no getting enough of Jonathan. The harder he takes it out on me, the more I meet him head-on. If he's a hurricane, I'm the wind that gets off on the damage he causes.

But it's not always damage, and that's what throws me for a loop. After he marks my arse with his handprint and wrenches one orgasm after the other out of me, Jonathan doesn't stand up and leave like when I first came into his life.

He doesn't look at me as if I'm an annoyance or something he's bent on breaking. There's acceptance in his steel eyes now, the sort that both frightens and intrigues me. Being on the receiving end of Jonathan's attention is like living in a high-alert mode twenty-four-seven.

Then he does things that make me pause.

Every day, he either makes us shower together, or he runs me a bath and takes special care with washing my hair. It's become so much of a habit that I get infuriated when I have to do it myself.

He also gets frustratingly protective whenever I hurt myself in any way.

Over time, he's eventually stopped being a blank board in front of his children. Jonathan will always be Jonathan; however, he sometimes follows my lead and doesn't purposefully act like a bastard.

I might be addicted to his harshness, but his tenderness strikes a completely different chord inside me. A part of me is slowly leaving my body and creeping to his side, and although I'm aware of it, there's no way I can stop it.

He's a steep cliff, and I keep rolling down, enjoying every bump and hit.

However, today, there's something wrong.

When he gave me an undecipherable look this morning, I brushed it off. Jonathan does a lot of watching and observing, and not all of his expressions can be explained.

After all, he didn't give me *that look* again, the 'You're crazy' one. We're past that phase, right? There's no way he'll bring that back up.

And yet, that doesn't alleviate the tension sinking to the bottom of my stomach. I caught myself touching my watch more than often today, and I barely pushed through the meetings.

I leave work early, opting to go home. Not that Jonathan will be there at this time.

My feet come to a halt in front of my car. Did I just call Jonathan's house *home*? Since when did I start considering it as such?

I shake my head, not wanting to think about it. Just when I'm about to open the door, a dark shadow passes in my peripheral vision.

My hand freezes as I search my surroundings.

H&H's car park isn't that big, but it's still underground and silent. The only sound is the buzzing from one of the defective neon lights.

This time, I don't stand there and wait for the hit.

I beep my car and reach out to open the door. When a hand comes from behind me, I startle, hitting blindly.

It's like I'm pushed back to that day eleven years ago. Soon, there'll be the crunch of the blade against my bones, then blood—lots of blood—followed by pain.

Uncontrollable pain.

I'll be buried alive in a grave. I'll be just like those women, where no one will hear my screams.

"No!" I shriek, then shove my hand in my bag and retrieve the pepper spray I started keeping on me since my most recent attack.

I whirl around and point it at the shadow. I don't care if he's a member of a victim's family. I shouldn't be the subject of his wrath.

My voice is strong and comes from the bottom of my gut. "If you want to attack anyone, go stab the fucker Maxim!"

"Whoa."

My hold falters on the pepper spray as I come face-to-face with none other than Ethan Steel.

My harsh breathing slows down and I glance behind him as if expecting to find the shadow. Sure enough, there's what resembles a shadow, but it's only Agnus.

"Sorry." I drop the bottle back into my bag. "I thought it was someone else."

"It's fine." He smiles, and it's kind of welcoming. Kind of, because there's something else behind it that I can't pinpoint.

"Is there something I can help you with, Ethan?"

"Yes, and I can't exactly visit you at Jonathan's place or he'll chase me away with a shotgun." He motions at his car. "Do you have a moment?"

I hesitate for a beat. It's not only due to Jonathan's warnings about staying away from Ethan—and the entire male population, per his words. I also want to go home tonight. It feels crucial that I be there.

Seeming to sense my hesitation, Ethan says, "It's about Jonathan."

That gets my attention. No matter how much Jonathan says he hates Ethan, he was once his best friend. One way or another, he knew him better than anyone else.

I follow to Ethan's car and Agnus joins in the front seat beside the driver. He's like Harris in a way, but without the latter's weird antics and snobbish sense of humour. He's kind of grown on me. Even Margot's and Tom's silence has grown on me, too.

Everything that I was wary of about Jonathan's entourage has eventually snuck its way into my life. Before I knew it, they became an inseparable part.

The car rolls down the streets. The bright city lights and the endless traffic are visible through the tinted window. No idea why all of it gives me a horrific premonition.

"What did you want to talk about?" I ask Ethan.

He leans an elbow on the armrest between us and pins me down like a lab researcher would do to his guinea pig. "Why don't you tell me, Aurora? What's your secret?"

My heart pounds at that word. *Secret.* Whenever someone says it, I feel like my past will come running in and ruin any type of stability I've been building for years. Not that Ethan would know anything about it.

Right?

Adopting my nonchalant tone, I say, "My secret concerning what?"

"Concerning how Jonathan treats you. He's never shown his true feelings about anyone—at least not until he crushes them. Hell, he didn't even act this way towards his father and brother when they were alive."

"Was he…close to them?"

"Yes, especially James."

My chest falls at what Jonathan must've felt when he lost his only brother. I know he died of an accident that also took away Astrid's mother, but that's not all. He was an addict prior to that. I could almost imagine Jonathan wanting to help him and not finding the right way to, because he sucks at offering emotional support.

"At first, I thought you were holding something over his head." Ethan taps his fingers on the armrest. "But we both know Jonathan is the type who holds things over people's heads, not the other way around."

"You can say that again."

"So what is it? The Alicia angle?"

"I don't know. You can ask him yourself if you're so curious."

"That would get my head on a platter, and I kind of need it. My head, I mean."

I clear my throat. "May I ask you something?"

"Of course."

"Elsa mentioned that Jonathan and you fell apart because he blames you for Alicia's death. Is that the case?"

"Not entirely. That was the final straw." He sighs, and his gaze seems to be trapped someplace in the past. "It all started with our loathsome rivalry and games. We used to play a lot of them when we were younger. Jonathan refused to lose and I was the same. When we graduated from university and each of us took reign of part of the family business, we rivalled each other in profit margin and stock value. Then it extended to other things. Gambling. Property. Women."

"Women?"

"Yes. We shared women. Occasionally at the same time."

"Oh." My lips fall open. I kind of find it hard to imagine Jonathan and Ethan doing threesomes.

"Is there a problem?"

"No, it's just that Jonathan is possessive."

"Of you, and of his wife, perhaps, but he wasn't in the past. He didn't care enough about anyone to be possessive."

"So you, like, had threesomes…right?" I whisper, not sure if Agnus and the driver should be privy to this conversation.

"We had. Don't get me wrong, we didn't touch each other, but we got off on the same things. Not to mention, we were somehow always attracted to the same type of women."

"Looks-wise?"

"No." A mischievous smirk tilts his lips. "Personality-wise. Both of us could sense their demons, their mental scars, and I guess we were attracted to the broken sides of them."

"Is that why he married Alicia? Aside from the revenge, I mean."

"You know about that."

"He told me."

He nods. "It's part of the reason, yes."

"And you married Elsa's mother."

"Correct. Both women were...how to put it? Beautifully broken. At least, Abby was. Alicia slowly disintegrated from Jonathan."

"What?"

"She pulled away from him after Aiden's birth. He became her world and Jonathan was second."

"That's not what Aiden said. He mentioned it was Jonathan who pulled away."

"Aiden was just a kid. He had no idea what was going on between his parents."

"And you do?"

"Despite our rivalry, Jonathan and I remained friends. We talked."

"Did you continue to share?"

He laughs, the sound light and amused. "Our wives? Absolutely not."

Phew. Then whatever Layla heard about Ethan's wife having an affair with Jonathan must've been a stupid rumour all along.

"So what happened? What caused you both to be at each other's throats?"

"They both fucked up," Agnus says from the front seat, making his presence known.

Ethan releases a breath that seems exasperated, but he nods. "We did. For net profit rivalry reasons, Jonathan arranged for someone to burn down my main coal factory in Birmingham. Due to a miscalculation, the factory caught fire while people were inside and many passed away."

"The Great Birmingham Fire," I gasp. It was all over the news back then. I can't believe Jonathan was behind that.

"So you kidnapped Aiden as retaliation?" I ask.

"Correct. Though, due to another miscalculation, he was tortured for more than a week by my unwell wife and almost died. Alicia figured he was with us, and drove to find him, and that's how she had her accident."

"That's why Jonathan blames you." It all makes sense now. His aggression towards Ethan is fuelled by the past, and although the man in front of me indulges him, there's something else to it.

He's not as closed off as Jonathan, and he doesn't hold grudges as long either. The reason he's been a thorn in Jonathan's side is probably because it brings back memories from when they were rivals or frenemies or whatever their relationship was.

"You want to be friends with him again." I don't voice it as a question, because I'm almost sure that's the case.

"Friends?" He chuckles. "Are we talking about the same Jonathan?"

"He's not a stone and you know it."

"But he's perfect at emulating one."

"That's because you keep provoking him."

"The only way he reacts."

"Yeah, you're right." I smile. "But I don't think he's that immune to emotions. He might not feel them like everyone else, but they're there, and I'm sure he also remembers your friendship."

"I wouldn't bet on it."

"I would, and you know what? I'm going to help."

He raises a brow. "And how are you going to do that?"

The car comes to a stop at a gas station for a refill. My grin falters as I stare out the window at the very familiar face on the TV screen inside the store.

Ethan is talking, but I'm not listening. Like a moth drawn to a deadly flame, I open the door with shaky fingers and step out.

My ears buzz, and the closer I am to the store, the more everything else is erased from my surroundings. It's like there's no one and nothing. No smells, no sights.

Just nothing.

I'm floating on air, unable to feel my legs. By the time I reach the counter, where the cashier and a few customers are focused on the news, I think I may fall.

I don't.

My feet keep me planted in place as the buzz in my ears gives way to the male news anchor's voice.

"Turmoil broke out in the juridical system today when Judge Huntington approved the parole hearing of Maxim Griffin." The image flashes from the anchor to an archived footage of when the police first arrested Dad. He was on his way home after that call he made to me when the police grabbed him. As they led him to the car, a conceited smirk tugged at his lips. "The most notorious serial killer in the UK's recent history has murdered seven identified women and ten others remain suspected. The ages of his victims ranged from nineteen to thirty and all carried the same physical description.

"Griffin is labelled as the Duct Tape Killer because he abducted his victims and suffocated them using silver duct tape for long periods of time that ranged from several hours to a day before he buried them behind his cabin. His daughter, sixteen years old at the time, was the one who reported seeing her father dragging a corpse out of their hunting cabin. The trial was messy and had a lot of public attention, both inside and outside of Great Britain." The screen flashes again to show Dad during his recent interview. "A few weeks ago, Griffin conducted an interview for the first time and accused his daughter of being an accomplice. He claims the only reason the police caught him was due to being betrayed by his partner in crime.

"The Crown Prosecution Service announced that it will re-open an investigation in regards of Clarissa Griffin, who also happens to be the only alleged witness of Maxim Griffin's crimes. The serial killer's daughter should be twenty-seven now. In an exclusive statement, her father's solicitor, Stephan Wayne, says that she has adopted a new identity and currently lives in London. It's notable to mention that Clarissa disappeared right after the sentencing of her father and escaped the Witness Protection Program." A headshot of me from eleven years ago appears on the screen. Even though it's old, if anyone looks at it hard enough, they'll recognise me. "The question remains. A victim or an assailant?"

My legs shake, unable to carry me as the screen switches to a statement made by the solicitor, Stephan.

I try to focus, but the world is closing in on me and all I can hear is the beeping in my ears and the sinking of my heart.

The cashier's attention shifts to me, and I jerk back. God. They'll recognise me. The nightmare will start all over again.

"May I help you, Miss?" The cashier watches me closely.

I lower my head as Dad's voice filters from the TV. "In the time I spent in confinement, I started believing in justice, its rules, and how it should be applied. I love my daughter, but she needs to pay for what she's done. Justice, Clarissa. I taught you that."

If someone stabs you once, stab them back ten times.

That's what he taught me. Those were the exact words my father said to six-year-old me when I came crying about a girl who stole my pens at school. He kept repeating them until they became my mantra.

The cashier is still staring at me, but before he can recognise me, I spin around and run out of the small store. They'll know who I am now, and everything will start again.

The name-calling, the trials, the poor police treatment, the accusatory looks.

Everything.

A hand grabs me by the arm and I yelp, coming to a screeching halt.

Ethan.

His brows scrunch. "Are you okay?"

No. Absolutely not.

He holds my phone that I left in the car, on which there are five missed calls.

"Jonathan has been calling nonstop." His gaze drifts behind me. "Also, why is everyone staring at you?"

No, no...

Agnus barges outside and kind of pushes me towards the car.

"What's going on?" Ethan asks, but he follows anyway.

"She needs to get out of the public eye." Agnus's features remain steady. "*Now*."

Ethan and I are both inside when the car revs its engine in the street. Then Elsa's father asks, "Are you going to elaborate, Agnus?"

"She's part of a public trial."

Again. I'm part of a public trial *again*.

I barely survived the first one. I can't go through that nightmare all over again.

EIGHTEEN

Aurora

I'M SHAKING BY THE TIME THE CAR STOPS. I HAVE NO CLUE about the destination. All I know is that I should stay far away from that place, those people.

From everything.

Ethan didn't try to talk to me, and I'm glad for that. I wouldn't have been able to converse with him even if my life depended on it.

I'm back to being that teenage girl who sat in a dark corner in the safe houses the police took me to. I pulled my knees to my chest and trembled all night, unable to rid the victims' faces from my mind.

At every trial, their families brought their happy pictures, their toddler albums, their graduation memories—all the things that made them human.

They thrust them in my face and demanded I see how their lives were stolen and could never be retrieved.

In that dark corner, I prayed for their souls. I even asked for forgiveness on Dad's behalf, but with time, I stopped everything altogether.

I think a part of me died during those excruciatingly long weeks. With every trial, every escape from the media, and every look in Dad's desolate eyes, pieces of my soul slowly chipped, then scattered.

For eleven years, I've been trying to gather them back together again, and just when I thought I finally could, the nightmare rushes back in.

The door opens, and I startle, pushing into Ethan's side. What if they found me so soon and will now finish what they started eleven years ago?

Maybe my attacker has returned and he'll drag me back to that eighth grave.

A breath leaves me when I get trapped in those grey eyes. It's a weird sense of relief, something I never thought I'd feel upon seeing Jonathan.

There's a crease in the middle of his forehead as if he doesn't approve of the scene. As proof, he clutches me by the elbow and pulls me out of the car. I stumble, but he catches me against him, his arm wrapping tightly around my waist.

He leans back into the car to glare at Ethan. "Get off my property and don't show your face here again."

"A thank you would be nice," Ethan shoots back.

"You're lucky that I'm not setting you and your car on fire."

"If it weren't for me and my car, Aurora wouldn't have gotten here in time."

I gulp, imagining what might've happened if I had been caught there on my own. Sure I could've escaped, but they could've recognised me first, or worse, filmed me and caused some sort of a media ruckus.

"That's why I'm allowing you to leave intact." Jonathan slams the door shut.

Ethan lowers the window. "Take care of yourself, Aurora."

And just like that, the car speeds down the road.

"That fucker." Jonathan stares at the retreating vehicle.

I'm still shaking, and as much as I want to, I can't stop. There isn't anything I want more than to pull myself together and then… what? Run? Disappear? Is that even an option anymore?

Jonathan holds me by my shoulders an arm's length away and leans down so he can stare me in the eyes. There's a slight furrow in his brow, only, it's not his usual disapproval; it's something similar to concern. "Are you okay?"

Tears gather in my eyes as I shake my head frantically. I don't attempt to speak, because I have no clue what to say, and something tells me I'd burst out in sobs.

I don't want Jonathan—or anyone—to see me that way.

"You will be." His thumb slides under my eyes, gathering the unshed tears and wiping them away. "Do you trust me?"

I stare at him, taken aback by his sudden question.

If he'd asked me that in the past, my answer would've been a definite no—especially after I heard Alicia's message. However, ever since that turned out to be null, there's been something morbid growing inside me for this man. Maybe trust is part of that?

When I don't answer, he grabs me by the hand, where the wound is almost healed. "You'll have to trust me on this one."

Before I can make out what he means, Jonathan drags me to his car. As soon as we slide inside, Moses drives out at full speed. I physically push back against the seat cushions from the force of it.

Jonathan straps a seatbelt across my chest, then asks Moses, "Is everything set?"

"Yes, sir."

"Did Harris confirm?"

"Yes, the flight is scheduled upon your arrival."

"Whoa. Hold on." I stare between Moses's bald head and Jonathan. "What flight? Where are we going?"

"Away from here," Jonathan says simply.

"Away, where?"

He runs his knuckles over my cheek, and I resist the urge to close my eyes and lean into his touch. He always gets to me when he does that. "A place where they can't find you."

"T-they?"

"My resources tell me the prosecutor will issue a warrant to bring you in for questioning, and there might be a travel ban."

"They can find me?"

"If Maxim's lawyer can, so can they. Besides, he's the one who revealed your new identity."

"Won't I, you know, be considered a fugitive if I leave the country?"

"There's no travel ban at the moment. This is completely legal, but even if it isn't, who fucking cares? I won't let them have you under custody until the trial—that's out of the question. Besides, you need to clear your head." His hand grabs both of mine before he lifts them and kisses my knuckles. "You haven't stopped shaking."

I'm breathless, caught in a trance by the way his lips glide over the back of my hands. He's not only kissing them, but in his own way, he's also comforting me.

Who knew there would be a day where Jonathan King comforts me?

"There. That's much better." He cradles my hands, which have stopped trembling, on his lap.

It takes everything in me not to wrap my arms around him in a hug. He's offering me an attentiveness that I never thought anyone, let alone he of all people, would show me.

"Then what?" I murmur now that I'm in a calmer state.

His thumb traces the back of my hand, eliciting small bursts of comfort. "I'll figure it out, but for now, we need to stay away from the media turmoil. When they find out you're no longer here, Maxim's lawyer will play a media game and fully expose your new identity. We're not only talking about where you're living and your company, but everything he already knows will be discussed by the entire country."

"Holy shit," I breathe out in a low murmur. The scenarios he's painting in my head form like a black doom.

"I know it's a difficult time, Aurora, but we need to get ready for all possibilities."

"Oh my God! What about H&H and Layla?"

"Harris is on it. I currently own H&H, so Layla should be fine, but I can't guarantee they won't harass her or her family. They should go stay someplace else. I have Harris arranging a safe hotel for them. Can you ask her to go with him?"

"Uh…yeah." I pull my phone and wince when I find about ten missed calls from Jonathan and five from her.

Jonathan's hawk-like attention doesn't miss what's on my screen and his tone hardens. "And next time, answer my fucking calls, Aurora."

"I'm sorry. I…wasn't thinking." I'm still not—not straight, anyway.

"You were with Ethan."

"I'm thankful he was there."

Jonathan's grip tightens around my wrist, but he says nothing. He also recognises that I shouldn't have been alone in the midst of people who most likely would've gotten my head on a stick.

I dial Layla and she answers after the first ring. "What the F, mate! Don't ghost me. That stuff gives me PTSD now."

"Sorry, Lay. Something came up."

"No kidding. Harris is at our house, saying we need to go, or something."

"Yeah, Lay, please go with him. I…I'm so sorry I got you, Kenza, and Hamza involved in this. I'm *so* sorry."

"What are you talking about?"

The whole case is public now, and she'll see it eventually. However, I don't want her to hear about it from strangers. "Maxim Griffin, the one who's currently all over the news?"

"What about that psycho?"

"H-he's my father, Lay."

There's no answer from the other side. It's the first time Layla's been speechless, and it's not the good type.

"A-are you going to say something?"

"Wait up. So you're, like, the daughter who reported him?"

"Yeah."

"Oh."

"I'm s-so sorry, Lay. I know I should've told you before and I'm sorry you guys will be implicated in this when my new identity is revealed, so just tell them you didn't know. Say I played you, lied to you."

"Bollocks. Where are you?"

"I'm leaving for a bit. Please follow Harris. It's for your own safety. *Please.*"

"We'll go to our relatives in Birmingham. Don't worry about us. You just take care of you, okay?" Her voice turns brittle at the end and she pauses before saying, "Remember, you're my ride or die, mate. I've got you."

"Lay..." I choke on my tears, gripping the phone hard.

By the time I end the call, I'm too emotional to talk. The fact that Layla is on my side without even hearing the full story squeezes my heart. I didn't know I needed her support until now.

Jonathan takes the phone from between my fingers and powers it off.

"Why are you taking it away?"

"Journalists will start bugging you."

The rest of the way is spent in silence as Jonathan holds my hand in his lap, still stroking my skin.

If it weren't for my loud thoughts that don't seem like they'll be cooling down anytime soon, I would've fallen asleep on his lap like I usually do when we're in a long car ride.

We arrive at a secluded landing area of an airport and a plane waits for us. When we come out, Jonathan places a hand on the small of my back and leads me to it. Moses carries bags, which I didn't know were already packed and loaded, from the car.

The flight attendant, a redhead with a blinding smile, welcomes us in. Jonathan doesn't release me until we're inside, and that's only because the entryway doesn't fit two people at the same time.

The luxury is clear in the furnishings, from the dark ceiling and flooring to the light caramel plush seats that appear custom-made.

The only flights I've ever taken were from Leeds to Glasgow, then from Glasgow to London. And those were the lowest classes available. I have no idea what first-class looks like, but something tells me this is a step further.

It isn't until we're completely inside that I notice no one but us is here.

"Did you book the entire flight?" I ask Jonathan.

"Didn't need to. This is my private jet."

Right. Not that it should be a surprise that Jonathan has his own jet. He travels around the world a lot. Or that's what he did before I came along, as Harris likes to remind me in his snobbish tone.

He lets me sit by the window as if he remembers when I told him that I'd never left the UK. I've never had the chance to look out from a window seat and have always wondered what it would feel like.

Jonathan fastens my seatbelt, then does his own as a suave male voice fills the space.

"Welcome aboard, Mr. King and Miss Harper. We'll be taking off in a few minutes, so please fasten your seatbelts. We will reach our destination in approximately thirteen hours. I wish you a comfortable flight."

The voice disappears and I'm about to ask Jonathan where we're going, considering the time we'll have to spend on the plane. Before I can open my mouth, the flight attendant reappears and nods when she makes sure the seatbelts are in place.

"Can I get you water? A drink?" She focuses on Jonathan and her smile widens as her voice drops. "Anything?"

I narrow my eyes at her as she blatantly flirts with Jonathan.

Is she one of his ex-fuck buddies? There could be no other explanation for the way she openly flirts.

The idea of Jonathan touching her in the same way he touches
me, kissing her, or even talking to her like he does to me turns my
blood hot, then cold.

"We're good," I say, glad I don't snap.

She's still focused on Jonathan as if my words don't matter and
I want to claw her eyes out.

It's only when Jonathan dismisses her with a finger that she
leaves, but she does so with a deliberate sway of her hips.

"I didn't know redheads were your type," I say before I get the
chance to measure my words.

"They aren't."

"Well, you obviously had a thing with her."

"Her?" he repeats, slight amusement shining in his eyes.

"The flight attendant."

"I haven't."

"Are you telling me women just flirt with you?"

"They do. Doesn't mean I pay them any of my attention."

I peek at him through my lashes. "Not even her?"

"No. I don't mix business with pleasure."

"But you did with me."

"True, though I never considered you business."

My teeth sink into my bottom lip at his unsaid words. The fact
that he considers me pleasure.

The plane starts moving, then ascends. My nails dig into the
plush armrest of the chair. Once again, Jonathan takes my hand in
his, and my nerves slowly calm.

I get lost in the early evening sky and the city lights as they get
farther away the higher we ascend. The view is mesmerising. I can't
believe how much I've been missing out in life. I'm twenty-seven
going on twenty-eight, yet I feel like a toddler in this world.

"It's so beautiful," I murmur.

"Indeed."

My attention snaps back to Jonathan, and just like the other time in the park, he's not watching the view, he's watching me.

"Right," I joke. "You've probably seen this scenery like a thousand times."

"It feels like a first with you."

My lips part, but no words come out. God. He sometimes says shit that turns me speechless and so utterly touched. How the hell does he do that?

"Are you comfortable?" he asks.

"Mmm."

"You might want to rest. Here." He fiddles with something on the side and both chairs fall back in a comfortable reclined position. Jonathan removes the seatbelts and pulls up the armrest so there's nothing between us.

I don't hesitate as my head rests on his chest, half my body covers his like we do when we sleep. His fingers caress my hair, and I lean farther into his touch.

It could be his soothing heartbeat or the peaceful atmosphere or that I'm putting a pause on the chaos back home, but sleep comes almost immediately.

"Where are we going anyway?" I ask in a half-sleepy tone.

"To my island."

NINETEEN

Aurora

J ONATHAN OWNS AN ISLAND.

No shit. He owns a fucking island.

I'm dazed during the entire drive from where the plane landed to wherever the hell he's taking me.

The early morning sun shines through the branches and leaves, almost like a welcoming ceremony.

The roads are narrow and tropical trees decorate the sideways as far as the vision goes. Moses drives with ease, knowing exactly where we're going.

That makes one of us.

"How did you get this island?" I inch closer to Jonathan. For some reason, his nearness always makes me feel safe in unknown places. Actually, that happens in all places.

He's leaning back against the car's leather seat, legs wide apart and his entire demeanour relaxed. My hand is nestled in his on his hard thigh. He hasn't let me go—not during the flight and not after we got into the car. "I won it ten years ago from a Saudi prince in a poker game."

"Poker?" I nearly shriek.

"Yes."

"He must be devastated for losing it."

"Not really. He has a few more islands scattered around the world."

"What did you bet?"

"Why do you want to know?"

"If he bet an island, you must've put up something of so much value."

He raises a brow. "And you want to know what I consider most valuable?"

"Sort of. What was it?"

"My son."

"W-what? You bet Aiden?"

His expression remains the same. "That's what I said."

"How...how can you even bet a person?"

"It's more common than you think."

"I...I can't believe you bet your own son—your only offspring. I don't think I want to talk to you right now, or ever. And I'm totally telling Aiden so he knows what you've done. What if you'd lost, huh?" I poke his shoulder. "Huh?"

A smile breaks free across Jonathan's beautiful lips. "I didn't think you'd be this easily deceived."

"You...you were joking?" That's as rare as witnessing a mythical being.

"You think I would ever bet Aiden? He's my only son."

Phew. Deep down, I didn't think he'd do that, but he also doesn't joke. That's the part that threw me off. "So what did you bet?"

"One of my subsidiaries."

"I didn't know you play poker."

"I don't."

"You just said you won it in a poker game."

"I only play when I know I can win. I don't like unsure gambles."

Considering Jonathan's control-freak personality, that makes complete sense.

My attention returns to the road and the way the trees part as we pass through. "What's the name of the island?"

"It's under King Enterprises."

"It should have a name of its own."

"The prince called it a complicated Arabic name. It's on the papers. If you're so insistent on knowing it, I can call Harris."

"You should name it something special to *you*. After all, not just anyone can own an island."

"Huh."

I'm not sure what he means by that, but it seems as if he's never thought of that possibility. Jonathan is the type who doesn't get attached to things like normal humans, and I guess that makes this whole suggestion pointless to him.

Oh well, at least I tried. I haven't gotten to see most of the island yet, and it already looks like a small space cut from paradise.

Thoughts of why we're here try to barge in. I think of Dad's interview and his accusations, about the prosecution, media, and victims' families.

The beauty surrounding me starts to vanish, its colours slowly turning to grey. This isn't a holiday.

I'm running away—it's as simple as that.

Jonathan releases my hand, letting it drop to his lap, and grips my thigh. It's like he knows exactly where my mind went and is bringing me back to the present.

A strange type of warmth engulfs me as I fall into his presence. There's something about his soft touch that, even if his features remain unreadable, I sense what he's trying to relay.

Right now, it seems that he wants me comfortable above anything else.

We stop by a house in the hills that's slightly hidden from below by tall trees.

It's smaller than the King mansion, and it has a modern feel to it with its two-storey round architecture. The interior stairs are visible from the outside through the shiny glass walls.

"It's different," I tell Jonathan as we step out of the car.

"It's the prince's creation, not mine."

The lack of Jonathan's grandiose touch makes sense then. If it were up to my tyrant, he'd make it appear as intimidating as he is.

In every sense of the word.

Power isn't only a tactic for Jonathan, it's his philosophy in life.

From what I understand about his past, the way he lost his father made him merciless. Seeing his dad die of weakness made him take a figurative vow to never be in that position himself.

In a way, he tamed power and made it his best friend. They're so intertwined now, as if they're one being.

Jonathan grabs me by the waist as he leads me inside. Moses remains still as a stone in front of the car, arms crossed in front of him, one hand over the other. I smile back at him with a nod.

"Eyes ahead, Aurora." Jonathan's voice holds a clear warning.

"I was just acknowledging him. I don't like ignoring people."

His lips thin. "You were *smiling* at him."

"So now I'm not allowed to smile at others?"

"Not if you can help it."

"And if I can't help it?"

We stop at the entrance, and he lifts my chin with two long fingers. I stare up at him with parted lips and he runs his thumb over the bottom one, back and forth, creating a sensual rhythm.

"Your smile, like everything else about you, is mine and mine alone. I don't share."

I'm trapped in the intensity of his grey eyes. In the storm lurking inside that he won't hesitate to unleash on the world at any second. The fact that he's willing to destroy the world for me shouldn't affect me this much, but a strange type of giddiness overtakes me.

Clearing my throat, I pull away from Jonathan to take a look at the house. Its interior is as modern as its exterior. There's nothing of the precise control and majesty that's clear in every inch of the King mansion.

Here, it's minimalistic but a bit cosier. I fall onto the plush sofa, throwing my head back. "This is so comfy."

"We can get a similar one for home."

Home.

No idea if he's calling it that on purpose, but somewhere deep down, in that wrong part of my soul, I believe it.

Whether I like to admit it or not, the King mansion has become my home. Jonathan's home is my home.

That's a scary thought.

I vaguely remember that I only have a few months left of the agreement we had, but I stopped thinking about that a long time ago.

I bite my lower lip as I open my eyes. Jonathan stands in front of me, his jacket slung over his shoulder, sleeves rolled up to his elbows. He lost the tie somewhere during the flight. Some strands of his black hair are tousled and falling over his forehead, making him appear the most ruggedly handsome I've ever seen him.

He's studying me intently. He's always doing that, watching me, pulling me to the centre of his attention as if I've always belonged there. "You should go rest."

"I'm fine." Rest is the last thing on my mind right now. I clench my thighs together, trapping the tingles in. I can't believe I'm turned on by just his appearance.

If Lay hears about this, she won't let me live it down.

"You must have jet lag, Aurora."

"I don't."

"You might not feel it now, but exhaustion will soon take over you. It'll be better once you sleep."

"I slept enough on the plane."

He sighs. "Must you have an objection to everything? Stop fighting me about your health and go rest."

I'm apparently doing a shit job at showing my interest, so I try again, this time lowering my voice. "Are you going to join me?"

I swear something shines in his eyes, but the blank façade returns all too soon. "I have to make a few calls."

"Fine." I huff, getting to my feet. "Whatever."

I bypass him and stomp to the stairs like an angry kid with issues. Damn him.

Upstairs, there are only two rooms, so I go into the first one. Sure enough, there's a large bed with white sheets, and the curtains are drawn, hiding the sun.

I kick my shoes off, then jerkily strip off my clothes. Disappointment sticks at the back of my throat like a foul aftertaste, but I refuse to acknowledge it.

Screw Jonathan.

I step into the glass shower and let the cool water submerge me. A full-body mirror is positioned in front of me, making me watch myself shower. It must be another one of the prince's creations—a weird as hell one. Who even does that?

I close my eyes and try to let the flow of the water rinse away my thoughts. But no matter how long I stand there, my mind keeps jumping back to the shitshow I left behind in England. This island is merely a temporary solution.

There's no way in hell I can escape forever. Besides, now that Layla and her family are involved, it's one more reason to not escape. It's not like I can take them all and smuggle them to Scotland or out of the UK with me.

A warm body envelops me from behind, his hard chest moulding to my wet back. He pulls my hair to the side, baring my throat before he wraps a hand around it.

Jonathan's lips graze the shell of my ear as he murmurs, "Is this what you meant by joining you?"

My thighs tighten as the earlier wave of arousal slams back into me with a vengeance. There's nothing I love more than the feel of Jonathan's body glued to my skin and his hot breaths mingled with mine.

His free hand comes down on my arse, and I yelp, my eyes shooting open. God. It hurts so good with the water like this.

My eyes meet his through the mirror. It's slightly foggy now with the steam, but I can make out the spark in those dark greys.

"What was that for?" My voice is so lustful, it would've been embarrassing if I wasn't so turned on.

"To get your attention. It needs to always be on me." He grabs me hard by the arse. "Not anyone else. *Me.*"

"Why?" I ask in the same voice, just to challenge him. Jonathan loves that—challenges, I mean.

His grip tightens on my arse. "This is mine. Everything you have belongs to me, and no one gets to touch or hurt you under my watch."

He spanks me again and I slap a hand against the mirror, the water forming a rivulet that runs down the condensation as his words leave the confinements of my ear and creep under my skin.

"No one?" My voice is soft, small, and filled with all the insecurities I've carried for endless years.

"No fucking one, Aurora." His voice drops. "Not even yourself."

"Jonathan…" I stare at him through the small visible space in the mirror.

He slaps my arse once more, making me shiver in both pleasure and pain. "What is it?"

"Ohh…I…"

"Those aren't words. Use actual ones." There's slight amusement beneath the order.

I place my other hand on the mirror to anchor myself. For some reason, it feels as if I'll fall if I don't.

My gaze meets his through the mirror. "Take me."

His eyes blaze, and I'm sure the needy tone in my voice doesn't escape him.

"Take you?"

"Jonathan, please."

"Fuck." Still gripping me by the throat, he slowly inches inside me, filling me to the brim.

My mouth parts as the water drips down my skin to where we're joined. I watch where his body meets mine, fascinated by the view. But that's not the only place we're joined. It's everywhere from my back to my arse to the hand gripping me by the hip.

Jonathan tightens his fingers around my throat, jerking my neck up. "Look at me. Watch me own you."

My light eyes clash with his darker ones in the mirror. I'm caught in a trance by the way he's thrusting in and out of me with measured strokes. But that's not the only thing that fills me with awe.

It's the look of utter abandon on my face coupled with the complete possessiveness in his features.

Oh, God.

Do I always look like that?

His lips find the shell of my ear and he bites before speaking in a husky tone, "Everything you see and don't see in there is fucking mine, Aurora."

He releases my hip and parts my arse cheeks with his strong hand. His thumb finds my back hole and I yelp, getting on my tiptoes.

"W-what are you doing?"

"I said everything you see and don't see." The tip of his finger pushes inside and I clench against his cock. "Mmm, feels virgin."

Oh, God.

Shit.

I'm not supposed to like having his thumb there, right? I've always thought that backdoor business wasn't allowed, or at least, that's how it was in my mind.

If normal sex didn't cut it, I didn't feel the need to put myself through the pain of anal. But that was before this man gave me my actual rebirth.

There's a pre-Jonathan era and post-Jonathan era, and I don't want to admit how fulfilling the second one is.

His teeth nibble on the sensitive skin at my throat, most definitely leaving a hickey. "Is it virgin?"

"Yes…" My moaned word is almost inaudible in the midst of the pouring water, but Jonathan seems to have heard it since a growl spills from this throat.

"I'm going to fuck it and own every inch of you, wild one."

"N-now?"

A dark chuckle invades the air. "No, you need preparation. I don't want to hurt you with my cock. But soon, though."

Before I can think about the stupid disappointment that hits me for the second time today, Jonathan pushes his finger a bit farther into my arse and picks up his pace in my pussy.

The feeling of being filled is so real, and there's even that slight burn of pain that's caused by his sheer size. It doesn't matter how wet or ready I am. He's so big and it always hurts so good to be pounded in by him.

My eyes droop at the intensity of his thrusts, and I'm transfixed by the image in the mirror. By the way I seem so small in his hold, but also by how closely we're joined, as if we can never be separated.

That view throws me over the edge.

Jonathan studies me with that usual focus of his as I come undone around him. My breathing hitches as pleasure rolls off me, making my legs unsteady.

The way I look at him is more than pleasure and lust.

It's more than orgasms and dirty fucks.

It's something I thought I would never feel again after that black day eleven years ago.

TWENTY

Aurora

I MUST'VE FALLEN ASLEEP AFTER JONATHAN CARRIED ME OUT OF the shower, because the next time I open my eyes, I'm on the bed.

A sheet covers me up to my chin and the towel is still wrapped around me.

I blink the sleep away from my eyes and glide my hand across the bed. Sure enough, Jonathan isn't here. My chest falls at that thought, and I curse myself for it. Since when did the need to see him next to me when I wake up become a habit?

The glass hints at the afternoon sun, shining through the trees. I stir and get up to search for my phone.

I need to call Layla and make sure she and her family are well-installed and protected. Then maybe I can take a look at what's going on in the news. That is, if there's an internet connection here.

I search through the bags on the chair and in the drawers, but there's no sign of my phone.

Ugh. It's Jonathan, isn't it?

A tender ache hurts between my legs every time I move, and

it brings back the memories of Jonathan taking me in the shower. It doesn't matter how much he fucks me, each one is an experience all on its own, and I've become so attuned to this feeling. To *him*.

It takes me a few minutes to put on a short summer dress I find in the bag he packed for me. How did he even come upon this? I bought it years ago and never actually got the chance to wear it.

I let my hair fall loose to the middle of my back, put on flip-flops, and descend the stairs. I search in the kitchen and in the lounge area, and then in an office situated near the entrance.

There's no trace of Jonathan.

My feet come to a halt as a dooming thought hits me across the face. Did he…leave me here?

I rush outside, my heart hammering in my chest. The car and Moses are also gone. The sound of the breeze slipping between the tree leaves is the only presence around me.

It's almost like a ghost island.

A shiver snakes up my body and wraps its meaty fingers around my throat. I instinctively rub my arms to drive away the goosebumps.

Wait, no.

There's also a faint sound of…waves. I follow the scent of the ocean, legs unsteady, and my heartbeat won't stop escalating. The idea of being all alone brings back memories of being utterly lost. Though I should be used to being lonely, I'm not. Not really.

Especially not now.

Sure enough, there's a beach down the cliff. Its shore expands into the horizon, creating a marvellous picturesque scene when combined with the sky. The clear, blue water sparkles under the afternoon sun, but that's not what causes me to stop and stare.

It's the man sitting on a chaise longue, a tablet in his hand.

Jonathan is wearing only shorts and a white polo T-shirt, which highlights his tall, muscular frame.

The sun shines on his black hair, which, for once, isn't styled. It falls across his forehead in a tousled and carefree way. His eyes are covered with black aviators as he scrolls through his tablet with his usual serious expression. His brows are slightly furrowed, jaw set and lips in a line.

I'm so used to those features, to the hardness and ruthlessness in them.

I'm so used to him.

When the hell did I become so used to this man?

The fact that he didn't leave me here on my own fills me with relief so strong, I nearly topple over from the force of it.

My feet lead me to him of their own volition. The flip-flops get lost in the white sand, so I kick them away and walk barefoot. It's not hot, but it's warm enough.

I stand beside his chair, my shadow falling across his face and chest, blocking the sun. Jonathan glances up from his tablet, and just like that, the serious expression slowly withers away.

There's still that usual harshness, the hardness of the man beneath. However, his features relax and his lips twitch in a heart-stopping smile.

God. I'll never get enough of his smile. It doesn't help that he's so stingy with it.

"You're up."

I'm still feeling relieved for finding him here. Add his smile, and I totally can't find my voice right now, so I nod.

He raises a brow. "You said you didn't have jet lag."

"I was tired."

"Is that so? Did I exhaust you, wild one?"

"A little."

"A little? We need to take care of that next time so that it's more than a little."

"Fine, a lot. Happy now?" I couldn't control the burning of my cheeks, even if I wanted to.

"Come here." Even though his eyes are covered with sunglasses, I can almost see the darkening of that grey colour.

"Come where? There's no room."

He clutches me by the wrist and pulls me down. I gasp,

expecting us both to topple over the chair. Instead, I end up half-lying atop of him, fingers splayed on his T-shirt.

"You were saying? Something about no room?"

For a moment, I'm lost in his sunglasses-covered eyes, in the way they watch me. The weird, yet overwhelming, sensation I felt while staring at our reflection in the mirror during the shower hits me again.

I shut the door on that thought and ask what I came down here for, "Where's my phone?"

"You don't need it."

"I have to make sure Layla and her family are safe."

"They are. Harris told me they arrived at Birmingham."

"I want to talk to her myself. At least let me call Harris."

"There will be no talking to Harris." He taps a few things on his tablet. "Here, call Layla."

I grin, taking the tablet from his hand, and dial Layla. I'm surprised it's saved in his SIM card, even if it is under 'Black Belt'. "Why do you have Layla's phone number?"

"She's an important part of your life," he says, as if that explains everything.

I try to get into a sitting position, because lying all over Jonathan is distracting as hell, and wait for her to pick up. It rings a few times before she answers.

"This is called stalking, Johnny. We are not going to stay at a hotel you're paying for. Save your money for charity."

I stare at him. He wanted to make her and her family stay at a hotel and even called her about it? Why didn't I know anything about this?

The shades cover his expression, but I doubt there's a reaction or an apology in there. He does whatever he pleases and is usually convinced that it's the right thing.

"Now, let me talk to Aurora," Layla demands. "Or I'm going to come out of the phone and strangle you—wait. Don't hang up. I won't actually do it."

I chuckle. "It's me, Lay."

"Mate! Are you okay? You're unharmed, right? Did that brute Jonathan do something to you?"

He did a lot of things, but none of them were brutish. If anything, they warmed my heart like nothing ever has.

How sad is my life if Jonathan is the highlight of it? Or maybe it's sad because I waited so long for something like this, and I got more than I bargained for in this impossible man.

He might be a tyrant, but he's the best to ever exist.

"I'm fine, Lay. We're at a beautiful island and I wish you were here. Are you guys okay?"

"As long as you're safe, we are." She sighs. "Mama and Papa send their love, and they said we'll all stand behind you."

"Lay..." My voice breaks.

"Hey, don't go sappy on me. We still need to talk about how you hid your past from me all these years. I demand compensation."

"A hug?"

"In your dreams. Okay, maybe this once."

I smile. "Are you guys comfy?"

"Totes."

My gaze trails to Jonathan, who could be either watching me or the ocean. "Maybe you should take Jonathan's offer."

"Nope. Not gonna happen."

"Are you at your relatives' in Birmingham?"

"We decided against it. We didn't really want to bring them trouble."

"Then where are you?"

"Somewhere better than Johnny's hotel."

"Where?"

"He came over as soon as we arrived here and told us we were welcome at his mansion. Told you, he's Daddy. Hold on."

Oh, God. No, she didn't.

There's a rustle at the other end of the line before a smooth, familiar voice filters in. "Hello, Aurora. How have you been?"

Before I can even attempt to greet Ethan back, Jonathan sits up, his arms enveloping me from behind as he snatches the tablet from my fingers. "What the fuck are you doing, Ethan?"

"Oh, Jonathan. What a surprise." He doesn't sound surprised at all. "I invited Layla and her family to stay at my Birmingham residence as long as they please. It's the least I can do to help Aurora in these difficult circumstances."

"Thank you," I say, even though I'm secretly planning to kill Layla.

Jonathan's eyes fix on me before he focuses back on the tablet. "Harris will come over to take Miss Hussaini and her family to the hotel."

"No, can do. We're cool right here!" Layla's voice comes from the background.

"You heard her," Ethan says. "I'll see you when you return. You, too, Aurora."

He hangs up before Jonathan can say another word. His hold tightens on the tablet and I suspect he'll somehow bend it in two.

The tension radiating off him could break something. He doesn't like that Ethan is meddling, and I guess Jonathan will always see him as some sort of a threat—even if he's helping.

"Are we alone here?" I ask to divert his attention as a wild idea springs to mind.

"Yes."

"What about Moses?"

"He stays near the plane landing." He pauses. "Why are you asking about him?"

I stand up and pull the dress over my head. I went commando, so when I let the cloth fall on the chair, I'm completely naked.

My nipples instantly harden; it's less to do with the air and more to do with the way Jonathan straightens, his entire focus zooming in on me.

His jaw clenches as he removes the shades, uncovering his darkened gaze. "Is that an invitation, Aurora?"

"No." I walk backwards towards the beach. "I'm going for a swim."

"A swim?"

"Catch me if you can, old man."

"Old man?" he repeats slowly.

"Yeah, show me your stamina."

"I did, not too long ago, and you were so exhausted, you fell asleep on me, remember?" He stands anyway, pulling his T-shirt over his head, then yanks down his shorts.

He went commando as well.

My feet falter in the sand at the view of him entirely naked, but I don't get to stare for long when he charges towards me.

I squeal as I turn around and run in the direction of the beach. The water envelops my toes and calves in seconds. It's a bit cold, and I shiver as it reaches above my knees, but I don't stop my escape from Jonathan.

A strange sense of excitement grips me. It's like those times when I used to hunt and stalk, but now, I'm not the predator, I'm the prey playing a game.

When I glance behind me, there's no trace of Jonathan. I stop when the water reaches my waist and search around. Where did he go?

Did he leave? But I'm sure I heard him come in after me—

My thoughts are suddenly cut off when something grabs my calf and I shriek just as I'm being pulled under. Then the cold shock withers away as strong hands grip me by the arms and lead me back to the surface.

I gulp in a large intake of air, gasping, my fingers holding on to a muscular shoulder. I blink away the water in my eyes to make out the sight of Jonathan's drenched face and his hair sticking to his temples. "Y-you!"

"Did you say something about stamina, wild one?"

"That's not fair."

"I never play fair." His lips brush over my nose. "I play to win, remember?"

I do, and even though the notion scares me a bit, I can't help but want more of it right now.

Splashing him in the face, I escape his hold and swim in the opposite direction.

He catches me in no time, but he also lets me go when he senses my need for a challenge.

It's always been there, no matter how much I've tried to smother it. Challenges are what make me thrive, and Jonathan offers me that in the best way possible.

Will he still feel the same if he finds out that I'm as much of a monster as my father?

TWENTY-ONE

Jonathan

"**W**HAT DO YOU MEAN BY, IT'S NULL AND VOID?" I ask Harris through the phone.

Aurora is taking a shower upstairs and I've come to the home office so she can't listen to the conversation.

During the past few days we've spent on the island, she constantly demands to speak to Black Belt. If it were up to her, she would be sniffing for details about the news from England.

Not that I would let her. Whenever she tries to ask Layla, I either take the phone away or tell her there will be no more calls. She stopped trying to get around me after that.

I brought her here for multiple reasons, and the most important of all is not allowing her to see the articles written on her.

Her name and face are all over the media, and some of the victims' families have come forward to say that she has the same look that's in her father's eyes. That they always thought she was unhinged like him.

I had Harris do some damage control, block articles and drive away the attention from Aurora's personal life, but there's only so much he can do. The media has always been obsessed with Maxim Griffin and his gruesome murders. The fact that he's finally talking is giving them the chance to bring back the past and fully investigate it.

Now, Harris is telling me that my solicitor, who's working on building a strong case for Aurora, says the whole prosecution's questioning, and even the trial, will be smoke and mirrors.

Correction, he's *not* my solicitor. I've never needed a criminal one before. Most of my hotshot solicitors specialise in corporate law. But I had my main law firm pick me the best criminal solicitor in the whole of the UK. Besides being known to have won all the criminal cases he's taken, Alan Sheldon took the bar exam at the same time as Stephan Wayne—Maxim's solicitor—and has also gone a few times against him.

From the outside looking in, that fact may seem trivial, but it's not. Alan is the best, not only because of his unbeatable record, but also because he's familiar with Stephan and his games prior to trials.

And Alan didn't get the perfect record by being a saint. He's been known to use every method under the sun to get his wins—moral or immoral. That's why he's a good fit.

While I don't trust people, I trust his need to keep his serial wins. When someone has ego as a driving force, nothing stops them.

"Alan told me the prosecution has absolutely no evidence against Aurora," Harris continues in his half-bored, half-sleepy voice. It's the middle of the night there, not that he minds—I don't think. He's a workaholic with zero life outside of King Enterprises. "They thoroughly investigated her eleven years ago. There was nothing that hinted that she knew or participated in Maxim's crimes."

"Are you telling me Maxim's solicitor is going after her as a ploy?"

"Probably. Alan says Maxim wants to drag her down, just to show his power."

"No. There's more to it." I take a sip of my cognac, savouring the burn. "If he only wanted to drag her down, he would've done it a long time ago. Something triggered him. Look into it."

"I did hear a tale some time ago."

"And why have you waited this long to tell me? You're losing your touch, Harris."

"I didn't think it was important at the time." He goes into defence mode. "I still don't, but it could be of value."

"Go on."

"When Aurora first entered your life, I met with a few of Maxim's inmates."

"Why did you do that?"

"I didn't trust her, okay? She came out of nowhere and could've played that entire thing with Ethan just to get close to you."

"What is this nonsense? You honestly think someone can use me?"

"No. But I don't trust people, especially new people. Better safe than sorry."

"And? What did your distrustful journey bring?"

"There was one of Maxim's inmates who was later transferred to a mental institute. Robert Hill. He was convicted for killing his wife and mother-in-law with a kitchen knife. He stabbed his wife twenty times and his mother-in-law fifty times, then went to the police station and handed himself in. Anyway, Robert told me that Maxim has a muse, and when I asked him what he meant by that, he said that Maxim gets inspiration by seeing his muse, and when he doesn't see her, he feels like he's missing something. Robert said that Maxim keeps her picture with him at all times."

"Is it Aurora?"

"No clue. Robert said he doesn't allow anyone to see it, and since Maxim is in solitary confinement, no other inmate has managed to take a look. He also said that Maxim is proud of his muse, saying it's because of her that he found his true self after years of floundering with no clear path. His muse is his freedom. Robert connected with that—the freedom part—because killing his wife and mother-in-law gave him his so-called freedom."

I scratch my chin. It must be Aurora. I thought Maxim was making this ruckus and asking for parole to take revenge against her, but if it's because he wants to see her, there's a problem.

He wouldn't just want to see her. Someone like Maxim will always want more. He and I are similar on that front. The need for more isn't a luxury—it's a biological need that cannot be stopped.

It's power.

For him, it's the fake god-like power that comes with controlling someone else's life before eventually ending it.

For me, it's the rush of control and the fact that I have so much ahead of me rather than behind me. The more I acquire, the more doors open in my way.

"Have you heard anything from your contact with Tristan?" Harris asks.

I down half my glass in one go. "Not yet. Tristan says Kyle does everything his way. It's a game of waiting now."

"How long are we supposed to wait for this Kyle to bring in results?"

"As long as it takes."

"We don't have as long as it takes."

"Your impatience is your weakness, Harris. School it."

"We have work to do. I've cancelled three important meetings since you left."

"Three meetings aren't the end of the world."

"With all due respect, it is, sir. I've never had to cancel such important meetings before."

"You didn't cancel them, you rescheduled them."

"Same effect. I'm getting anxiety attacks."

"You don't even know what an anxiety attack means."

"I do now. I googled it."

"Stop whining, Harris."

"If you come back, we can hide Aurora and—"

"No."

"You didn't hear me out."

"Any option that includes putting her life and mental state in jeopardy is declined."

"Levi is right to say you're smitten," he mutters under his breath.

"Since when are you friends with that punk?"

"He gives me free football game tickets."

"You don't even like football."

"They're still free tickets."

I shake my head. "Let me know if there are any changes."

"Let me know when you decide to finally return."

"Won't be happening in the near future. Do you have anything on Jake?"

"I'm close."

"Good. I need him to pay. I don't care which methods you use." The accountant who stole Aurora's hard-earned money doesn't get to live his life as if nothing happened.

He might've given me the opening to sneak into her life, but he, like anyone who hurts her, won't escape my wrath.

The door opens, and I pause with my drink halfway to my mouth. Aurora comes inside wearing a light blue summer dress. Her hair is loose and falls over her shoulders and down her back. Judging by the peaks of her nipples, she's not wearing a bra.

That's a sight I can become accustomed to.

She's been freer lately, wearing as little as possible and getting rid of the clothes whenever she sees fit.

Not that I'm complaining.

In the past few days, I've fucked her in all positions possible. It doesn't matter if she's trying to read a book or cook or exercise, whenever I get the chance, I seize it.

Then sometimes, she'll take my hand and we'll go on long walks at dusk or dawn. She's revisiting her passion of hiking and discovering. I'll never get used to the way her eyes shine whenever she witnesses some picturesque scenery. It's like she stops breathing and gets lost in the moment.

I've never found things beautiful, per se. The first and only thing I think about concerning the outside world is whether it's useful in my end goal or not.

Aurora is different. She stops and stares. She appreciates the little things and doesn't take anything for granted. And, in a way, her strong passion about living life to its fullest has been rubbing off on me.

Or perhaps it's because I get to see the spark in her eyes and the brightness in her features that haven't been dimmed by her past.

The contradictions in her persona are fascinating. On one hand, she's so sure of herself that she started her own business. But on the other hand, it seems as if she's still a toddler when it comes to the world.

The number of things she's said are 'her first' is higher than I would've thought. I use it to my favour, though, and make all those firsts happen so that I can watch her face light up in wonder.

Like the plane, the island, and everything in between. I'm taking that woman to every corner of the world so she can live her life as she was always meant to.

But for now, I'm keeping her occupied here by the exotic views and hikes. Aurora also loves swimming in the night, but she holds on to me, afraid something will catch her in the dark.

Despite her adventurous nature, Aurora still tosses and turns during her sleep. She still shivers whenever I touch her scar and tattoo. She still can't purge the past from her head, no matter how hard she tries.

"Won't be happening in the near future," I tell Harris and hang up.

Aurora stops in front of me, and I turn the chair so I'm facing her. "What won't happen?"

"Nothing you should worry about."

If hiding the truth will keep her temporarily safe, then I'm ready to buy more time.

"Tell me."

"I'd rather do something better than talking." I wrap a hand around her arse and pull her so she's standing between my legs.

A smile grazes her full lips as she clutches me by the shoulders. "Jonathan, stop it."

"Are you wearing the plug?" I've been making her wear different butt plugs for the past few days, and while she whines, she hasn't taken any of them out unless I tell her to.

She bites her lower lip. "What if I'm not?"

"Then I'll punish you."

"Punish me?" The subtle arousal in her voice as she says the word 'punish' gets my dick hard against my trousers.

"Disobedience gets you in trouble, so yes, Aurora. I will."

"How?"

"How do you think?"

"You'll spank me?"

"Amongst other things." My voice drops. "By the time I'm finished with you, you'll scream the whole house down."

Her breathing visibly hitches and her nipples turn as hard as pebbles against the dress. I sink my teeth around one over the cloth and tug. Aurora's nails dig into my shoulders as she moans, her chest thrusting into my face.

"Bend over," I order.

She pulls back and gulps a few breaths. "J-Jonathan, w-wait..."

"There will be no waiting. Bend over and show me that arse. Let me see if you've been a good girl today."

"Jonathan. *Please.*" Her nails sink deeper into my skin, and it's obvious that she's fighting her arousal.

The desperation and anxiousness in her dark blue gaze stops me. That's an expression I don't ever want to see on her face again.

The need to ravage her slowly dissipates, replaced by the urge to wipe away that expression. "What is it?"

"What were you talking about before I came in?" Though she's still touching me, the look in her gaze is numb—like the one she had in the footages of Maxim's trial eleven years ago. I recently watched them after Harris sent them over and I can't erase the expression from my brain. She appeared like someone so damaged, they were done with life.

"It's about my dad, isn't it?" she asks in a small voice.

"He has no case. It's his word against yours and all evidence points at him."

"Just because I didn't commit the murders of those women, doesn't mean I'm not an accomplice."

I lift my hands so they're resting on her waist. "What are you talking about?"

The spark that always shines in her face slowly dims until it's non-existent. "We hunted together—Dad and I, I mean. I got off on it, and I looked forward to it. The reason I followed him that day was because I thought he was hunting without me. True, I didn't like killing the animals, but stalking, following trails and blocking their exits? I loved all of that. I might have loved it a bit too much. So what if I didn't hurt those women? I have my father's sadistic nature, and I'm…a monster like him. I just never got the chance to fully grow into my character. So maybe I deserve this—the trial, the media, the unwanted attention. It's been long overdue."

"Nonsense."

Aurora blinks away the moisture gathering in her lids. "W-what?"

"You're not a murderer. Hunting is allowed by law. Thinking you're just like Maxim because you enjoyed hunting with him doesn't make you a monster, it makes you a daughter. He was your only parent, and it's natural that you were attached to him and picked up his hobbies. The fact that you didn't get off on killing the animals and that you reported him means you're cut from a different cloth than him. Don't let his media games mess with your head. That's exactly his purpose behind this entire masquerade."

She blinks again, and this time, the light slowly returns. Those dark blues that shouldn't be allowed to lose their spark. Not eleven years ago, and certainly not now.

My fingers trace over the cloth where I know her scar and tattoo are. She shivers, her lids slightly drooping.

"Why did you get the closed eye over the wound?"

"When I was stabbed, I fell into the eighth grave—the same one you got me out of. I was delirious when I finally regained consciousness and got myself out. When I first looked at the wound, it felt like I was looking at Mari-Jane's eyes—the one I witnessed being dragged. The wound felt just like her eyes, along with every other victim's. At the time, I couldn't sleep because their vacant gazes always visited me. I still can't sometimes."

So that's the reason behind her nightmares. I don't stop stroking her scar and Aurora leans into me, her nails digging into my shoulder again as if she's afraid she'll lose her balance.

"After I sutured that wound, I got the tattoo of the closed eye. I thought that…after Dad was sentenced, they could rest in peace, you know?" Her voice cracks. "Not now, though. They can't be in peace if he gets out."

"He won't. He has no evidence against you."

Her attention shifts to the block of books behind me, to the window, and even the table. She stares at any place but at me.

"Aurora, look at me."

Her gaze slowly finds mine, and it's only when she's fully focused on me that I say, "You did nothing wrong. Do you hear me?"

Her lips tremble and she lets her fingers intertwine at the back of my head. "I never thought anyone would ever tell me that."

"I will—every day if I have to—until you believe it."

"God." She smiles, but it's not exactly joyful. The pain still lingers there like a ghost ready to pounce. "You're nothing like how you were in the past."

"How was I in the past?"

"I don't know. When I first met you at the wedding, I thought you were too distant and too untouchable. You still are, in a way."

"The wedding wasn't the first time I met you."

"What do you mean the wedding wasn't the first time we met? I didn't even live in London."

I could tell her about that time in the cemetery, but that will only bring on Alicia's memory and I don't want her sad, so I change the subject. "You didn't. You had a Yorkshire accent."

Nostalgia covers her features. "I did."

"You lost it. Why?"

"I…" She clears her throat. "I had to so I wouldn't be identified. It was so hard at first."

I can imagine her struggling to lose her accent. She was always a proud northerner, but because she needed to shed everything that had to do with Maxim, she ditched that part of herself, too.

Aurora's head seems to be heading in that direction, considering how her gaze gets lost in the distance.

I won't allow that to happen.

"Bend over." My order, though calmly spoken, gets her immediate attention.

Heat blossoms in her cheeks. "Why?"

"Don't make me repeat myself, Aurora. I hate it and you'll get spanked more for it." My hand trails down and I grab her arse, causing her to yelp. "But you like that, don't you?"

"I don't know what you're talking about." Her voice is breathy.

"Are you going to do as you're told?"

She lifts her chin, that challenging streak rushing back in. "Make. Me."

Tugging on her wrist, I flip her so her chest meets the desk and her arse is in the air right in front of me as I stand.

I yank her dress up to her waist and my cock strains against my trousers when I find her naked. Completely, utterly naked and splayed out for me.

She came prepared. Aurora rarely goes commando, and when

she does, it's because she wants me to have easy access. She confessed that herself after our swim at the beach.

Her porcelain flesh is reddened by my handprints from last night. I don't spank her hard enough to cause a bruise, but I always leave my mark.

My hand comes down on her flesh and Aurora gets on her tippy-toes, her moan echoing in the air.

"When I say bend over, you bend the fuck over." My fingers caress her skin, admiring my handprint on her, then I spank her a few more times until she's whimpering and begging for more.

"J-Jonathan..."

"Stay still." I part her arse cheeks and she tenses up when my thumb connects with the black plug in her butt. "You put it in."

"Mmm."

"Was it hard? Did you struggle like the first time?" I fucked her then to make her aroused enough for the toy to fit inside her.

"N-no. But I liked the first time better."

"Why was that, wild one?" My hand wraps around her nape. "Because your cunt was filled in the process?"

She releases a needy sound but says nothing.

"Answer me and you might get a redo."

"Yes." Her voice is barely audible, but it's the only answer I need.

I use my other hand to unbuckle my belt and don't bother undressing. As soon as my dick is out, I drive balls-deep inside her, making her shift against the desk. Even though I take it easy, I know I'm too big for her, considering how she strangles me every time.

"Holy shit," she moans, her body moving in synergy with mine.

For someone who was dead for so long, her body comes undone around me in no time.

My hand keeps her caged against the wood as I thrust into her. My free fingers tease the plug in her arse, pulling it out the slightest bit before driving it back in. The movements of my dick match that of the toy, causing her to writhe against the table

"Oh, Jonathan... Aahh!"

She falls apart all around me, her tight cunt strangling my dick and wrenching out my own release.

I empty inside her with a grunt, my seed filling her pussy and dripping between her thighs.

A wave of possessiveness hits me at the way she continues clenching around me, milking me until there's nothing left.

She's mine.

Fucking mine.

And always will be.

I'll keep owning her until I put a fucking baby inside her.

In the past, Aiden was the only offspring I needed, but now, I'm chaining Aurora to me, and if a baby is what it'll take, then that's what it will be.

TWENTY-TWO

Aurora

"I'M NOT BORED AT ALL, MATE. I GET TO BE WITH DADDY."

I laugh at Layla's tone. She almost sounds offended that I suggested she might be bored out of her mind at Ethan's place. Since it's been more than a week, I'm starting to get restless, so I thought she might feel the same.

"Besides, there's also Agnus," she whispers. "And he's, like, totally Daddy material, too. I'm going to collect them all."

"You need help, Lay."

"Shut up. You've got your Daddy-in-practice."

"I do not." My cheeks heat as I say the words. Jonathan is sitting on the sofa opposite me, and even though his attention is on the tablet, I have no doubt that he's also focused on the conversation.

There's no way in shit I can ask Layla about the state of things in England. He won't hesitate to snatch the phone away and end the call.

He's a tyrant about that—amongst other things.

I tuck my hair behind my ears. "So is everything else good? Are you comfortable?"

"Absolutely. This is like a holiday and Daddy's mansion is the best."

"It is?"

"Totally. He's taking good care of us."

"I'm so glad. Thank Ethan on my behalf."

"He's right outside. Do you want to talk to him?"

"Yeah, sure." I've barely finished the sentence when Jonathan stands up and towers over me, extending his hand.

I sigh, glaring up at him. "On second thought, I'll thank him in person, Lay. Talk to you later."

As soon as I hang up, I shove the phone into Jonathan's hand, seething on the inside.

He tucks it in his pocket and sits beside me, still cradling his tablet. "You will not thank Ethan, on the phone or in person. The next time you see him, you'll walk the opposite way."

And just like that, he returns to his tablet. Now that he's issued his order, his job is done.

Well, screw him.

I take a few moments to suck in deep breaths, because if I speak while agitated, it'll just backfire on me. Jonathan's level of conniving intelligence doesn't hesitate to use people's emotions against them.

"If I'm thankful to Ethan, I'll express it."

He doesn't lift his head. "You will not."

"Well, you wouldn't know if I meet him behind your back."

I realise the severity of what I've just said too late. Jonathan's attention zeroes in on me, his jaw clenching under his five o'clock shadow. "What did you just say?"

"I said I'm free to meet whomever I like." I stand my ground, yet my fingers tremble. To say Jonathan looks scary right now would be an understatement.

"Repeat your exact words, Aurora."

When I remain quiet, he abandons the tablet. I don't notice it until he grabs me by the throat and tugs me to his side. His touch is firm, merciless, and while it usually turns me on, the expression on his face terrifies the hell out of me.

"Did you just say you'll meet Ethan behind my fucking back? Is that it?"

"Well, if you don't let me—"

"It's a yes or no question," he cuts me off.

"I won't do it," I whisper. Even though I like challenging Jonathan, stirring up his ugly side is an entirely different thing.

He gets weird about anything that includes Ethan, and I sure as hell don't want to get in the middle of that.

"You won't do what?" His grip tightens on my throat, and this time, arousal expands across my skin.

During the days we've spent on this island, I've gotten used to his touch more than ever before. It might have to do with the different toys he keeps shoving up my arse. Whenever he fucks me with one inside me, I feel like my orgasm hits me from a dozen different places all at once.

But deep down, I know it's not only because of the toys, punishments, or exotic positions. It's because of him—Jonathan. The way he listens to me, the way he keeps telling me that the past isn't my fault. I never knew I needed to hear those words from him until he said them.

Whenever we walk or lounge on the beach, we talk about everything. Our lives, our visions, and our goals. For Jonathan, it's his pursuit of power. For me, it's proving my artistic streak. The ability to somehow grasp the uncatchable time through design. He raised an eyebrow when I told him that was part of the reason why I chose watches. It might have started with the present Alicia brought me, but it was my fascination with the notion of time that became my driving force.

When I was little, I took time for granted. But after my life flipped upside down, I wanted to commemorate every second possible. When I told Jonathan that after losing my inhibition due to alcohol, he said he was proud of me. And I might have climbed him and demanded he take me then and there.

The fact that he's turning out to be more than I ever thought I needed is pushing buttons I didn't know I had.

I don't know how it happened or why, but Jonathan has effortlessly become an undivided part of my life. I couldn't get rid of him even if I wanted to.

That's both terrifying and exciting.

Instead of answering his question, I deflect, "Why do you hate Ethan so much?"

"You know."

I shake my head in his hold. "It's not only because of Alicia's death. If anything, he also lost his factory, wife, and nine years of his life. If you compare things, Ethan had endured more damage than you."

He traces my jaw with a deceptively tender thumb. "Are you taking his side, wild one?"

"I'm just stating facts. I...I want to get to know you."

"And you think decoding my relationship with Ethan would do that?"

"Whether you like to admit it or not, he's the only one you consider a worthy rival."

"Worthy isn't the word I would use. Try infuriating."

"Come on, tell me what it's all about."

His thumb continues gliding up and down my skin, creating maddening friction. "All you need to know is that I don't like him close to you."

"Why?"

"Because."

"That doesn't answer my question."

"It wasn't supposed to."

"Wait. Is it because of your attraction to the same type of women?" I can't believe I haven't thought about that before now. It makes complete sense that Jonathan wants me away from Ethan because he thinks Ethan also sees me the way he does.

His thumb halts as he narrows his eyes. "How do you know about that?"

"Ethan told me."

"Ethan told you," he repeats with a lethal edge. "What else did he tell you?"

"He said you used to have threesomes and share women, and that you're attracted to the same type."

"And then he said he could be better than me, didn't he? I'm going to fucking murder him."

"He didn't say that."

"He always said that to the women." His lips twists. "In fact, he didn't need to. They gravitated towards him anyway."

"What do you mean."

He pauses, and I suspect he won't answer my question, as usual, when he feels pressed, but then he speaks quietly. "In the past, I was always the one the women wanted to fuck, but the one they envisioned a relationship with was Ethan."

Oh. Jonathan feels like I would be like them. Far from it. It's crazy, but I wouldn't choose anyone above him.

"In case you didn't notice, you're intimidating, Jonathan."

He narrows his eyes on me again. "Right."

"I mean it. You have a god-like presence that no one dares to come near."

"You did."

"I would always choose you."

"Always?"

"Always."

He smiles a little before he schools his expression. "Ethan is still dead for putting the idea in your head."

"Stop it."

"Don't try to protect him. His life is over."

"I'm not." I smile tentatively. "He really didn't make that suggestion."

And if he had, I would've definitely protected him. Judging by Jonathan's reaction, he really wouldn't hesitate to hurt him.

"Ethan is guilty until proven innocent."

"It should be the other way around, Jonathan."

"Not in my book." His facial expression is hard as granite. "What else did he run his mouth about? Don't leave anything out."

"Just that and the fact that you prefer broken women. How come the two of you are attracted to the same type?"

He remains silent for a beat before his calm voice drifts all around me like a halo, "It's a challenge."

"A challenge?"

"Ethan and I don't like normal. Normal is boring. Back in university, we had no problem having girls fall at our feet, but the high soon withered away. Broken women, on the other hand, were interesting. We got to explore them and bring them to heights even they didn't think was possible. It was thrilling for the three of us."

My throat dries at the image of Jonathan and Ethan worshipping a woman. I don't like it—not that I shouldn't. It was way back. I still don't like it, damn it.

The fact that Jonathan also considers me a challenge is what sits badly at the bottom of my stomach.

Is that all I am to him?

"You shouldn't be mad at Ethan, then," I murmur. "He must think there'll be sharing like in the past."

One moment I'm sitting, the next, Jonathan drags me over. I fall all over his lap with a gasp. His fingers are still wrapped around my throat as his eyes darken to a frightening colour.

I'm staring up at him and trapped in that gaze that's able to not only dissect me, but simultaneously reach inside me.

"That won't be fucking happening." His voice is clipped with an edge that's meant to cut.

"N-no?"

"No one but me gets to fucking touch you. If anyone attempts to, they'll disappear and never return."

His pure male possessiveness could be scary at some level, but for some reason, it cools the fire burning in my chest.

"You would do that?"

"I would do more than that, Aurora. Do you think I was joking when I said you're mine?" His fingers cup me over my shorts, eliciting a rush of pleasure. "I'm going to put a baby in you to prove it."

My smile falls at his words.

It all makes sense now, the fact that he's never used a condom and that at some point, he started coming inside me and often fucks his seed into me. Or the fact that he nodded with approval when I told him I don't use any birth control.

The tyrant has been trying to impregnate me all this time.

It should make me angry or something, but I can't get past the bitter taste lingering at the back of my throat.

"You can't," I murmur.

"I can't what?"

"You can't put a baby in me. I'm barren, Jonathan." My voice chokes on his name and I sit up, needing the distance.

He lets me go, and I'm thankful he's allowing me to breathe in something other than his woodsy scent. Maybe he'll hate me now that I can't give him the baby he wants. At the beginning, I swear he was against it, which made sense, considering he has Aiden and Levi, and to an extent, it made me comfortable.

The fact that he changed his mind to wanting babies is messing with my head. I hate this feeling, the fact that I'm defective in so many ways. The fact that I can do nothing to fix it.

"How did that happen?" His voice is the same, with that edge of control and firmness, and, in a way, I'm thankful for it.

"I was born this way. I discovered it in my late teens when I went to the GP for birth control. She ran some tests and told me I was born with a genetically damaged ovary, so I can never have children of my own."

Silence.

It stretches between us for a second before I chance a peek at Jonathan. He's watching me with the same intensity as usual.

Before he can say anything, I blurt, "So it won't be happening—children, I mean. If you want those, then you should search elsewhere and find someone else—"

I'm cut off when he grabs me by the throat again and kisses me with an intensity that robs my breaths, thoughts, and words. I fall into Jonathan, my fingers gripping his T-shirt, and my eyes screwing shut at the raw power and sensuality in his kiss.

It's like he's driving a point home with his mouth, and although I can't exactly pinpoint it, I feel it. I fall into it. I become one with it.

His lips wrench away from mine as both of us pant, sucking in each other's air. "Fuck that. Fuck anyone who's not you, wild one."

An overwhelming sensation explodes in my chest so hard, it's almost painful. But at the same time, it's the relief I never thought I needed. "B-but you said you wanted a baby."

"I only wanted to glue you to me with that. Now, I'll just find another method."

"R-really?"

"Have I ever lied to you?"

"No, but..."

"I already have Aiden, and I practically raised Levi, so he's basically my son, too. Believe me, having those two punks is like fathering a dozen children."

A small smile grazes my lips. I can totally see that.

"But if you want kids, I will make it happen." His expression turns determined. "I don't care which doctor I have to threaten."

"Stop it." I smile. "I don't want them."

"Why not?"

"Because psychopathy is genetic and I'll never take the risk of having a child inherit Dad's qualities."

"You haven't."

"Just because I escaped that fate, barely, doesn't mean my

offspring won't—or the following generation, or the next. Being born without the ability to procreate is a blessing in this case, not a curse."

"It is what you make it to be, Aurora." He strokes my hair back. "The world is at the tip of your fingers."

"It is not."

"It is now. I'll bring the world to its knees in front of you. All you have to do is ask."

"Why?" I whisper.

"Why what?"

"Why would you do that for me?"

"Because the world needs to bend the knee for my queen."

My queen.

My mouth falls open and my eyes nearly bug out.

Holy shit. I think Jonathan just called me his queen. I didn't hear that incorrectly, right? It's not a sadistic play of my imagination.

Right?

"Now." His fingers sneak under my shorts, and my legs willingly open. "Have you been a good girl?"

"W-what?"

"Are you wearing the plug?"

No.

Shit.

I was so excited about the phone call with Layla, I came down without putting in the stupid toy.

"What will you do if I say no?" I murmur.

"If I spank you, you'll like that so I'll go a step further." His fingers sink into my folds and I arch my back against him.

"A step further?" I moan.

His lips find my earlobe and he whispers, "There will be no orgasm."

"Jonathan!" I protest.

"Only good girls get orgasms."

"I won't do it again." I cradle his face with my fingers and brush my lips against his jaw, knowing how much he likes it when I kiss him. "Please?"

"Try harder."

I plant kisses all over his cheek, his lips, his chiselled jaw, and even his nose and his eyelids. It's the first time I've been so forthcoming about kissing him, but Jonathan doesn't stop me. If anything, he loosens his hold a little to give me room to worship him.

To take my fill of him like I never have before. As I continue my ministrations, he fingers me slowly until I'm writhing in his hands, begging for more.

"Jonathan..."

"What?"

"More..."

"More what?" He twists his fingers inside me and I arch my back against him.

"T-that...that...please..."

He pulls out his fingers and I groan against his face, but I don't have to wait for long as he unbuckles his belt and slides his huge, throbbing dick inside me. We moan at the same time as he fills me whole. His fingers slide my wetness to my back hole using them instead of the plug as he thrusts slow and measured. His metal gaze never leaves mine as he fucks both my pussy and my arse.

But those aren't the only things he's owning. He's claiming me body, heart, and soul, and it's completely out of my control. I can't stop it, even if I wanted to.

Jonathan might be feared by the world, but as I stare into his sombre eyes, I find safety, belonging—feelings I never thought I would find again. And because this is out of my control, it scares the shit out of me. At the same time, I don't want to run away from it.

"J-Jonathan..." I moan, gripping his neck like it's a lifeline.

"What, wild one?"

"Harder."

He complies, his hand surrounding my throat as he brings me to the edge. He doesn't stop, though. Not when I scream his name.

Not when I writhe against his body.

Not when I beg—no idea if it's for more or for him to stop.

He takes me in countless positions as if he can't get enough of me. As if we'll lose the connection the moment he's out of me, and I wouldn't be surprised if that's the case.

When he finally comes inside me, I'm so deliciously spent and sore.

As I lie limp in his arms, a satisfied moan leaves my lips, and before I sleep, I murmur, "I want to go home."

He strokes my hair away from my face, his voice quiet as he repeats, "You want to go home?"

"I'm sick and tired of running away." A shiver runs through me. "It's time I finally stand up in front of the monster of my past."

TWENTY-THREE

Aurora

ECIDING TO GO HOME AND ACTUALLY DOING IT ARE TWO entirely different things. All I want to do is dig a hole and hide in it.

However, the thought of running away like in the past cripples me. I can't do that anymore. I can't start anew, pretend I have a rebirth and go on with my life.

The memories of lonely nights, trembling under the blankets, cause me to shudder.

Besides, I can't give up the life and the balance I've found. It's not just about Layla and H&H. It's also about Aiden, Levi, Astrid, and Elsa. It's about Moses, Margot, Tom, and even Harris. It's about the sense of family I've refound. And at the top of that chain, there's Jonathan.

The man who held my hand through it all and didn't judge me, even when he thought I'd lost my mind. If anything, he promised to protect me—including from myself.

For as long as I can remember, I've only had myself to rely on.

Protection could've only been provided by me. Having Jonathan there brings a certain peace I've never experienced before.

But it's not just about the sense of protection he brings. No. It's also about how he doesn't allow me to get lost in the maze in my head. It's almost as if he knows how dark it gets and pulls me out every time.

I'm not sure what it is about him that allows him to read me so well. I doubt it's because of the age difference, which, ironically, I don't think about anymore, and when I do, it's more with awe than anything else.

Not only does Jonathan know me, but he also recognises my needs before I come to terms with them myself. He's taught me that recognising one's own strength and weaknesses is what makes you strive higher.

With him, I feel both vulnerable and powerful. I can take on the world, but at the same time, I'm scared he'll pull the carpet from underneath my feet one day.

Because right now? I seriously cannot imagine my life without him. The fact that he was once my sister's husband barely gives me pause anymore.

I'm so sorry, Alicia. I'm the worst sister to ever exist.

Our first stop as soon as we arrive in England is Birmingham.

"I could've come to check on Layla on my own," I tell Jonathan as the butler welcomes us inside Ethan's Birmingham mansion— or palace. It's a lot bigger than the one in London, and Moses had to drive a long time before we were able reach the entrance with its majestic lion statues and high towers.

"You think I'd let you come to Ethan's house alone?" The question is clearly rhetorical since Jonathan continues in that haughty tone of his, "Nonsense."

"Don't be a jerk to him, okay?" I whisper in case someone is around. "We're in his house, after all."

"Depends."

"On what?"

"On whether or not he looks in your direction."

I chuckle. "You can't be serious."

He fixes me with one of his uptight glares. "I'm dead serious, and if you want me to prove it in front of him, I will."

"I don't see what the big deal is. After all, you used to share women in the past." And no, I'm still not over that.

"The key phrase in your sentence is 'in the past'. I wouldn't even share a table with him willingly."

"So I've been wondering... If you guys weren't fighting, would you still be sharing women?"

He grips me by the waist, his fingers digging into my side. "Why the fuck are you asking these questions? We already established that Ethan, or anyone else, is off the fucking table. I wouldn't share you for the rest of your life."

"You mean your life?"

"*Your* life. Death won't stop me, wild one. I'll find a way, even as a ghost."

"I have no doubt about that." The masculine voice coming from our right pauses our conversation.

Instead of letting me go, Jonathan keeps me planted to his side with a possessive hand at the small of my back.

Ethan stands at the base of the stairs, placing a hand in his trousers' suit pocket and smiling amicably. "Welcome to my Birmingham residence, Aurora. Jonathan, it's been a long time since you've come here. More than twenty years, I believe."

"Not long enough."

I elbow him and whisper, "Play nice."

"He's looking at you, so that's a no," Jonathan says in a voice loud enough for Ethan to hear.

"Always a charmer, Jonathan." Ethan smiles at him, but there's no welcoming in it.

The latter returns it with a scowl.

The amount of testosterone around here is high as hell. I can almost taste it on my tongue.

"Where are Layla and her parents?" I ask to dissipate the tension.

"Mr and Mrs Hussaini went for a stroll, and as for Layla—"

Ethan's words cut off when a door opens from the other side of the room, and in comes Layla carrying basket of roses, throwing the petals at a solemn-faced Agnus. He doesn't seem to enjoy it in the least, but he remains silent as she grins. "I could totally turn you into a princess, Agnus. If anyone can do it, it's me."

Ethan laughs, and even Jonathan is about to smile before he seals his reaction, as usual. I'm beginning to see a pattern between Ethan and Jonathan. One is more open and the other is closed off. However, they have a lot of traits in common—the most important of all, their hunger for power. The more they have, the more they want. That's why they clicked a long time ago.

Jonathan is just more forthcoming about it. Ethan doesn't show it as much, but that doesn't deny his desire for it.

Upon seeing me, Layla pushes the basket of roses at Agnus's chest and runs towards me.

I open my arms and she hugs me without protest. "I missed you so much, mate. Don't you dare leave me again."

"I missed you, too, Lay."

"Come on." She grips me by the hand. "We have so much to catch up on."

Ethan motions at the stairs and raises his brow at Jonathan. "My office?"

"Play nice," I mouth at Jonathan.

"No," he mouths back and I shake my head as Agnus abandons the basket of roses on a table and follows them.

With the three of them there, I can only imagine what will happen in that office. Definitely not something I want to witness.

Layla and I sit on a bench in the garden. The trees here are so tall, they block the horizon.

"So?" she asks impatiently. "Details."

"Promise you won't hate me?"

"Never. Ride or die, remember?"

I let it all out and tell Layla about my life ever since I was brought up in Leeds, and all the way to witnessing that crime, losing my sister, and the whole trial nightmare.

While I speak, Layla's expression falls and I think she hates me by the time I finish, but she hugs me again. Two hugs in one day is a first.

"I'm so sorry you had to go through all of that on your own. You were so young."

I hold on to her and let the tears loose. It's the first time I've talked about the whole thing and I'm so grateful that Layla is the one I got to tell everything that happened.

She pulls back and wipes my tears with the back of her sleeves. "Johnny gets brownie points for taking you away from here so you could clear your head. His Daddy status is reinstated."

"You're awful." I smile through the tears.

"Can I ask you something?"

"Sure, Lay."

"Which name do you prefer? Clarissa or Aurora?"

"When I was Clarissa, I was happy, but it was at the expense of other people's suffering. I don't like being her anymore. I don't like the memories associated with her or the fears she went through."

"Aurora it is, then. It'd be super weird to call you anything else." She grins tentatively. "Why did you pick that name?"

It's my turn to smile as the memories of summer and marshmallow scent filter back in. "Alicia said if she had a baby girl, she would've named her Aurora. I guess it's stayed with me."

"I'm so proud of how far you've come, mate."

"Are you being sappy right now?"

"Who? Me? Never!" We laugh and she scoots closer, her expression morphing into one of seriousness. "What are you going to do now?"

"I'm still thinking about it. Hey, Lay, don't you miss work?"

"Honestly? I'm going out of my mind here. You know I hate staying still, but it's okay. I can take it."

"Well, I can't."

"What do you intend to do?"

"I'm going to stand tall like I was supposed to sixteen years ago."

The following day, I go to the prosecutor's office. I don't tell Jonathan, because he'd stop me.

I refuse to live my life in fear, scared about when they'll come knocking on my door, or when they'll catch me while I'm walking down the streets.

Although I don't share my plans with Jonathan, I make my way through the building, armed with his words to me.

You did nothing wrong.

He's right. I haven't. And now, I'll own up to it.

They take me to a white room with a grey table in the middle. I keep my cool as the prosecutor tries to intimidate me with his questions.

The prosecutor, who introduced himself as Joffrey Dale, is an older man with a few decades of experience under his belt. It makes sense that they're assigning him to an important nationwide case like this.

His bushy brows are drawn together as if they were made to judge people. His suit is a size too big and his head is half-bald with a few streaks of hair combed in the middle. But that doesn't take away from the sharp look in his light brown eyes.

After a long silence, which he spends reading the file in front of him, Joffrey finally lifts his head. "We'll start with the basics. What's your name?"

"Aurora Harper."

"Your legal one, Miss."

"Aurora Harper. I registered it."

He nods as if the information is new to him, when it's most

likely a tactic. Even the white room we're in, which seems sterilised, must be some psychological trick. The police played them a lot on me back in the day, but I was too young to recognise them.

"Why have you come here, Ms Harper?"

"Voluntary questioning."

He fixes me with his bland eyes. "For what?"

"Maxim Griffin's parole hearing." My hands grip each other on my lap, but I force them to loosen.

"What's your relationship with Mr Griffin?"

"He's my father."

"And you're the Clarissa he's accusing of being his accomplice?"

I nod.

"Are you admitting to his accusations?"

"I'm admitting to being his daughter that used to be named Clarissa. That's all. His accusations are entirely false."

He focuses back on the file, retrieves images of the murdered women, crime scene ones, too, and lays them in front of me. I force myself to stare at their faces, even though tears start rushing in.

"Do you remember them, Ms Harper?"

"Of course I do. I dream about them all the time."

"Who are they?"

"My father's victims."

"Do you remember their cause of death?"

I swallow a deep breath, the air sticking in my throat. "Suffocation by duct tape."

"Do you know how long it takes for death by suffocation?" The question is clearly rhetorical since he continues in his flat tone, "Normally, it's twenty minutes, but in their cases, he left a small opening in the duct tape to slow the process. Their death processes ranged from four to twenty hours. They spent all those hours begging for air, only to find death."

"I know that! I also know he stalked them and made them feel like he was their dream on earth before he lured them to the cabin. I also know he cut their arms, played with their bodies while they suffocated, then kept the duct tape as a trophy before he buried them. I also know those seven reported victims weren't his only ones, and that many other cases were closed for lack of evidence. So why don't you look into those instead of this entire masquerade? Why the fuck are you allowing that sick bastard the right for parole?"

Despite my outburst, Joffrey's voice and expression remain cool. "Because, Ms Harper, we might have evidence that he wasn't the only one involved in those murders."

"What evidence?" I laugh with a bitter edge. "I testified against my own fucking father. I brought him to you the day I lost my sister. If you have something against me, show it, but I know you don't. All of you are playing into his hands."

"Then why did you escape the Witness Protection Program?"

"I didn't trust the police. They were aggressive and careless, and I didn't feel safe in their company."

"Or you wanted to run and hide."

"If I wanted to run and hide, why would I come here of my own volition?"

He opens his mouth to say something, but a knock on the door cuts him off. Before he can stand up, it barges open, and in comes a man looking to be in his early fifties. He's slim and short, wearing an elegant striped suit and carrying a leather briefcase.

"Who are you?" Joffrey asks.

"Alan Sheldon. I'm Ms Harper's solicitor. The voluntary questioning is over, effective immediately, Dale."

Wait. I have a solicitor? When did that happen?

"Ms. Harper was ready to answer more questions." Joffrey doesn't hide the irritation in his tone, but he also stands his ground.

"Not anymore. My client needs to rest before the trial." Alan motions at me and I rise.

I was done anyway. I came here to urge them to investigate the other victims and to warn them of Dad's manipulative nature, but if they'd rather play into his hands, then it's all on them.

"Ms Harper," the prosecutor calls when I'm standing beside

Alan. "Mr Griffin said you were never innocent. What's your reply to that?"

"You don't have to answer that question," Alan tells me.

"It's okay. He should know that Dad doesn't even know the meaning of innocence. He spent his entire life tarnishing it."

And with that, I'm out of the room. Alan walks closely beside me. We're about the same height, but since I'm wearing heels, I'm a bit taller than him.

"Don't show up for any voluntary questionings anymore, and if it somehow happens, please call me beforehand, Miss."

"I'm sorry, but who hired you?"

"Mr King."

"Oh." Of course, it's Jonathan. Did I mention that he's always one step ahead?

"Word got out that you were here." Alan's voice turns critical. "The press is just outside."

Shit. Fuck.

Sweat trickles down my spine at the thought of facing them. I'm sure the victims' families are there, too. Despite my pep talk, I can't handle restarting the nightmare all over again.

"We can wait, then go through the back," Alan suggests.

"Running away would mean I admit to doing something wrong. I haven't."

"Remember, you don't have to answer anything."

I nod, but I'm not in the right headspace. My feet hesitate at the revolving doors as dark memories of the trial rush back in.

It's okay. I can do this. I'm not that sixteen-year-old girl anymore.

Snapping my spine into a straight position, I march right outside.

As Alan had forewarned, the press is waiting. As soon as I come out, a horde of people rush towards me. Cameras flash in my eyes as phones and microphones are shoved in my face.

It's a complete shitshow and I'm caught right in the middle of it.

Alan tries to shield me, but he alone can't ward them all off. Bodies bump into me, and eager, slightly judgemental eyes bore into mine.

The questions rain on me from all directions.

"Ms. Harper, is it true you escaped?"

"Why change to Aurora Harper? Did you erase your family history along with Clarissa Griffin?"

"Is it true you picked the victims for your father?"

"Why have you come to questioning?"

"Is it true that you escaped the Witness Protection Program to join an extremist jihadist group?"

"What's your comment on your father's accusations?"

"Will you stick to your initial statement or are you going to change it?"

"Were you diagnosed with an antisocial disorder when you were young?"

Their words muffle into each other, and it takes everything in me to stay in the present. The flashing of cameras keep throwing me back to eleven years ago.

"Murderer! Murderer!" A group of people protest at the side of the road. They're holding pictures of the women who lost their lives because of Dad.

I recognise their faces, even though it's been a long time ago. The families. The people left behind.

Sarah stands with them, carrying the toddler I saw her with at the charity event. She's glaring at me and screaming with the others. "Murderer! We want justice!"

One of them throws rotten tomatoes at me and I close my eyes, letting them hit my face. I retrieve a napkin from my bag and try to wipe it away, but they hit me with another one.

Tears sting my eyes, but I refuse to let them out and I force myself to remain completely still.

I force myself into a numb state. That's the only way to get through such scenes.

On the third tomato, a few buff men dressed in black surround me and Alan. We're in such a small circle that their heights and developed physiques block the press and the victims' families.

They block everything.

I stare with a stunned expression as Jonathan strides to my side with that innate confidence of his. Relief as I've never felt before engulfs me as he wraps an arm around my waist and pulls me into the crook of his body. I inhale his woodsy scent, using him as an anchor to dissociate from the hell surrounding us.

Jonathan faces the press and says in a loud voice that everyone can hear, "This is my first and final warning. If anyone harasses my fiancée again, I'll sue and destroy them in court."

He then leads me towards an awaiting car. My legs barely carry me and he has to half-lift me. Only one word stays stuck in my head.

I'm not becoming deaf, right? Because I think Jonathan just called me his fiancée in front of the entire world.

TWENTY-FOUR

Aurora

MY FIANCÉE.
   My fiancée…
   My. Fiancée.

Maybe if I say those words once more in my head, they'll somehow make sense. But will they really?

I can't stop staring at Jonathan as he uses the wet napkins Moses passes him to wipe my face and my clothes.

His jaw is set and he seems angry. It's not even directed towards me, but I somehow feel it in my bones.

"Aurora!"

"W-what?" *Was he talking?*

"I asked you if you're okay." He's studying me intently, as if that will manage to snap me out of my daze.

It doesn't.

Since there's no way I'll be able to speak, I nod.

"I need words, wild one."

"I-I'm fine." But am I? I don't think so. Not after the bomb he's just dropped out there for the entire press to hear.

"Why the fuck did you even go in there? Why didn't you tell me first?"

Because I thought he would pull something like this. I mean, not exactly, but yeah, something similar.

I've read about Jonathan's brutal ways with the media. He shows them no mercy when they overstep their boundaries or try to get their noses in his private life—or his family's. The more he blocks them, the more they become obsessed with him, though.

He wraps a hand around my throat and pushes me so my back is pinned to the leather seat. His woodsy scent rushes into my lungs and it's all I can breathe. His presence is all I can see. His touch is all I can feel.

I love it when he does that.

"I'm waiting for an answer," he insists, and I know his soft phase is coming to an end. Jonathan might be protective, but he also has a no-nonsense, ruthless streak that demands to be obeyed.

"I'm done running away," I murmur. "I have no reason to hide. I'm not him. I'm *not* my father."

His lips pull at the corners in what I assume is approval. "Still, you do *not* go behind my fucking back ever again. If Alan didn't have acquaintances in the office, we might not have gotten here on time. Do you know what that means, Aurora? You could've been attacked."

I gulp. "It wouldn't have been the first time."

"Fuck." He hits the side of the seat. "It won't happen under my watch. *Never*. Is that understood?"

I believe him.

No idea why, but I believe the words coming out of his mouth as strongly as Layla believes in her religion. *He* is my religion.

When he showed up earlier, all I could think about was safety. It's weird, isn't it? That the man I call my tyrant is also my safest place.

"I said, is that fucking understood, Aurora?"

I nod.

"There will be no more putting yourself down for others, whether it's victims' families or what-the-fuck-ever. They're not your victims and you will not take their shit."

"Okay."

"No one hurts a fucking hair on your head, Aurora. No one touches you but me. Do you hear me? I'll burn them all down before they put you through the hell from eleven years ago again."

"Jonathan, don't hurt them. They're just in pain." I have no doubt that he'll crush them under his shoes if he chooses to.

"How about you? Aren't you in pain? Weren't you in pain eleven years ago? You were sixteen, for fuck's sake. They had no right to blame you for Maxim's crimes, and if they continue to do so, I will show no mercy. I'll burn them until no one is left."

"Jonathan..."

"That's final, Aurora. You might've tolerated that and gotten fucking stabbed for it, but I'll never let it happen. I will protect you."

My heart warms at his words, at the force behind them, because I have no doubt he'll do as he says. But I need to get a point straight, "You don't have to protect me. Just because I'm a woman doesn't mean I can't protect myself."

"I'm not protecting you because you're a woman. I'm protecting you because you're *my* woman."

Holy. Shit.

My mouth hangs open for the second time today, but this time, my heart is about to go into overdrive. Jonathan just called me his woman.

His. Woman.

That should offend me in a way, but that's the last emotion gripping my heart.

The car comes to a stop in front of the mansion before I can say anything. Jonathan releases my throat, only so he can carry me in his arms out of the vehicle.

I grip his shoulder. "I can walk."

"And I can carry you."

This man is a serious tyrant.

We pass by Margot and she watches us for a second, probably because of the tomato stains on my jacket. "May I get you anything, sir?"

"Food, Margot," Jonathan says while breezing past her. "Leave it in front of my room."

He doesn't wait for her reply as he ascends the stairs, not caring about the weight he's carrying. He really doesn't have the stamina of an old man. I can only imagine what he was like young.

Or not.

That means imagining him with Alicia, and I feel so guilty towards her right now. I feel so guilty for wanting her husband for myself. For feeling safe with him like I never have with another human being.

He's like the fortress inside of which I know nothing will come near me, let alone hurt me.

In the room, Jonathan lowers me to my feet and peels the jacket off me, then throws it behind him. "Those fuckers."

"Jonathan..."

"Not a word, Aurora. I won't stand by as they do this to you."

"No, I meant...what you said earlier. Why did you?"

"What part?"

"The part about how I'm your fiancée?"

He raises a brow. "Aren't you?"

"W-what?"

His expression remains blank, and I hate that I can't see past it. "You are, in a way."

"No. We had a deal, remember? I only have a few weeks left here, then each of us will go our own way. There certainly was no fiancée clause in there." Even as I say the words, my throat closes around the part where we'll separate.

Jonathan watches me for a beat too long, which makes me

fidget. When he finally speaks, his voice is lethal, "Is that what you think?"

"That's what it is. It's what we agreed on." I don't know why I keep emphasising the point I hate. All I want is an explanation for the whole fiancée thing and why the hell he brought it up in front of the press.

It could be a camouflage tactic recommended by his solicitor, or even Harris. No clue why I'm mentioning the forgotten agreement. Maybe I want confirmation of it, because I sure as shit am starting to forget it exists. And when I do remember it, my stomach sinks at how little time there is left.

Jonathan continues his unreadable study of my face. I hate his closed features so much right now. Of all times, he can't seal himself from me now.

"Huh."

That's it? *Huh.* What is that supposed to mean?

I see?

I agree?

It's nothing?

We should talk about this?

Before I can ask him just that, he points at the bathroom. "Take a bath, then eat. You have to begin preparing for your trial with Alan starting tomorrow."

Then he turns around and strides to the exit with his usual confident steps. The door closes behind him with painful finality.

My heart falls to my feet as I watch where he stood only seconds ago. He'll return, right? He'll just make calls, as usual, listen to Harris's snobbish voice, and come back.

Right?

Refusing to think of the alternative, I drag my heavy feet to the bathroom and take a shower instead of a bath. It feels wrong to take a bath without him doing it for me.

Margot brings me supper and I barely manage to take a few spoonfuls of soup. Again, it's weird to eat without Jonathan either sitting me on his lap or staring at me across the table with that raised brow so I'll eat.

When I'm finished, I lie in bed and read Layla's texts to distract myself from Jonathan's scent that's surrounding me like a vice.

The fact that he's not here yet causes my stomach to dip.

Layla: Mate! Guess what? Jake the piece of S turned himself in.

My eyes widen.

Aurora: Jake, as in the accountant Jake, who stole our funds and ran off to Australia?

Layla: Uh-huh. That Jake. Jessica was notified a few hours ago about how he turned himself in. He spent the funds, but at least we'll have our justice.

Aurora: But…how?

Layla: No clue, but I heard he was coerced into it. Whoever did it, I love him.

Jonathan.

This has his fingerprints all over it. This must be what he talks about with Harris in private, not wanting me to hear.

My heart aches at that realisation. He's been searching for Jake all this time and finally made him pay.

The need to go to him and thank him, kiss him, hug him, hits me like a ton of bricks.

Layla: Anyway, enough about that sucker. Don't think I didn't see the news. Since when are you engaged to Johnny?

Layla: I need details, mate. And I'm totes not jealous that you have a Daddy and I don't. *crying emoji*

I smile, but it's sad at best. Layla doesn't know that I might've ruined this entire thing with him altogether.

After we're done texting, I toss and turn all night in bed.

Jonathan doesn't return.

TWENTY-FIVE

Jonathan

A DEAL.

She said we had a deal.

A fucking *deal*.

I grip my phone so tightly, I'm surprised it doesn't crack into pieces. I'm even more surprised that I'm able to function after the whole fucking show that happened today.

While I was planning the future Aurora and I will have together after the drama with Maxim ends, she's been thinking about the fucking deal.

As in, during all the months we spent together, her sole purpose has been to leave me.

Running is constantly the first thing on her mind no matter what I do.

It doesn't matter if I paint the world gold for her or if I pluck the bloody stars from the sky and scatter them at her feet. She'll just step over them and run.

Like she always does.

Like she has been doing for the past eleven years.

But here's the thing. She didn't have me in the past. She didn't belong to me body and soul. I don't care how much her heart fights me, it'll eventually crumble like the rest of her.

Will it, though?

I was never one to receive affection. Being incapable of it turned me into a solid wall against it. Even my own mother didn't think I needed such a thing. To make it even worse, Alicia completely withdrew from me and my own son cares more about challenging me than anything else.

Why would Aurora be any different?

That isn't the problem, though. The problem is that I want her to be different when I never wished for it in my entire existence.

"Where to, sir?" Moses asks from the front seat.

"The headquarters," Harris says on my behalf. He followed us here after the media show and was about to leave for a meeting when I told him I'd join.

He has barely stared at his tablet for the last minute. That's a record.

"Didn't you say you're staying in for today?" he asks slowly, almost cautiously. I must appear like I'm on the verge of combusting, and Harris is smart enough to pick on exterior changes.

"Don't you always bitch that I'm constantly absent? You should be happy I'm coming along." My voice is calm, but it's the deceptive type that hints at a fucking storm brewing underneath.

"I am, but...you wouldn't usually leave Aurora's side. Especially after what happened today."

"She's Ms Harper to you."

"I can't call her Ms Harper now. That's like calling Grams Mrs Willis."

I release a breath but say nothing.

Harris readjusts his glasses with his index and middle finger. "Trouble in paradise?"

"Shut it."

"I was wondering when she'd snap."

"She?" I give him a side-eye. "*I am the one who's supposed to snap.*"

"With all due respect, sir, you're not the one who was dragged into a foreign world all of a sudden and forced to deal with...well, someone demanding—for the lack of better terms."

No. But I might as well be.

"She was bound to rebel against you."

"Do you have a point, Harris?"

"Do you want my advice?"

"Since when are you an expert?"

"I've been Googling things to stay ahead."

"*Googling?*"

"You would be surprised at what you can find there. Anyway, all I'm saying is, give her time, sir."

"That won't be happening."

"Suit yourself."

"What the fuck is that supposed to mean?"

"It means, you might lose her once and for all."

My breathing turns harsh and rugged as I resist the urge to punch Harris' snobby face. "That won't be happening either."

"It will, unless…"

I stare at him. "Unless *what?*"

"Unless you give her space. If you want her to fall back into you willingly, then you should leave her alone for a while."

"How long is a *while?*"

"As long as it takes."

"What if she never comes back?"

He sighs and readjusts his glasses again. "Then it's better to let her go."

Let her go.

I know what that means, and despite my black mood, I recognise it's probably the best option for her.

But how the fuck can I let go of the piece of myself I finally found?

TWENTY-SIX

Aurora

THE FOLLOWING WEEK PASSES IN A BLUR.

It's the longest period of my life.

Part of it is because of the upcoming trial and the imminent doom of facing my father again. Alan and I have been practising what I should and shouldn't say, how I should react, and even what I should wear.

My solicitor is sure that the prosecution has nothing to bring me down, but I can tell he's wary of the other solicitor pulling something from his sleeves.

However, that's not the part that unsettles me the most. The reason I'm out of sorts is mainly because of the cold shoulder Jonathan has been giving me lately.

He doesn't sit me on his lap anymore, although he does give me that severe look so I'll eat. He runs me baths but doesn't stay when I take them. He brings me meals but doesn't linger. He's in the know about all my meetings with Alan, but he doesn't talk to me about the trial.

Jonathan doesn't talk to me. Full stop.

When we had a family dinner the other day, he remained

completely silent, listening to Aiden and Levi throwing jabs at each other. He didn't stay for their usual chess game, and as soon as the meal ended, he went straight to his office.

Elsa and Astrid asked me if something was wrong, and Aiden said they're getting back the Jonathan they all recognise.

He didn't return that entire evening and stayed the night in his office. He does that a lot now, pulling all-nighters in his company, with Harris and a usually-tired Moses.

In the beginning, I thought the phase would wear off, and he'd eventually return to being the Jonathan I know—the man I grew accustomed to. He hasn't.

Now, whenever Ethan is in sight, or one of the boys says something about me or to me, he doesn't hesitate to tell them off, but his attention is never directed at me.

I hate how I can barely sleep anymore—if ever. The bed feels so cold and desolate without him. Before, nighttime used to be my favourite, but now, I dread it like nothing else. It means I'll go home and sleep without him. It means I'll continue watching the door, waiting for it to open, then sleep with tears in my eyes when it doesn't.

The only times Jonathan talks to me is to tell me to eat or to not leave the house without security.

They follow me around everywhere now, especially to H&H. There are usually many reporters waiting there and making everyone's lives a nightmare. Layla threatens to give them hell, but I manage to stop her by saying it'll only make it worse.

By the end of the week, I'm so mentally exhausted, I want to curl into a ball and disappear.

But I don't do that. Instead, I go one step further in a last-ditch attempt to get Jonathan back. Though talking to him would probably be a better option.

But have you seen Jonathan? It's not like I can walk up to him and he'll listen. He's so hot-headed, and when he erases you, it's hard to even look at him in the eyes, let alone talk to him.

So I invited Ethan over for afternoon tea. I mean, this is where I live too and Layla has been coming over the entire time. I also consider Ethan a friend, so he should be welcome to where I live.

Or at least, those are the excuses I tell myself.

Margot watches us peculiarly as she serves us tea near the outside pool area. Almost as if she's asking me if I've lost my mind.

Perhaps I have, but I'm so sick and tired of Jonathan's silent treatment. If Ethan is what it'll take to have him talk to me again, so be it.

It's a rare sunny Friday afternoon, and Jonathan is still at the office, so maybe he'll pull another all-nighter.

I take a sip of my tea while Ethan twirls the ice in his scotch. There's been a small smile on his lips ever since he stepped inside.

"What?" I ask from above the rim of my cup.

"I'm imagining Jonathan's reaction. Fun."

"You do realise that antagonising him isn't the way to get back into his good graces, right?"

Tell that to yourself, hypocrite.

"It is. Jonathan lives for challenges instead of sappy emotions. On the day of his father's funeral, which was only a few days after his mother's, his older brother, James, was devastated. Guess what Jonathan did?"

I lean closer in my chair, the thought of him losing his parents so close together spreads an unusual ache through my chest. The pain I feel for him is mind-boggling, considering he has no emotions under his radar. "What?"

"He plotted how to bring down the man who caused his father's death. That was his form of grief."

"Alicia's father."

He pauses with the glass halfway to his mouth. "You know about that."

"Jonathan told me."

"That's…interesting. You're not her replacement, after all."

"What do you mean?"

"At first, I thought he brought you in to alleviate his guilt about losing Alicia since the two of you look so much alike. Now, I'm sure that's not the case."

My heart picks up speed and the thing won't slow down, no matter how much I try not to get caught in Ethan's words. "How do you know?"

He takes a sip of his drink, his features relaxed, and he appears completely in his element, despite being in another person's house.

But considering his history with Jonathan, he probably came by a lot in the past. The King mansion isn't a strange place to him.

"Jonathan never opened up to Alicia. In his mind, it was unnecessary to worry her, and although he thought he was protecting her, he was only sealing himself off. The fact that he shows his emotions freely to you is, as I said, interesting."

"He opened up to you too in the past, no?"

"Not by choice. I bugged him for it and I usually ended up getting cursed."

An involuntary smile grazes my lips, imagining one of their bickering scenes. "I'm glad he had you."

And I mean it. Ethan has the ability to deal with emotions, unlike Jonathan who purposefully keeps them in a vault.

"I'm the one who's glad *you* are here, Aurora."

"You'll be less glad when I drown you in the pool."

Both of us freeze at Jonathan's strong voice. My hand gripping the cup trembles and I try to steady it to no avail.

Planning this was one thing, but having it become reality is entirely different.

He steps beside me, all tall and powerful in his sharp black suit. Tingles erupt all over my skin from just seeing him. Will there ever be a day when I don't get tangled up by his presence?

"Jonathan." Ethan smiles. "Always a pleasure to hear your threats."

"Get out of my property."

"I'm afraid I can't. I'm Aurora's guest."

Jonathan's jaw clenches, but he doesn't look at me. Shit. If even this tactic doesn't work, I'm completely lost here.

I stand in a frail attempt to dissipate the tension. One moment I'm up, the next, Jonathan wraps a hand around my throat and slams his mouth to mine.

A gasp leaves me, but he swallows the sound and everything I had to say. His lips claim mine in a possessive kiss that leaves me with no breaths, thoughts, or balance. There's no use in trying to keep up with the powerful strokes of his tongue. They're too fast and dominant for me to reciprocate.

A feeble whimper is the evidence of my surrender as I freely give the reins over to him. Jonathan devours me in the most passionate, deep kiss he's ever given me.

I still can't breathe by the time his lips leave my mouth. My nerve endings tingle on my skin with the need for more.

Jonathan doesn't release my throat, holding it firmly but not painfully. His harsh voice is directed at Ethan as he speaks, "Aurora and I aren't accepting guests. You know where the door is."

I don't get to focus on Ethan's expression, or the fact that Jonathan has just claimed me in front of him. My whole being is focused on Jonathan's skin on mine, the fact that he's touching me, kissing me. It's been only a week, but it's felt like a decade.

Being so used to his touch, only for it to be abruptly taken away, is the worst type of torture he could've inflicted on me.

Jonathan releases my throat and clutches me by the waist. He practically drags me by his side to the lounge area and slams the French balcony's doors closed.

As soon as we're out of Ethan's view, he backs me against the wall, his fingers finding my throat again.

I stare up at him, my vision invaded with his sheer savage presence and the storm brewing in his metal gaze.

"Do you want to be fucked in front of Ethan, Aurora? Is that it?"

"What? No."

"Then what the fuck was that show all about? Your guest? Your fucking *guest?*" Gone is the Jonathan who ignored me with a calm expression. Right now, he seems on the verge of burning everything in his path and leaving ashes behind.

Why the hell am I excited for that?

Even though his hold has me hostage, I manage, "He's my friend."

"Fuck that. He's not your friend. He's not your anything."

"Why?"

He narrows his eyes. "Are you doing this on purpose, wild one? Is it because you know that Ethan and I are attracted to the same types of women?"

I haven't thought about that, but since he mentioned it, his reaction makes sense now.

"This is your final warning. Provoke me with Ethan or any other man again, and I'll fuck you in front of them. After I kill them, of course, because no one gets to see you naked but me."

I swallow because I have no doubt he'd do it. Jonathan doesn't have limits like everyone else. His moral compass is screwed in more ways than one.

And I know this is my chance to finally get a rise out of him after such a long time of the silent treatment.

"Why would you care?" I lift my chin. "You pretended I didn't even exist this past week."

"Isn't that what you want?"

"W-what? What *I* want?"

"You want out, no? You're only thinking about the deal and how soon you can leave, remember?"

I bite my lower lip. "I was only asking."

"Only asking?"

"Forget it."

"I can't forget it." His fingers trace my lower lip and it parts involuntarily. "Here's the thing, Aurora. You won't leave."

"I won't?"

"There's no way in fuck I'm letting you go."

My chest flutters. "But the agreement—"

"Fuck the agreement. What do *you* want?"

"I…if I want to go, will you let me?" I guess that's what I really want to know. I need the confirmation that Jonathan respects my need to have my own choice, that he won't force his opinions on me because of his control freak nature.

While I can't get enough of him, I'm neither his property nor his toy. I want to be his equal.

His expression remains the same, hard as granite and unreadable. His tone is calm, composed. "What do you think?"

"I don't know."

We stare at each other for a beat too long, our breaths mingling. His woodsy scent fills my nostrils and creeps under my skin. His whole presence winds imaginary fingers around my heart.

Only Jonathan has the ability to reach into my ribcage and barge through as if he were always meant to be there.

He lifts me up, and I squeal as he drops me on the edge of the sofa. The leather creaks underneath me as my breasts meet the surface and my knees land on the floor.

Jonathan kneels behind me, bunches my skirt up to my arse, and yanks my underwear down, letting them fall to my knees.

The sound of his belt buckle comes from behind me as he thrusts two fingers inside me in one go.

A loud moan leaves my lips and I muffle it against the cool leather. A wave rushes through me with supersonic speed. Maybe it's because it's been a long time without his maddening touch, but the moment he slaps my arse, I come.

Just the slightest stimuli and I'm on the edge.

"You don't know? You should know, wild one. The answer should come easily to you." His voice is hard, but there's something else underneath that I can't put my finger on.

His cock slips between my arse cheeks and I tense. Despite all the preparations and the toys, Jonathan is big—more like, huge. There's always a delicious sting of pain whenever he fucks me. Imagining that size in my arse causes uncontrollable shivers to break out on my skin.

"Relax." Still moving his fingers inside my pussy, he circles my clit with his thumb. Small bursts of pleasure grip me and I let myself fall slack against the leather.

"Good girl."

I moan at the sound of those words out of his mouth. After last week's fuck-up, I thought I would never hear them again.

"You'll be able to take me, won't you?"

"Mmm."

"What if my dick is too big for this tight arse?"

"I can take it."

"You can, huh?"

"Mmm."

"You want me to confiscate your last virginity for myself?"

My thighs clench at the thought, and I'm so turned on that I can't see straight. "Y-yes."

"What was that?"

"Fuck me, Jonathan."

"Fuck you where?"

"In the arse. Fuck me in the arse."

A low grunt fills the air as Jonathan uses my juices as natural lube. He takes his time prepping me that I wiggle my arse against him so he gets on with it.

He then thrusts his cock an inch inside me, and although he's been preparing me since the island, the stretching sensation is real.

"Oh…G-God…" My voice is broken by both pleasure and pain. They always come hand in hand with Jonathan, and I've become so accustomed to it that the mere thought of having one without the other depresses me.

"I'm going to own every fucking inch of you."

It could be his words or the way he's stimulating my body, but I relax even further, my nails digging into the sofa until he's fully inside.

With his fingers deep into my pussy, I feel so utterly full, like

I've never experienced before. His cock doesn't compare to the plugs. It's so much more real, and the sparks of pleasure feel like they're shooting from all places at once.

The mere brush of my hard nipples against my clothes and the leather sends an additional bolt of arousal to my core and arse. Everything in me is attuned to the feel of him inside me, at my back, and all around me.

But it's not only about the physical connection. Being with Jonathan is like free-falling without a landing. It's finding oneself after years of being lost. It's peace after a war. And it's all because of him.

He called me his queen once, but what he doesn't know is that there's no king to my kingdom but him.

It might be a small kingdom compared to his empire, but mine is more intimate, and he's the only person I would ever allow inside my bubble.

He's the only person who's made me feel safe, even though the world is scared of him.

My calculative tyrant and skilled lover.

"Fuck, you're so tight." Jonathan moves slowly, both in my pussy and in my arse, letting me get accustomed to him.

A whimper rips in the air and I realise it's mine as he picks up his pace. Sparks of pleasure like I've never known crowd in my nerve endings with a crippling force.

"J-Jonathan...I-I..."

He wraps strong, masculine fingers around my nape, giving me the anchor I need. "That's it. Fall into me, wild one."

I turn my head towards him and he holds my eyes hostage as the orgasm rips through me with a strength I've never experienced. It's a shattering. A fall with no chance of hitting the bottom.

Jonathan continues his onslaught, powering into me, and as he promised, he owns every fucking inch of me. His cock meets his fingers through the thin barrier and my lids droop to soak in the sensation. I can't stop watching him filling me, even with the uncomfortable angle.

His shoulders tense under his jacket as he stops. Then a grunt spills from his sensual lips as his cum warms my insides and drips down my thighs.

I whimper at the loss of him when he pulls out of me, his cock and fingers leaving wet trails on my inner thigh and arse.

But before I can ponder on the loss, Jonathan turns me around, backs me against the sofa, and takes my lips in a slow, hungry kiss that steals my breath more than the one from earlier.

It's like he's cementing the connection we just had and sealing it with a kiss. I soften against him, my fingers digging into his hard chest for balance.

"In case you haven't figured out the answer, listen carefully, Aurora," he whispers in dark words against my mouth. "I will *not* let you go."

TWENTY-SEVEN

Jonathan

I CARRY A SLEEPING AURORA IN MY ARMS FROM THE BATHROOM to the bedroom.

I keep telling her that falling asleep in the bathtub is dangerous, but she mumbles that I'm there.

It's true. I *am* there. I don't take the fact that she trusts me enough to fall asleep in my arms for granted.

Since I took her a few days ago, I've been trying to spend as much time with her as physically possible.

Not having her sleep next to me on an everyday basis has been torture. Needless to say, I've been having blue balls for all the times I didn't fuck her or spank her until she begged me to come.

But here's the strangest part. It's not only about the physical connection—even if it started that way. While I love how she comes undone under my touch, I enjoy how she curls into my embrace more. How she wraps her arms and legs around me while she sleeps. How she holds on to me when she has nightmares. How my name is the first thing she whispers when she wakes up. How she grabs my arm and invites me to the baths I run for her.

Most of all, I enjoy how she tells me about her days and her work. How she retells one of her and Layla's adventures with a huge smile on her face. How she keeps urging me to get in touch with Aiden and Levi because they're my family.

Aurora barged into my life, wreaked havoc in my order, and disrupted my chessboard. At first, the moves she made were insignificant, but they kept escalating with time. By the time I noticed the changes, it was already too late to kick her out.

Not that I would.

If anything, I'm keeping her.

All of her.

She smells of her apple lotion that I've become lowkey addicted to. It's not even about the scent of apples—it's about her natural body warmth mingled with it. It's a trademark that no other human being would be able to replicate.

I can't get enough of it no matter how long I fill my nostrils with it.

She moans softly when I place her on the bed. I cover her with a sheet over her bathrobe and spend a few minutes watching her.

It doesn't matter how often I see her soft face with the tiny features, full lips and long lashes. It doesn't matter whether she's asleep or awake.

I can't get enough of watching her, of wanting to get so close that she won't be able to leave.

Am I being overbearing? Probably.

But I honestly can't imagine my life without her in it. If anything, I've forgotten how I used to live before she came along.

I brush my lips against her forehead before I begrudgingly leave her side and step into my closet.

After putting on a tuxedo, I stand in front of the mirror to do my bowtie. While I hate to leave Aurora's side, I have a banquet to attend.

She's out for the night after the thorough fucking and bath massage.

Besides, if I even attempt to skip tonight, Harris will show up here and bitch for an hour about meetings like the workaholic he is.

It's strange that I used to be exactly like him—if not more demanding—but now, the idea of leaving takes all my self-restraint.

Tiny hands wrap around my chest from behind as her warmth glues to my back.

Aurora's head peeks from the side and she meets my gaze in the mirror. "Going somewhere?"

"Work."

"What happened to 'we'll stay in bed all day?'" She tries to hide her disappointment from her overly expressive eyes and fails. She can be so adorable sometimes.

"Didn't we, wild one?"

"Well, not really."

"I think your arse and pussy would testify otherwise."

She hides her face against my jacket to camouflage the flaming of her cheeks. I get the urge to grab her and kiss the fuck out of her.

So I do just that.

Spinning around, I wrap my hand around her throat. Her dark blue eyes meet mine, wide, expectant, and I meet those expectations when I slam my lips to hers.

I lost count of how much I've kissed her but each time she melts against me, her tiny fingers wrapping around my bicep or nape, it feels like a first.

And like every first, I feast on her luscious lips, grabbing her by arse and pulling her against my trousers.

I'm rock hard again. Fuck.

Pulling away, I breathe against her mouth without releasing neither her arse nor throat. "Go back to sleep."

"Do you not want me with you?"

"What the fuck is that nonsense?"

"Well..." she stares at her feet. "You don't take me with you to events or even invite me."

I place two fingers underneath her chin, forcing her to stare up at me. "Didn't you say you don't want to take part in anything that has to do with 'my world?'"

"That was before. I thought…"

"You thought what?"

"I thought you were embarrassed to have me on your arm."

"Why would I be embarrassed?"

"You're not the type to be embarrassed, but, you know."

"No, I don't know. You're not my dirty little secret, Aurora. I'll shout at the top of the world that you're mine if that's what it will take."

Her delicate throat works up and down with a swallow. "But people will talk about my resemblance to Alicia."

"Fuck people, and Alicia has been dead for eleven years. I don't think she minds."

"So you're not keeping it a secret?"

"Why the fuck would I announce in front of the world that you're my fiancée if I was keeping it a secret? Stop having those thoughts, okay?"

"Okay." A smile grazes her lips as she tiptoes and kisses me on my cheeks. "Have fun."

I grab her by the arm before she can leave. "Where do you think you're going?"

"Back to sleep."

"Forget about that. You're coming with me."

"I am?"

"If you want to. I would be happy if you came with me and made the night less boring." I rephrase so it doesn't come off as if I'm ordering her around.

Aurora is a strong, independent woman, and needs her choices. I think part of the reason why she acted up the other time was because I completely took that will away.

It's hard to give a choice when I'm used to my orders being met, but for her, I will learn. Eventually.

"I would love to." She wraps her arms around my neck and seals her lips to mine.

As I kiss her, I know, I just know that there's only one choice I would never give her.

The choice to leave me.

TWENTY-EIGHT

Aurora

S OMETHING FEELS WRONG THE MOMENT I ARRIVE AT MY office and receive a phone call from an unknown number.

Since the media attention started, Jonathan changed my phone number so that only he, his family, and Layla have it.

He even deleted Ethan's number when I added it. No kidding.

Jonathan has been more severe about his possessiveness since he took me against the sofa a week ago. He's been more tender, too, whether we're alone or with people. I still haven't asked him what he meant about the whole fiancée business, but I'd rather not ruin it.

At least, not for now.

I need his closeness more than anything as I deal with this whole fucked up situation. I need to sleep in his arms and feel like I'm in a castle and no one will ever be able to hurt me.

It's weird how I handled it all alone eleven years ago, but I don't want to think about that option now. Having Jonathan, Layla, and even Aiden and Levi and their wives, brings me a long-lost sense of peace that I'm ready to fight for with all my might.

At first, I don't answer the phone, thinking it's a reporter. They don't stop. At all. They keep bugging me, Layla, and even our employees for stories about me.

Jonathan wasn't kidding when he said he'd crush them, though. Aside from the security that surrounds H&H on a daily basis, Harris is keeping King Enterprises' solicitors busy by having them file countless lawsuits and restraining orders.

My screen lights up with a text.

Unknown Number: Hello, Ms Harper. This is Stephan Wayne, Mr Griffin's solicitor. I have one final message to relay from my client. There's a threat to your life and Mr Griffin can protect you from it. Your father is ready to take back his accusations if you visit him.

I sit down on the sofa, staring at the text. He's willing to leave me in peace?

No. I internally shake my head. This is one of Dad's games. He loved those—games, that is. There's a reason why I never visited him. Aside from the pain and trauma I feel whenever I think about him.

Dad is a master of manipulation, and although I could see through it, I'm not completely immune to it. If I do visit him, I have no clue what type of person I'll be when I walk out of there.

The day the court sentenced him for life, our eyes met, and I couldn't stop crying. All the pain and disappointment I experienced back then translated into tears that I couldn't hold back.

As the officers were taking him away, Dad stopped in front of me and whispered the words I've never been able to forget, "Next time we see each other, either I kill you or you kill me."

My phone lights up with another text from Stephan and I open it with unsteady fingers.

Unknown Number: You should be receiving a gift from your father.

A knock sounds on the door and I stare up as my assistant,

Jessica, walks inside carrying something in her hand. "This came for you, Ms Harper."

My eyes widen as I make out the wooden box. It's so similar to the ones I received Alicia's messages in.

Oh, God.

No.

All this time, I've been coming to terms that the entire debacle with the messages was a hallucination. I've become paranoid and had to check things twice and even take pictures so that type of incident never happens again.

If there's another box, then...it's real. It wasn't my imagination, after all.

Was this my father's game all along?

"You saw me with the box, Jessica, okay?" I take it from her fingers, and she nods with a quizzical expression before leaving.

My fingers shake as I unclasp the box, and sure enough, there's a flash drive. However, what's different this time is the note neatly folded underneath it.

I open it and read the writing I would recognise even a hundred years from now. The neat writing and his way of curving his S's and C's are still the same from when he helped me with my homework.

Dear Claire,

You must've received similar packages to these in the past with Alicia's voice on them. I have, too. Probably at the same time as you. That's why I'm breaking my silence.

I dislike being shoved in a corner, just like I'm sure you do. Someone is after us, my little muse. If you want evidence, listen to my own recording of that day.

Then we'll talk.

If I had any doubts, they vanish after reading Dad's letter. He received Alicia's messages, too? But why would he? They were directed at me.

It takes me a minute I don't have to spare to plug the flash drive into my laptop. Soon after I hit Play, there's a rustle of sounds, like a car revving to life or something. Then there's the sound of a crash, a loud one that deafens my ears.

"Fuck."

Dad. That's Dad's voice. The sound of a car door opening, then slamming shut echoes in the air. I assume it's his truck.

The rustle of running and the harsh gliding against a surface is the only thing that can be heard. It's like he's sliding down dirt or a harsh surface.

More rustling comes through before Dad's booming voice fills the air, "Alicia! Give me your hand!"

Alicia? My sister?

"Alicia!"

"N-no..." Her voice is brittle and she sounds far away and in pain. "You're the reason behind this."

"I'm fucking not. I would never hurt you or Clarissa."

A small chuckle comes from her before she coughs, and her distant breathing catches as if she's gurgling blood. "Why? Because we're Mum's daughters? Your original muse? I know, she left it for me in her will. She told me to cut all ties with Clarissa because of *you*. My own mother wanted her daughters apart because of no one other than *you*! She said that something unlocked inside of you after you met her and that she created a monster. You told her that you loved the challenge of killing people who looked like her because you couldn't hurt her. You can't hurt me and Claire either, because we look like her, but we inspire you to kill, don't we?"

"And yet, you kept coming back." Dad's voice is stone cold. "You came to Leeds all the time when you could've stayed away."

"I didn't want you to use Clarissa as a muse instead of me."

"Give me your fucking hand, Alicia. You'll die in there."

"Maybe it's better if I do—just like Mum did. I thought she killed herself because of Dad, but it was because of *you*, Maxim," she snarls. "She willingly left this world to not carry on your sins with her."

"So you'll leave your role for Clarissa?" His voice turns calm in an almost manic way.

A sob tears from her throat. "Leave her alone. She's your daughter. At least she's your daughter."

"Which will make her a better muse than you and your mum ever were. After all, she shares my and Bridget's DNA."

"M-Maxim…leave her…"

"Then give me your fucking hand, Alicia. Take responsibility for both Bridget and her."

"I can't." She sounds defeated, numb almost. "My own husband thinks I'm crazy, and even my son believes it sometimes. And now, he left me. Aiden and Clarissa are the only bright things in my life, but I'm not theirs."

"You're not crazy—you were made to believe that. I think I know who's behind this."

"I-is it Jonathan?"

"You don't want it to be him?"

"Tell me. P-please."

"Give me your fucking hand first."

"Y-you'll leave Claire alone?"

"I will."

"And Aiden?"

"I couldn't give two fucks about him. He looks nothing like you and Bridget."

"F-fine." There's the sound of a pained moan as a rustle of clothes comes from Dad.

"Oh…" Alicia breathes heavily. "I c-can't move. T-there's so much blood…"

"Fuck! Fuck!"

"M-Maxim…I…I d-don't feel so good…"

"Don't you dare go!" he shouts at her, voice more enraged than worried.

"C-Claire… D-don't do this to her… D-don't make her me and Mum… P-please…*please*…"

"Shut the fuck up, Alicia." More friction of clothes come from Dad's side.

"T-tell Aiden and C-Claire that I love them so much and I-I'm sorry I couldn't take them far away and p-protect them." She's full on crying now, her voice turning weaker with every second. "Tell J-Jonathan I forgive him if he did it. Tell him that he should pick up his life and move on."

"I said shut the fuck up." Dad groans as he seems to be trying to lift either the car or her.

"This must be how those women felt…" Her voice is far away, barely audible, but sounds serene. "The helplessness. The…end. I'm paying for staying silent and playing a part in their deaths. Isn't it ironic that you, of all people, get to see me go? I-I'm cold, Maxim. S-so cold…"

Dad curses a few times more, but Alicia's voice disappears, and soon enough, the recording ends.

Tears stream down my cheeks as I stare at the screen through blurry eyes.

The sound of Alicia's voice plays in my head like a haunting song on repeat. Her words, her helplessness, her final moments.

That's where Dad had been that morning. He was chasing Alicia before she crashed, then he returned to bury his seventh victim.

He was there with her as she spit out her last breaths.

I grab my bag, and I'm on autopilot as I leave the office.

This recording confirms a few things.

One, I'm not crazy. Alicia did say that Jonathan was poisoning her.

Two, this is a lot bigger than I thought.

And there's only one way to figure it all out.

TWENTY-NINE

Aurora

THIS IS THE LAST PLACE I EVER EXPECTED TO WALK INTO WITH my own feet.

But now that I think about it, the reunion was meant to happen sooner or later.

There's too much black water between us, and I was never going to move on without having this confrontation.

The security Jonathan has following me around is waiting outside. I have no doubt that they called him, so I don't have much time before he barges in here and drags me back home.

The room I'm in is sterile with bland grey walls. A few armed guards stand at the corners and cameras blink from every angle possible. Prior to coming inside, I was searched thoroughly and even got sniffed at by dogs. This is what it feels like to be the offspring of a dangerous criminal and to carry his sins on my shoulders.

A large glass with a few holes separates me from him as I sit facing the man I once called Daddy. The man who held me and raised me on his own. The man who taught me everything and nursed my colds. The man who took me to festivals and on hunts and hikes.

The man who was my superhero but other people's monster.

Seeing him in that interview doesn't lessen the impact of meeting him face-to-face. Or, more accurately, through the glass.

He's wearing elegant trousers and a matching striped shirt. His blond beard is trimmed short but not gone. His eyes have some lines underneath them, but he doesn't appear much older than the last time I saw him—in court, eleven years ago.

He's gained some muscles, and considering he's tall, he's always appeared as a bodybuilder champion of some sort.

Maxim Griffin is still the same man from my memories. Once a father, now a devil's spawn. Or maybe he was a devil's spawn before he was even a father?

A small smile paints his lips, making him appear normal, approachable even. The guy next door, who'll eventually kidnap you, strap duct tape on your face, and watch you slowly die as he cuts you.

I push those images away because if I get lost in the memories of those vacant eyes, I won't be able to keep my cool and address the reason I'm here.

"Clarissa. Long time no see." His voice is still the same—suave, posh, welcoming. He rarely spoke with the heavy Yorkshire accent. His mum, my grandmother, was a Londoner, and he somehow kept that accent. However, he switches to a northern accent whenever he feels it can get him closer to people. His ability to blend in with others and attract them with the sheer power of his charisma is the scariest thing about the Duct Tape Killer.

"I'm not here for a reunion." I'm surprised my voice is calm, considering the jittery emotions sinking at the bottom of my stomach.

"Then what are you here for?"

"You know. You sent me that recording on purpose."

"It was the final attempt to bring you to me. And here you are."

"Why haven't you sent it before? Why now?"

"Because you're stubborn. You take after me, in that respect. We share DNA, Claire—I know how to push your buttons. I thought the interview and the media attention would be enough to make you crumble, but you're not that sixteen-year-old kid anymore, you're stronger." I don't miss the pride in his voice as he says the last word.

"No thanks to you."

He laughs, the sound long and a bit deranged. "It's all thanks to me, Claire. I made you, and you were only able to grow because you rebelled against your maker."

"I reported the truth. I saved people."

"And how did that feel, my little muse?" His humour disappears as he leans closer on the table, his fingers intertwined while he watches me closely with unhinged eyes that match mine in colour. "Did they worship at your altar, or did they bite the hand that fed them? They attacked you, cursed your existence, and are currently plotting your demise. Didn't I tell you that humans only exist to be used?"

"I'm *not* you." The words clog my throat before they come out.

"You are in many ways. That's why you turned me in, Claire. You did it because you were afraid you'd become like me, and that type of freedom scared you. It still does. Admit it, we're one, my little muse. We always were."

My fingers shake and I grip them together on my lap. "I did nothing wrong. *You* did. So don't you dare put me in the same category as you."

"But we are. That's why you're here. You were always meant to come see me and apologise for the misjudgement you made by turning me in."

"The only reason I came here is because of the recording of Alicia's last moments. You said someone was trying to make her believe she was crazy. Who was it?"

"Oh, that. It's the same person who sent us the recordings of Alicia's messages. They also knew about my fixation on Bridget and Alicia. See, the first time I met your mother, I was…experimenting, but no matter what I did, it always fell short. Bridget came to

Yorkshire for a festival and was sitting alone in a pub. The moment I saw her, it was as if I'd found purpose, inspiration, beauty, and madness. She was the muse that I'd spent so long searching for.

"I planned to suffocate her after I fucked her that night, but I couldn't. The light in her eyes kept me going and going and...*going*. We spent the weekend together, then she went back to her husband. I followed her from afar, and she was different in London—boring almost. She was nothing like the woman who threw away all her inhibitions and showed her true colours at that festival. However, she did inspire me, and for that, I kept her alive.

"My obsession with her bled into women who resembled her, and let's say, she suspected it. When she gave birth to you, she dropped you at my doorstep and disappeared into the night. I was so busy with you, I didn't pay her many visits. Then Alicia came for you of her own volition. She was a carbon copy of Bridget, so when your mum killed herself, I latched onto Alicia for inspiration. She became my new muse, and I assume the one who poisoned her knew that fact."

My lips tremble and I set them in a line as I absorb what he's said and hear the confirmation that he's a monster with his own words. "Who is it?"

"I have my theories."

"Who?"

"Why do you want to know, my little muse? Do you suspect they're after you now?"

"I want justice for Alicia." My heart dips in its cavity as I murmur, "Is it Jonathan?"

A part of me has already started mourning the fact that it could be Jonathan. After all, Alicia named him, and he made me feel as if I were insane when I mentioned the flash drives. He could've easily bribed Paul, the concierge, so that he'd lie and say he didn't receive any packages.

If he hurt Alicia in any way, I won't be able to forgive him. I don't care that she did. I'm not her, and deep down, I'll always hate him.

It'll destroy me in the process, but I won't be able to trust him ever again.

"Jonathan." Dad raises a brow. "What is it about him that got you both tangled up? I didn't raise you to take other people's leftovers, Claire."

"Is it him?" I insist.

"Apologise first and I might consider forgiving you and telling you."

"What?"

"You heard me. Say, *I'm sorry I turned you in, Dad. I'm sorry I fucking betrayed you.*"

"I didn't betray you, Dad. *You* betrayed *me*. You painted the world for me, then you turned it all black. You became my hero just to pull the carpet from beneath my feet. The world shattered in front of my eyes the moment I saw you dragging a corpse with complete nonchalance. I was sixteen, Dad! Fucking *sixteen*. I hadn't even lived yet and you killed me. I hadn't breathed yet and you smothered me. I spent the past eleven years gasping for air and finding smoke. The moment I start to pull my pieces together, the memory of you scatters them apart all over again. So don't you dare sit there and say I betrayed you. *You betrayed me.* You were my world, but you metaphorically buried me alive in that eighth grave. I'm finally digging my way out, and I will *not* allow you to push me in that hole again."

Tears soak my cheeks by the time I finish, but they're not sad or weak tears. They're angry tears. Injustice tears. Because I was finally able to tell him what I think, what I've always thought.

The reason I felt so guilty towards those victims was because, even though I hated him for what he did, I couldn't stop considering him as my dad. The little girl in me still loved him. She still saw him as the father who picked her up, after her mother threw her away, and raised her as if his world revolved around her.

But he tarnished that world. He smashed it to pieces.

Maybe that's why sixteen-year-old me thought I needed to take the jabs and the hits. She even thought being stabbed was karma for not being able to hate my father as much as I should. For secretly still loving him. For secretly missing him.

I needed to come to terms with the fact that it's okay to consider your father a father, despite him being a monster. I just have to move on from those memories where I considered him my world.

He isn't.

He's just a monster who doesn't deserve respect.

Dad remains motionless. His expression doesn't change, but his jaw clenches. "You will not get anything from me unless you apologise, Claire."

"I'll never apologise for turning you in, Dad. That was the best decision I made in my life, even if it flipped it upside down."

I stand up because it's useless to try to extract information out of him. He's right. We're both too stubborn, and he won't give me anything unless I comply with his condition.

"They're only after you because you're my muse now, Claire. They're after me, not you."

"Then I hope they get you." A tear slides down my cheek as I stare him in the eyes that are identical to mine and, in a way, it feels like I'm bidding farewell to the little girl I always saw in those eyes. To the me from the past. "This is our official goodbye, Dad. I'll never visit you again. If you still want to go on with the parole process, I'll stand there again and tell them you deserve every second you spend in prison."

I take one last look at his face, at the drawn brows and the golden beard and hair and I finally grieve my father.

When I get out of the building, I inhale a deep gulp of air.

Real air.

Actual air.

The feeling of being alive hits me straight in the chest and it's so strong, I have to brace myself against the wall for a second.

I'm finally alive.

Finally breathing.

I'm finally out of that grave. Literally and figuratively.

"Are you all right, Miss?" One of my security men clutches me by the elbow.

I straighten, clearing my throat. "I'm perfect. Thank you."

"Mr. King has been calling nonstop," he says as he leads me to the awaiting car.

Of course he has.

Once I'm in the back seat, I check my phone, and sure enough, there are a dozen missed calls and emails.

From: Jonathan King
To: Aurora Harper
Subject: Answer The Fucking Phone
Refer to subject. Don't make me come find you from fucking Oxford.

Then another one.

From: Jonathan King
To: Aurora Harper
Subject: I'm On My Way
You better be ready for that arse to be turned red.

I power off my phone. Dad didn't deny that Jonathan could be the one behind Alicia's poisoning. If he is, this will get ugly.

"Miss." The bodyguard hands me his phone with a pleading expression. "Please answer or he'll fire us all."

The fucking tyrant.

I swipe the green button.

"If you don't put her on the fucking phone right now, consider your future ruined."

My heart picks up speed at the sound of his voice, and I want to murder that heart. I want to bury it with Alicia so it never beats again.

"I'm on my way home," I say in a bland voice that I don't even recognise. "And stop threatening people."

I hang up before he can say anything.

By the time we reach home, Jonathan has called the guards' phones a few more times, but I took them and powered them off.

"Tell him I did it," I say to the men as I leave the car and stride into the house.

They nod, but their expressions remain unsure.

My steps are long and confident. Jonathan better be ready for the hell I'm going to bring him the moment he walks through the door.

He'll tell me everything, and he better be convincing, because I'm not in the mood to be trifled with today.

A shadow passes in my peripheral vision, and I freeze. The screeching sound of my heels echoes in the silence.

Oh, no.

No, no, no.

I make a run for the entrance. The security guys are there and—

A body hits me from behind and we both crash to the ground. I scream, thrashing and clawing at them. A hand covers my mouth from behind, muting any sound I have to make.

I manage to roll onto my back and claw at the mask covering his face. I remove it, my nails pulling at his hair, then I freeze. The dragon tattoo. How come I didn't see it before?

"*You*," the word falls from me in a murmur.

Renewed energy rushes through me and I hit him in the crotch. He wails and I use the chance to jump to my feet. Adrenaline tightens my muscles and I'm about to make a run for it again when something prickles my nape.

I fall into the shadow's hand, eyes rolling to the back of my head.

"J-Jonathan…" I whimper as the world turns black.

THIRTY

Jonathan

"**F**UCK!"

    I grip the phone tightly as my security guy hangs up on me.

I'm willing to bet it's Aurora again, not him. She has that fucking attitude that drives me insane.

But she had no business visiting the fucker Maxim. If he tells her anything that will worsen her state of mind, I'll murder him in his cell.

"Faster, Moses."

My driver speeds up, not caring if we get a few tickets in the process. As long as I reach Aurora, nothing else matters.

I try calling my security again. This time, Arnold picks up. Fucking finally.

"Where is she?" I bark.

"She just went inside the house, sir."

"Don't let her out. I don't care if you have to chain her to a fucking tree."

"Yes, sir."

"Don't hurt her, though. Leave a scratch on her skin and I'll cut off your balls."

"Yes, sir."

I hang up, releasing a breath. Sometimes, I don't know what goes on in that woman's head. It doesn't matter how submissive she gets under my hand or in bed. Out of it, she's a tigress ready to rip the world a new one—me included.

Maybe that's what made the challenge of taming her all the more thrilling. The feeling of utter control and empowerment I get from owning her is something I've never experienced before.

Even the feelings I have for this woman are entirely different from what I know. It's that strange sensation that creeps up on you, then completely owns you.

Contrary to what everyone thinks, I do feel. I loved my parents and my brother in my own way. Aiden and Levi, too. But all of them are family—they're people who hold the King name and my blood.

Aurora is different.

It's not even a sense of duty and mutual understanding like it was with Alicia. There's no mutual fucking understanding with Aurora. She does what her head tells her and tests my control every step of the way.

Yet she's the only woman who's fit to be the queen of my empire.

With Aurora, it's…belonging. Yes, I believe that's the right word. She's the first person who's spoken to my soul without words. Which is weird as fuck since I always thought I lacked that—a soul, that is.

At first, I didn't understand how she brought out that part of me, but the more time I spend with her, the more certain I am that she's slowly but surely becoming an indispensable part of my life.

The thought of living on without her punches a hole in my previously impenetrable chest.

That's why her suggestion of ending it per the agreement pissed me the fuck off. It still brings on incomparable rage to the front of my head.

There's no way in fuck I'm letting her go, or worse, standing by to watch her move on. I'll kill every last fucker before that happens.

The car rolls to the mansion and I release a long breath.

Is the confrontation with her going to be easy? Probably not, but that's the thing about Aurora, I'm ready for her tantrums and provocations and everything in between.

Hell, I even strive for them now.

My phone vibrates in my hand, and I expect it to be one of the guards who'll tell me she's trying to leave—or that she has already left.

I'll chase her to the ends of the earth if I have to.

The unknown number that flashes on my screen gives me pause.

I answer with my curt tone, "Jonathan King."

"Kyle Hunter."

"Right, Kyle. Have you figured out the identity of the attacker?"

"I've done more than that and I'm on my way. Give me access inside." His cool voice filters through the phone with ease.

"Who is it?"

"Not only is he under your roof, but his game is a lot bigger than you think."

I stop breathing as Kyle continues speaking. The name he says, the dates, and the events that occurred are all connected. But it's not his words that make me barge out of the car before it properly stops.

It's the woman inside.

Aurora's life is in danger.

THIRTY-ONE

Aurora

VOICES REACH ME AS IF I'M AT THE BOTTOM OF THE SEA AND they're somewhere at the surface. Distorted, far away, and barely audible.

My tongue sticks to the roof of my dry mouth and it takes me a considerable amount of energy to swallow.

My pupils move behind my eyelids, but I'm not seeing anything… *I don't think*. It's like I'm back in that grave. My side open, blood pours from me and I can't lift myself to come out.

Tears pool at the corners of my eyes. No. I'm not that sixteen-year-old girl anymore. I said goodbye to my nightmare. I mourned him.

Slowly, too slowly, my eyes open. The walls are turning and I'm about to fall.

Only…I don't.

I'm bound to a chair by thick ropes around my torso and others strain my arms behind my back.

Blinking twice, I start to register my surroundings. The counter, the clean white flooring, the table in the middle.

The kitchen. I'm in the kitchen at home.

My eyes widen when I make out the man behind a camera that's sitting on a tripod. The man who has a mask falling around his neck. The scratch marks I left earlier run diagonally across his face.

The man who stabbed me eleven years ago and attacked me a few weeks back.

Tom.

The reason I haven't picked up on the dragon tattoo is because he has hair now. He was bald back then—eleven years ago, I mean.

Despite the taste of acid and fear at the back of my throat, I hold my ground. I have no doubt that he plans to hurt me, and that camera is probably a way to record it.

Shit.

Fuck.

During my stay here, I thought he was silent because it's a part of his personality. He's actually grown on me for his kind nature, but I had no clue he'd been plotting my demise.

But he wasn't the one who drugged me earlier...right? I scratched him and was running...then I somehow got punctured by a needle and fell back into his arms.

Someone else was there.

"The princess is finally awake."

I jolt at the voice coming from my right. My eyes nearly bug out of their sockets as she joins Tom.

"M-Margot?"

"Yes, Miss?" Her tone is flat, her green eyes stone cold.

"B-but how? Why?" I stare between her and Tom. "He was the one who attacked me."

"With my help." Her Irish accent becomes more prominent. "As for why, maybe you should've asked your father during today's visit."

"Y-you're a victim's family member?" It's hard to speak, and it's not because of who's standing in front of me. My tongue is heavy and so are my limbs—probably due to the drugs.

"The first one," Margot says. "The forgettable one because she didn't get suffocated and buried in a grave. My sister, Megan, was the Duct Tape Killer's first victim, but it happened more than twenty years ago. She was kidnapped, but since she had issues with drugs, the police categorised her as a runaway. Your father made her death seem like an overdose and dumped her under a filthy bridge. He never admitted to that murder, and when Shelby, my sister's boyfriend at the time, went to prison a few years ago, he asked him if there were any women he'd never mentioned. Maxim said he never talked about the ones who happened before his muse came along. Those were forgettable, *mere practice,* as he called them. The ones who happened after he met Bridget and Alicia were his real masterpieces. He didn't even remember her name. My sister and only family was a nobody to him. He called her *practice!*" Margot's voice raises at the end before she releases a breath and smooths it.

"So Tom and I decided to make him pay in the best way we knew how. Tom is my nephew and I raised him after Megan died when he was only ten. We'd already tracked down Maxim before you turned him in. We learnt his patterns and his obsession with his pretty little muses. Bridget had already killed herself at the time, so we paid extra attention to you and Alicia. We were going to make him suffer, and killing him wouldn't have sufficed. He had to lose the two people most precious to him."

I gasp as the pieces of the puzzle fall into place. "Y-you…you're the one who poisoned Alicia?"

"Her mind was fragile anyway. It was a piece of cake to slip her something here and another thing there. In no time, everyone, Jonathan and Aiden included, believed she was losing it. The bitch even thought Jonathan was poisoning her since she decided to be smart and test the tea he brought her. She never suspected me or how I made her think she was losing track of everything. Her hallucinations were mostly caused by elaborate plots Tom and I concocted over the years. We recorded whispering voices and made her think she was hearing things. A lost book here, a missed item there, and she started talking to herself in order to remain sane. Which, of course, only made her more insane. It was her payment for being Maxim's willing muse."

Angry tears fill my eyes at the thought of what Alicia went through. That must be what they did to me, too. Those voices I heard the morning after I thought I was suffering from hallucinations were hers and Tom's doing. These monsters made my sister believe she was insane. "She did that to protect me."

"Yawn. And what's so special about you, Clarissa? Aside from the fact that you're the final chink to Maxim's armour? I admit, you're not as easy to break as Alicia was. Shelby paid your previous building concierge to turn a blind eye on all the packages we sent, but you still wouldn't give up."

Fuck. Shelby. I should've known there was something off about the standoffish old man who used to live next door to me.

"Why didn't you kill me eleven years ago?" I glare at Tom. "Does she have to answer that for you, too?"

"You didn't suffer enough," he says in a monotone voice. It's probably the first time I've heard him speak, and his tone is as quiet as his silence.

"Besides, no offence, but you're not important. The role you play in Maxim's life is." Margot clicks on the camera. "We're going to record you being killed by Tom. It'll be live and an insider will show the footage to Maxim. Once he loses his final muse, it'll be his downfall and the best revenge Megan could've gotten."

Despite the heaviness of my head and my tongue, I meet both their gazes. "I'm sorry you lost a sister and a mother, but that doesn't give you the right to blame it on me. I'm a victim, too. I turned him in, even though he was everything I had."

"Shut up." Tom reaches me in a few steps and slaps me so hard, I reel in my chair. "She was my world. He took her and I will take you."

"Use the knife, Tom." Margot motions at the glinting blade on the counter and he retrieves it.

My chin trembles, and I start seeing the ending, but I don't lower my gaze.

I did nothing wrong.

But as he brings the knife to my throat, a shudder goes down my spine. Regrets rush to the forefront of my mind. Most of them are about how I haven't really lived, and now that I'm ready to, it'll be taken away.

It's about how I can't say goodbye to Lay, her family, and *my* family. Because, in a way, Aiden, Levi, Elsa, and Astrid have warmed their way into my life and become my family.

But most of all, thought, it's about Jonathan.

I regret not saying the words I've felt for so long but have denied or thought I was no longer worthy of feeling.

There's a need to close my eyes, but I don't. I'm going to die with my chin held high.

A tear slides down my cheek as I realise it's over before it even started.

It took eleven years, but it's finally over.

Just when I'm about to surrender to my fate, the door barges open.

THIRTY-TWO

Aurora

J ONATHAN IS HERE.

The moment my eyes fall on him, a sudden urge to cry hits me out of nowhere.

I didn't know how much I needed to see him in my final moments until now.

His tall frame nearly blocks the entrance as he breathes harshly, and just like when I was a kid, he looks exactly like a god. Only, I'm not scared of him now. Was I even scared of him back then?

A forgotten memory hits me straight in the chest.

My small hand tugs on Alicia's full wedding dress. She smiles down at me, her dark eyes nearly closing with the motion. "You don't have to hide from Jonathan, Claire. He's family now."

"Family?"

"Yes."

"Cuz you're marrying him?"

She nods.

I pull on her dress some more, which is our secret signal for her to come down to my level.

Alicia is so tall, and I can barely reach her thighs. She says I'll grow up to be tall like her one day, but that's obviously not happening.

She crouches and gives me her ear so I can whisper, "When I grow up, can I marry him, too?"

She laughs, the sound making Jonathan stare at us, and I hide behind Alicia again, my cheeks flaming.

My sister ruffles my hair and whispers back, "If I'm not here, you have my permission."

I'm thrust back to the present with tears hanging on to my lashes. Oh, God. I can't believe I asked Alicia that. Jonathan is right to call me a wild one.

My gaze follows him as he slowly approaches the scene, his attention set on the knife Tom is holding to my throat.

He might've shown up, but it's too late. Margot and Tom have no care for the consequences of their actions. That's what happens when you live only for revenge. It becomes your start and your end. Everything else is collateral—their own lives included.

They don't care if they die at the end of this.

"Let her go." Jonathan's voice is clear, hard, and leaves no room for negotiation.

Margot stands in front of him. "This has nothing to do with you, Mr King. Leave and we won't hurt you."

Jonathan's guards follow after him, their tall, broad frames filling the entrance. Some of them have guns, but they'll make no difference to my fate, considering that Tom's knife is already slicing through my throat. A hot liquid trails down my neck.

Jonathan's face turns into granite as his stormy eyes fixate on Tom. "You're going to die."

"Not before her." Tom's voice is as expressionless as his face. It's like he lost the ability to feel when he was young.

"Go," I whisper in a barely audible voice at Jonathan. "Aiden and Levi need you."

"Shut up, Aurora."

"I'm lucky I found you again—or you found me. Y-you gave a different meaning to my life and taught me how to rise above myself, and I'm so thankful for that, Jonathan."

"Stop saying your goodbyes," he snaps.

"Try to compliment the boys more often. They don't show it, but they love your approval. Try to forgive Ethan. I know you need his friendship as much as he needs yours. Take care of Layla, and tell her I love her and I'm so lucky to have found her." My voice breaks at the end as tears fall unchecked down my cheeks. Blood soaks the hem of my jacket and I try to ignore how I'm shaking all over. How tiny shocks of fear wrap like thorny wires around my heart.

No matter how brave my words are, I don't want to die.

I fought with death for eleven damn years. Why does it get to win now, when I'm so close to beating it?

Jonathan approaches me, his jaw clenching under the stubble. Tom tightens his hold on the knife and Jonathan stops in place, his lips thinning into a line.

"You're not going to die," he says with so much conviction, I almost believe him.

I almost think that I'll come out of this chair and I'll be able to hold him again. I'll be able to tell him what I haven't been able to all this time.

"You'll watch her die." Margot levels him with her haughty glare. "Just like Maxim."

"My men are on their way to Shelby." Jonathan's gaze drifts from Margot to Tom. "If you don't remove that knife right now, I won't hesitate to kill your father, Tom. So what's it going to be?"

"He's in prison," Tom says. "He'll finish Maxim off after Aurora dies."

"I'll finish him anyway." Jonathan's posture is calm, despite the tension in his shoulders. I don't know how he remains so calm under such circumstances. I'm on the verge of a breakdown.

"Small price to pay." Margot smiles. "Do you think death scares us?"

"Then you leave me no choice." Jonathan steps aside, and a part of me is glad that he's putting his life first. His family and many people's livelihoods depend on him.

I ignore the bitter taste sticking to the back of my throat and try to gather the influx of thoughts scattering through my head.

"Jonathan…" I murmur. "I lo—"

My words are cut off when something punctures the kitchen's window. The knife that was previously held to my throat clutters to my lap and the body behind me disappears. There's a loud thud and Margot shrieks, the haunted sound echoing in the space.

My eyes widen as I make out Tom lying on the floor, his eyes staring up at me—or rather, at nowhere. A hole settles in the middle of his forehead.

Margot falls to her knees in front of him, sobbing and calling his name. There's no answer. No movement.

Holy shit. I think I'm going to throw up.

A shadow appears at the window, and I flinch against the chair, the ropes tightening around my skin. For some illogical reason, I think Tom's shadow has returned as a ghost and that he'll finish what he started. The continuous bursts of adrenaline seem to be drawing energy from my life essence.

The shadow slowly comes into full view. He's wearing elegant slacks and a dark blue shirt that matches the hypnotic colour of his eyes. The rest of his face is covered with a mask. He nods at Jonathan, who nods back. The masked man winks at me, laugh lines appear under his eyes as he stares at Tom's corpse, and with that, he disappears.

Did he just kill Tom and smile about it?

I'm still focused on the window when strong hands cut off the ropes using the knife. My heart flutters and soars to life as Jonathan kneels in front of me, his gaze hard and focused.

He runs his fingers over the wound in my neck and they come away with blood. "Fuck!"

"I'm okay."

"I'm not. Fuck, Aurora. What would I have done if something had happened to you?"

The moment I'm free of my bindings, I wrap my trembling arms around his neck. My first inhale of his woodsy scent brings fresh tears to the forefront, but this time, they're happy tears. Grateful tears. "Thank you."

Jonathan kisses my forehead and my cheeks, then brushes his lips against mine in a brief, soul-shattering kiss. With every touch of his mouth against my skin, it's like he's reviving me back to the life that was nearly stolen away from me.

He carries me in his arms, and I don't protest since my legs wouldn't be able to hold me up anyway. I snuggle my body into his embrace so effortlessly, as if I was always meant to be there.

And I was.

There's no doubt in my mind that I always was.

Jonathan's security wrenches Margot from above Tom's corpse. I don't want to look at him or the vacant look in his eyes.

"T-Tom!" Margot sobs. "Come back, honey. You can't leave."

Still carrying me in his arms, Jonathan stops in front of her and levels her with one of his wrath-inducing glares. The look of a god about to destroy everything in his path. "You raised him on useless revenge and eventually killed him, Margot. You'll rot in prison for the rest of your life thinking that. You'll regret the second you were born. Now, that is *my* revenge."

He doesn't wait for her reply as he strides out of the kitchen, her pained sobs and wails following after us like arrows.

My eyes are barely able to stay open, and my head feels wrong. What did they inject me with anyway?

I thought the heaviness in my head would loosen after being released from the ropes, but it's getting worse.

"J-Jonathan...I...d-don't feel so good..."

"Aurora."

His voice turns hollow and distant.

"Aurora!"

My grip on his shirt slackens as my head rolls back and everything turns black.

THIRTY-THREE

Aurora

LIFE HAS NEVER BEEN THE SAME AFTER THAT NIGHT.
    I think that's a given, considering how Jonathan's 'man' sniped down Tom as if he were a fly. When I asked Jonathan who the sniper was, he told me it was no one I needed to worry about. Something tells me his type might be even worse than the monster I spent my childhood with.

It took me a few days to regain my strength with the amount of propofol Margot and Tom injected into me.

Jonathan, being Jonathan, admitted me to a private clinic. When I told him there was no need, he gave me that look—the one that says 'you don't get to argue with me when it comes to your health'—and I eventually kept my mouth shut.

Layla came over, brought me her mum's couscous and hugged me to death. I joked, telling her maybe I should get hurt more often so she'd hug me. That earned me harsh glares from both her and Jonathan.

Ethan and Agnus showed up, too, and for the first time,

Jonathan didn't kick Ethan out. It might have something to do with how I begged him not to, but I believe this is a start to rekindle their friendship. I meant it when I told Ethan I'd help.

Aiden, Levi, Elsa, and Astrid visited, too. The boys were shocked about Margot's involvement, considering that they've known her their entire lives, but after a one-on-one talk with Jonathan, they seemed to have accepted it.

My nephew begrudgingly said he's glad I'm safe, and by begrudgingly, I mean, everyone said it first, then stared at him so he'd follow.

Aiden and I might have started off on the wrong foot, but I have faith in the future. After all, we're the people Alicia loved the most. I cropped the clip of her last moments and sent him the part where she said she loved him so much.

Elsa's eyes filled with tears as he listened and re-listened to that part. I think both he and I needed that goodbye from Alicia. Jonathan knew what my sister's opinion of him was before her death, the part where she thought he was poisoning her, and that she forgave him. I could tell he didn't like that she had those thoughts about him, but on the other hand, the closure gave him and Aiden a much-needed fresh start.

They're revisiting their father and son relationship that was basically non-existent after Alicia's death.

The small cropped parts are the only thing Jonathan and Aiden heard—I would never let him them listen to the entire clip of her death. I'll bury that painful experience between me and Maxim.

My father got attacked that night by Shelby. He was saved at the very last minute by a guard and he's currently in a coma that he might never wake up from.

When I learnt the news, I didn't grieve or feel sad. I didn't feel relief either. I'd already mourned my father, so whether he stays alive or dies doesn't really make much of a difference to me.

It's ironic that he tortured people until they died slowly, and now, he might receive the same treatment. He's neither dead nor alive—just floating in between.

Due to that fact, the parole case was dropped, and I didn't have to stand in trial. The media attention slowly withered away after Maxim's attack. The victims' families who were thirsty for justice all these years stopped protesting, too.

I'm slowly but surely getting back my life. Layla and I will finally launch our new product next month, and so far, we're having great prelaunch attention. It might also have something to do with the whole press interference.

Layla says any publicity is good publicity and it's only fair we use the suckers who harassed us.

Taking a deep breath, I hold the box in my hand and tap on Jonathan's office door. I don't wait before going inside.

Since Tom's death and Margot's arrest three weeks ago, the two of us have been on our own in the house. Harris arranges for a cleaning staff to come, but they're supervised by the security team. Needless to say, Jonathan doesn't trust anyone anymore. Not that he ever has in the past.

He sits behind his desk, focusing on his laptop. I stop and stare at the way his shirt is rolled to his elbows, revealing his strong forearms. He's not wearing a tie and his top shirt buttons are undone, hinting at his chiselled chest and the raw masculinity he exudes by just sitting at his desk.

I doubt there will be a day when I won't stop and stare at him. He owns me in every single way—just like I own him. And it's the best type of belonging I've ever felt.

Jonathan and I might not have started as a fairy tale, considering his tyrant behaviour, but I wouldn't have wished for a different beginning. If he hadn't cornered me the way he did, if he hadn't chased me after I ran, we wouldn't be where we are today.

During the past few weeks, he's been treating me like his queen—bathing me, feeding me, and even driving me to work because he doesn't trust any other 'fucker'. At night—and in the mornings—he owns my body in every sense of the word. He dominates and pleases me. He sets my skin on fire with every touch until I've turned into a complete addict.

He lifts his head when I round the table and stand in front of him. He stares at his watch. "You're here."

"Is that a problem?"

"You were supposed to return in an hour and I was going to drive you."

"I can drive on my own."

"No."

"Stop being a tyrant."

He raises a brow. "You like that about me."

"No, I don't." Okay, maybe I do, but he'll never know that. "Give me your hand."

He doesn't protest as I remove his watch, open the box, and retrieve the dark grey one I've been working on for months. I've probably had the idea for it since the first day I stepped into this house.

Its masculine design and size fits Jonathan's wrist perfectly as I strap it in place. I stare with admiration at my work, but then I realise I didn't ask for his opinion.

"It's one of a kind, so you better like it. Or pretend to," I blurt. "No, don't pretend. You *have* to like it."

He smiles, his features easing with the motion. "Are you going to mass-produce it for others?"

"No, it's specifically made for you. I mean, I only had you in mind when I was working on it."

"Then I'm not removing it for life."

I bite my lower lip. "Does that mean you like it?"

"I like everything you make, but since this is specifically for me, let's say it's your best work yet."

I wrap my arms around his neck, fingers getting lost in his hair as I brush a kiss on his forehead.

"I have a present for you, too."

I pull back at his words. "What type of present?"

"I fully transferred H&H's stocks back to you and Layla."

A huge grin pulls at my lips. "You did?"

He nods.

The overwhelming joy is crushed by a dooming realisation. My smile drops as fast as it appeared.

Our agreement said that he'd only transfer the stocks back at the end of the six-month period.

Those six months are almost over.

No idea why I thought that didn't matter anymore. I swear it's because that dick Layla has been ramping up my hopes. Two weeks ago, when I went back to my flat to get some of my things, we discovered that Jonathan now owns the building. Actually, he bought the thing soon after the start of our agreement.

The fact that he was able to waltz into my flat that day I fainted made more sense. Then Layla told me that if he bought the fucking building I live in, Jonathan has long-term plans for me.

Apparently, that's not the case.

"So what now?" My lips tremble as I drop my hands from around his neck. "Is this my ticket to leave?"

"Your ticket?"

"Well, aren't you giving me back the stocks so I'll go?"

"Is that what you think?"

"Isn't that why you did it?" My voice is broken and hurt, even to my own ears.

He grabs me by the waist and tugs so that I end up sitting on his hard thighs. The position has become too familiar. The thought of never having it again is more painful than being stabbed.

Jonathan's fingers dig into my hipbone, tender but firm. "It's the other way around."

"The other way around?"

"I gave you back the stocks so you wouldn't stay just because I'm holding them over your head."

A deep breath heaves out of my lungs as his grey eyes hold

mine hostage. "Does that mean you're giving me the opportunity to choose whether I leave or stay?"

He gives a sharp nod. "But if you do choose to leave, I might not play fair."

"When have you ever?"

"You already know my methods, so choose wisely. I'll give you some time to think about it."

"I don't need time."

He narrows his eyes, fingers tightening into my hip. "If you're in the mood to be chased, I'm happy to oblige."

I lean over and whisper in his ear, "I'm not going anywhere."

"No?"

"I've kind of gotten used to you. It'd be weird to get a different roommate."

"Is that so?"

"I think so. I love you, Jonathan."

He smiles, a genuine one that lights his grey eyes and threatens to stop my heart. "You do, huh?"

"I do. I thought I was incapable of love after losing Dad and Alicia, but you wrenched it out of me so easily. In the beginning, it was frightening, but it soon became exciting. I'm so glad I met you—or more like, re-met you."

His hand wraps around my throat, and my breathing hitches like every time he does it. "And I'm glad I kept you, wild one. You flipped my world upside down and I enjoy every second of it. I don't only love you, I'm obsessed with everything about you, and I'll spend the rest of my life proving how much your presence means to me."

"Jonathan..." My voice shatters with adoration and utter passion for this man. My tyrant. My love. My life.

"You're staying. It's final."

"I'm staying. After all, I have Alicia's permission."

"Alicia?"

I lift my chin. "It's a secret between me and my sister."

"Fascinating." He shakes his head. "I've known you were a wild one since you were five."

"Since I was five? I first met you when I was seven."

"Mmm. Maybe."

"Jonathan. What do you mean?"

A sadistic gleam covers his eyes. "A secret."

"You're awful."

"You still love me."

"I do."

"Say it."

"I love you, Jonathan." I sigh. "I love you so much."

Still grabbing me by the throat, his lips find mine in a kiss that seals my fate.

EPILOGUE 1

Aurora

Six months later

YOU KNOW WHEN YOU THINK YOU HAVE IT ALL, AND THERE'S a nagging feeling at the back of your head that maybe something wrong will happen and take all the good away?

I've never stopped thinking about that possibility since the attack. Not even after Dad went into a coma, taking most of my childhood memories with him.

But in another way, I learnt to move on.

My nightmares have slowly started to disappear, and it's all thanks to the man who sleeps beside me every night.

Jonathan holds me to him or above him, and the moment I get lost in his warmth, the world ceases to exist—nightmares included.

We go out on long walks, and I've gone back to hiking. I love the thrill of climbing and knowing I'll reach the top at the end of the journey. The fact that Jonathan is there every step of the way gives me a sense of empowerment I wouldn't have found any other way.

That's why I'm here today. A year ago, if anyone had told me I would be wearing a huge white dress and walking towards the man I once thought was a god, I would've pegged it as another hallucination.

Now, it's far from it.

All eyes turn to me as the music changes. We're on Jonathan's private island for our wedding. The island he named *Aurora* right after he told me I was staying with him and that was final.

He can be so swoony, despite his tyrant nature.

For him, the proposal was simple. He slid the ring on my finger and said, "You agreed to stay, what did you think it would be?"

Not that I would've said no. From the beginning, Jonathan was never a fling. He was a beautiful disaster waiting to happen and I just fell into it. Then I changed him as much as he changed me.

I put my mark in him as deep as he put his mark in me.

Ethan walks me down the aisle, as per my suggestion. He and Jonathan are slowly building back their relationship, so if my tyrant sees that I consider Ethan a father figure—a friend—he'll lower his guard. It won't be easy, but it's worth the shot.

Everyone I love and care about have been brought here by Jonathan's private jet. Layla sits amongst her parents and brothers, tears in her eyes. Aiden and Elsa are intertwining their fingers while sitting in the front row.

Jonathan and I took them to Alicia's grave as soon as we got engaged to get his permission, in a way. Aiden said Alicia wouldn't have an objection, so he didn't either.

Levi and Astrid are beside them, grinning, and Levi keeps winking at me. He can be such a charmer, which is a King thing I guess.

Harris, Moses, Agnus, and Jessica are all here. There are also some of Jonathan's closest associates like the Duke, Tristan Rhodes, the Earl, Edric Astor, and the Prime Minister, Sebastian Queens.

I don't focus much on the guests, though. My attention is stolen by the man standing at the end of the aisle. He's wearing a sharp black tux that matches the colour of his styled hair and reflects the heat in his grey eyes. He's watching me with so much love, obsession, and adoration, it makes my toes curl.

It's like the world has disappeared and we're the only people left in it. Jonathan always has that effect on me. But this time, it's different, almost as if our lives will become one.

The moment I stop in front of him, he glares at Ethan, who smiles when putting my hand in Jonathan's. "Take care of her or you'll have me to deal with."

I can tell Jonathan wants to cut him, but he lets it go when my fingers are interlaced with his. The huge engagement ring glints under the afternoon sun.

We say our 'I do's' in the midst of our family and friends, and I feel like I made the best decision of my life by choosing this man.

My love.

My tyrant.

My everything.

He lifts the veil, eyes darkening with heat. "You're officially mine now, Mrs King."

"And you're mine, Mr King."

EPILOGUE 2

Jonathan

Three years later

"**W**HAT DID YOU SAY ABOUT STAMINA, WILD ONE?" I GRAB Aurora by the throat as she holds on to my hand. "How about a redo?"

"I take it back," Aurora pants, pulling herself to crawl onto my lap.

Her lips fall open as I let her snuggle into me while we sit on the warm sand. We're both naked after I fucked her on all fours, then with her legs over my shoulders and my hand around her throat until she begged me to stop.

That got her a few more spankings before she came for the third time.

Her long legs tuck into my lap as she kisses along the line of my collarbone, inching up to brush her lips over my jaw.

She now has this habit of kissing me anywhere possible. No idea why she developed it, but I'm not complaining.

"Do you have to always prove me wrong?" she whispers

against my skin, her voice breathy and the smell of sex lingering in the air.

I love marking her as mine and having her smell like me. This will be her scent until the end of our lives.

"If you call me an old man again, I'm tempted to retaliate, and yes, Mrs. King, proving you wrong is a pleasure."

"Aiden and Levi call you an old man, too."

"Behind my back because they're cowards." I lift her chin. "Besides, I don't have to prove anything to them."

"And you do to me?"

"Abso-fucking-lutely. All the time."

A small chuckle falls from her lips as the blue in her eyes brightens to a thousand megawatts. "You will never change."

"Is that a good or a bad thing?"

"Both." She sighs, hiding her head in the crook of my neck. "I love it here."

It's our downtime after working for long months, and we always come to the island for a detox. I had to kick Aiden out because he was planning on bringing Elsa here.

Aurora said we could have a family holiday, but I hardly tolerate the lot of them during weekly dinners. I don't like sharing Aurora with them, and since Aiden and Levi figured that out, they've become dicks about it on purpose.

Ethan does that, too, and I'm still secretly planning his murder. Doesn't matter that we picked up our strange friendship-turned-rivalry again.

I don't like anyone in Aurora's vicinity. Full stop. Even Layla plays with fire when she steals her time from me.

I waited so long for this woman, and now that I've found her, there's no letting her go.

Not now.

Not ever.

Since Aiden graduated from university, he's been getting more involved in the company. Harris likes the level of challenge he brings to his workload, and they get along more now than when Aiden used to consider him my minion.

I loosened my grip a little in Aiden's favour. He still has a long way to go, but he's like me when I was younger, and I have no doubt that King Enterprises will prosper under his rule.

Besides, I need more free time to spend with my wife. Whether it's getaways like this one or the hiking that she picked back up or even dinners at the Hussaini restaurant.

Aurora runs her fingers over my chest, releasing a soft sigh that creeps straight under my skin and into that place she's carved out for herself in my heart. "We should've let Aiden and Elsa join us."

"And have them ruin our time? No."

"They wouldn't have ruined our time. Besides, I miss Eli."

Aurora is so obsessed with Aiden's boy, and he uses her love for his son to his advantage by throwing him in our direction whenever he wants alone time with his wife. Whenever he decides to bring Elsa here, he calls me or Aurora and says, "Hey, how about grandchild time?"

Not that I mind. Being a grandfather has brought new meaning to my life, and although Aurora can't have children— and won't, as per her decision—she's content to raising Aiden's and Levi's.

The night Eli was born, Aurora led me to a closet in the hospital and told me the fact that I'd become a grandfather was a 'turn-on', fumbled with my belt, and didn't stop until I was inside her. I had to place a hand over her mouth to muffle her screams.

"We can bring Eli, but not his parents."

She laughs. "I have the perfect gift for him."

"How about me?"

"Are you jealous of a toddler, Jonathan?"

"I don't like being left out."

"You're my world." She plants a kiss on my mouth. "How can you be left out of it?"

"And you are mine."

I pick her up and she squeals, holding on to me with all her might as I carry her to the ocean.

Time to prove my words.

THE END

WHAT'S NEXT?

Thank you so much for reading *Rise of a Queen*! If you liked it,
please leave a review.
Your support means the world to me.

If you're thirsty for more discussions with other readers of the
series, you can join the Facebook group, Rina's Spoilers Room.

If you're looking to what to read next, jump into *Royal Elite Series*
to read Aiden & Levi's books.

Next up is an epic duet set in the world of the Russian Mafia.
Throne Duet features the assassin Kyle who made an appearance
in *Rise of a Queen*.

ALSO BY RINA KENT

For more books by the author and a reading order, please visit:
www.rinakent.com/books

ABOUT THE AUTHOR

Rina Kent is a *USA Today*, international, and #1 Amazon bestselling author of everything enemies to lovers romance.

She's known to write unapologetic anti-heroes and villains because she often fell in love with men no one roots for. Her books are sprinkled with a touch of darkness, a pinch of angst, and an unhealthy dose of intensity.

She spends her private days in London laughing like an evil mastermind about adding mayhem to her expanding universe. When she's not writing, Rina travels, hikes, and spoils cats in a pure Cat Lady fashion.

If you're in the mood to stalk me:

Website: www.rinakent.com

Newsletter: www.subscribepage.com/rinakent

BookBub: www.bookbub.com/profile/rina-kent

Amazon: www.amazon.com/Rina-Kent/e/B07MM54G22

Goodreads: www.goodreads.com/author/show/18697906.
Rina_Kent

Instagram: www.instagram.com/author_rina

Facebook: www.facebook.com/rinaakent

Reader Group: www.facebook.com/groups/rinakent.club

Pinterest: www.pinterest.co.uk/AuthorRina/boards

Tiktok: www.tiktok.com/@rina.kent

Twitter: twitter.com/AuthorRina

Printed in the USA
CPSIA information can be obtained
at www.ICGtesting.com
LVHW091946170624
783329LV00066B/30